## "Brand,
**The words sp**
**but Sybil**

He grunted, and any welcome she might have imagined in his eyes disappeared into a stone-hard look. "Exactly what you see. A cowboy with a horse and a dog."

"But you must have a name besides Brand. You must be more than that."

His eyes grew harder, colder, if that were possible, and she shivered.

He might have well said, "Goodbye, this conversation is over."

She had enough for her story.

*He was known only as Cowboy. He never did give a last name before he rode into the sunset. He didn't welcome any questions about his true identity. But he was the best bronc buster in the territory. A reputation well earned.*

*It began when he was ten…*

But she wasn't satisfied.

She wanted to know what caused the pain she had glimpsed before he pulled his hat lower.

**Books by Linda Ford**

Love Inspired Historical

*The Road to Love*
*The Journey Home*
*The Path to Her Heart*
*Dakota Child*
*The Cowboy's Baby*
*Dakota Cowboy*
*Christmas Under*
  *Western Skies*
  "A Cowboy's Christmas"
*Dakota Father*
*Prairie Cowboy*
*Klondike Medicine Woman*
*\*The Cowboy Tutor*
*\*The Cowboy Father*
*\*The Cowboy Comes Home*

*The Gift of Family*
  "Merry Christmas, Cowboy"
†*The Cowboy's Surprise Bride*
†*The Cowboy's Unexpected*
  *Family*
†*The Cowboy's Convenient*
  *Proposal*
*The Baby Compromise*
†*Claiming the Cowboy's Heart*
†*Winning Over the Wrangler*

\*Three Brides for
  Three Cowboys
†Cowboys of Eden Valley

## *LINDA FORD*

lives on a ranch in Alberta, Canada. Growing up on the prairie and learning to notice the small details it hides gave her an appreciation for watching God at work in His creation. Her upbringing also included being taught to trust God in everything and through everything—a theme that resonates in her stories. Threads of another part of her life are found in her stories—her concern for children and their future. She and her husband raised fourteen children—four homemade, ten adopted. She currently shares her home and life with her husband, a grown son, a live-in paraplegic client and a continual (and welcome) stream of kids, kids-in-law, grandkids and assorted friends and relatives.

# Winning Over
# the Wrangler

## LINDA FORD

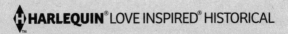

Recycling programs
for this product may
not exist in your area.

LOVE INSPIRED BOOKS

ISBN-13: 978-0-373-28254-8

WINNING OVER THE WRANGLER

Copyright © 2014 by Linda Ford

www.Harlequin.com

**Printed in U.S.A.**

The Lord shall guide thee continually, and satisfy
thy soul in drought, and make fat thy bones:
and thou shalt be like a watered garden.
—*Isaiah* 58:11

Prejudice comes in many forms.
It can be against the color of your skin, your heritage or, as it is in this story, your family reputation. Although I will name no names, this book is dedicated to those of my children who deal with prejudice. May you find grace and strength in those kinds of situations, and may you know the assurance of both God's love and the love of your family.

# Chapter One

*Eden Valley Ranch, September 1882*

Stampede!

Brand knew what was happening before it took place. He saw the horses press against the corral gate, frightened by something beyond his vision. It could have been anything from a stalking cougar to a tumbling tumbleweed. Wouldn't take much to alarm a bunch of wild mustangs. Wood creaked. The gate wouldn't hold under the pressure of frightened horses.

Brand's fists tightened so hard on the reins his knuckles cracked. His heart squeezed his blood out in a flash flood.

He would shout a warning to those along the fence, tell them to stand back. But he barely had control of the horse under him, which until a few minutes ago had never been ridden.

The gate snapped. The horses reared and screamed and pushed at each other, as frightened by the noise of the breaking fence as they had been by being confined. Brand held his mount with a firm hand. The horse was not ready to ride in tight quarters, but from the first,

he'd sensed a willingness in it that was absent in many
of the others he'd worked with. With no choice but to
trust himself and the others to the green horse, he rode
in the direction of the escaped animals. He had to turn
them away from the people, get them back into the pen
before anyone got hurt.

He saw a little boy and one of the women who had
been watching. They stood only a few feet from the
kicking, screaming, twisting animals surging in their
direction. Choking dust clouded the scene.

He kicked his mount, raced for a gate, slipped it open
with lightning speed and galloped toward them.

The stampeding horses were ahead of him. Before
them, the boy scampered toward a fence and rolled under
it. But the woman stood frozen, her mouth hanging open.
Brand couldn't tell if she screamed, couldn't have heard
it in the uproar if she did.

Out of the corner of his eye, he caught the movement
of other cowboys racing for their own horses. No one
else was close enough to rescue her. Brand leaned over
the horse's neck and urged him onward, closing the distance between them and the woman.

Ten more feet. He dared not look to the right or the
left. All that mattered was that frightened woman.

Five feet.

One more leap of his horse and Brand reached her
side. He leaned down and swept her into his arms,
clutching her to his chest as they raced onward, out of
the way of danger as pounding hooves thundered past
and dust-laden air swirled.

He slowed, grateful the horse cooperated. "You're
okay now. You're safe." He pressed her trembling body
closer.

He'd noticed her earlier as she stood by another

woman, watching him at work. How could he not keep stealing glances at her? She was the most beautiful woman he'd ever seen, with her golden curls flashing in the sunshine. He could describe everything about her in detail…the autumn-gold top she wore, the brown skirt that swung about her legs as she moved. The way she walked, as if life held nothing but promise for her. The way she smiled so sweetly at others.

It had taken all his concentration not to be distracted by her presence. It was his single-minded attentiveness that gave him his reputation as the best bronc buster in the West, and he wasn't about to lose it.

And now she rested in his arms, holding his shirt-front as if it was a lifeline, and lifted her gaze to him. His world tipped at the way her cobalt-blue eyes caught his in a pleading look. How was he supposed to keep his mind off her in this situation?

Cowboys turned the herd of wild horses back to the corral amid more dust and more shouting.

"You're safe," he murmured again, as fierce protectiveness filled his insides. He wanted to promise both himself and her that he'd make sure she was always safe.

Then his world righted and reason returned. He could never make such a promise. In fact, he carried more risk than any woman deserved, and certainly more than he meant to give one. He warned himself to stay away from her before he brought danger into her life.

A mahogany-haired woman rushed toward them— the woman he'd seen earlier with his golden beauty. And then Eddie Gardiner, the ranch owner who had hired him, raced up on his horse. Already the dust had begun to settle.

"Are you hurt?" Eddie asked.

"No. I'm fine." The woman had a gentle, soft voice

with a sweet English accent. A voice full of music and peace, despite the danger she'd just been in. Was her life really as peaceful and perfect as her voice caused Brand to think? From what he'd seen of her, he knew her to be a high-class lady. Likely she had never had reason in her privileged life to deal with the harsh realities of a place like his.

Realizing he still held her tight, Brand forced his arms to unfold, and lowered her to the ground, where her friend took her hand and pulled her close.

"That was exciting," the other woman said.

The golden beauty shivered. "A little too dangerous for my liking."

If she thought a herd of wild horses was dangerous, he could not imagine what she'd think if she knew the truth about him.

Eddie glanced about. "Where's Grady? Wasn't he with you?"

The woman gasped. "He was right here." She and her friend spun around, looking for him.

They must mean the boy who had wisely taken himself out of harm's way. Brand's smile formed as he looked toward where the boy had hidden.

"I'm here, Papa." The little fella crawled from under the fence and dusted himself off.

Brand would have guessed the blond-haired, blue-eyed child to be about five or six.

Grady swiped at his runny nose and looked up at Brand. "I wasn't scared."

Brand laughed at his bravado. "I was."

Grady hung his head. "Maybe I was a little."

"It's a good thing to be scared sometimes." A message he wished he could send to the woman he'd rescued and who now looked up at him with big trusting eyes.

He touched the brim of his hat and reined around. Already others had the horses contained and were moving them back into the corral. He should have checked the enclosure better. His oversight had put people at risk.

Eddie's wife raced down the hill, her skirts held in one hand. He'd seen she was in the family way, and hoped she wouldn't fall.

As soon as she was close enough, she caught Grady and sank to the ground, cradling the boy in her lap. "Thank God you're safe." She glanced up at Brand. "I saw the whole thing. You saved Sybil's life. You're very brave."

Brave! This woman was called Sybil. As if that could cancel out danger. It couldn't.

Brand wanted to ride away, avoid all this fuss, but he was surrounded by people.

He felt Sybil's gaze on him. Felt its warmth and watchfulness. He tried to avoid looking at her, knowing her blue eyes did something funny to his resolve. Made him weak and vulnerable.

"I don't think you have met Brand." Eddie pulled the woman close. "This is my wife, Linette, and my son, Grady." He turned to the other two ladies. "Mercy Newell." The darker of the pair. "And Sybil Bannerman, our guests from England. Ladies, this is Brand, best bronc buster in these parts."

"Pleased to meet you." Brand touched the brim of his hat. His dusty clothes and hat had seen better days. Normally he didn't care, but Miss Sybil was so neat and proper, he felt grubby.

"Mr. Brand, you are indeed a hero."

Her gentle words drew his gaze and he smiled despite himself. "No hero, ma'am. Just in the right place at the right time and glad I could be." He doffed his hat and edged away.

"Wait," Linette called. "You must let me do something to show my gratitude. Please join us for supper."

"Appreciate the offer, ma'am, but I got a dog back at my campsite and he's waiting for me." Dawg would be fine on his own, but Brand grasped at any excuse to avoid joining the others. Again, he vowed to ignore Miss Sybil. Again he failed to do so. He met her gaze. She flashed a bright smile that caused his heart to shift sideways, and almost made him lose his balance.

He touched the brim of his dusty hat again and turned his attention back to his job. The horses milled about, upset at their sudden escape and equally sudden corralling. The one he rode picked up the tension. "Enough for today," he said to the men fixing the fence. "No point in trying to work with them when they are riled up like this." He dismounted and turned his horse into another pen, away from the mustangs he hadn't yet ridden.

Cal, the young cowboy who'd given Brand nothing but dark glances since he started work on the horses, looked him up and down. "Guess you think you're pretty special, having rescued Miss Sybil."

No mistaking the challenging tone in the other man's voice. "Nothing special about doing what a man can do. I'm sure you would have done the same if you'd been on a horse at the time."

"You got that right. And I could break these horses if the boss would give me a chance."

"Yup. I figure you could, all right." He had no mind to start a disagreement. "Maybe next time the boss will let ya. Seeing as I won't be back here again."

"Huh. Figures." Cal stalked away.

Brand had no idea what bothered Cal and didn't

rightly care. He would be here long enough to do the job Eddie had hired him for, then be gone, never to see any of them again. It was how he must live his life.

At that knowledge, he turned and stared up the hill. Linette and Eddie, with Grady between them, entered the house, Mercy on their heels. But Sybil had paused halfway to the house and stared toward him. He couldn't see her eyes at that distance, but nevertheless, felt the intensity of her look. Wondered at it. For a moment, he couldn't tear himself away.

Then, with a great deal of effort, he pushed forward all the reasons he had to ignore her.

Dawg would be waiting for his supper. "I'll be back in the morning to work on the rest of those mustangs," he said to any of the nearby cowboys who cared to listen. He didn't glance about to see if anyone acknowledged his words.

His gaze lingered two more seconds on the beauty up the hill. Then he jerked around and strode to the clearing he'd chosen as his home away from home. Not that he had any home to be away from. Hadn't had one since his ma died six years ago. Even before that their homes had been temporary at best, as Ma tried to keep ahead of Pa and Cyrus, Brand's older half brother.

Brand had asked her often why she'd married a man who robbed houses, banks and stagecoaches. She said he hadn't done that until later, when things went wrong once too often.

"He said it didn't make sense that the rich got richer and the poor got poorer no matter how hard a poor man worked," his ma had said. "So he decided to even things out."

Only the way Pa and Cyrus went about doing it put their faces on wanted posters as the Duggan gang. And in order to protect Brand from the shame and the danger, Ma took him and fled.

At the memory he pressed his palm to his chest—the same spot where Sybil's head had rested—then jerked his hand to his side. He crossed to the fire-pit he'd built out of river rock, and lit a fire. His memories flared along with the flames.

Brand had continued to run for the same reasons—to avoid the shame and the danger. He avoided friendships for the same reasons, plus more. One thing he'd learned well in his twenty-three years: associating with Brand Duggan put others at risk. Pa and Cyrus didn't hesitate to threaten his friends in order to try and force Brand to cooperate with them. Besides, simply being associated with the Duggan name spelled ruin, and shunning by decent people.

He'd once allowed himself to grow fond of a young lady, but when he'd grown bold enough to tell her his last name she had reacted in anger and firmly informed him she'd have nothing to do with a man bearing such a stained name. She'd made sure he understood all the risks and shame she could face simply by being allied with him.

And she was right. Knowing him put her at risk from his family and at risk of censure from the community. People like Sybil, Eddie and the others at Eden Valley Ranch could live where they chose, in a big house, open and free, while he must always be on the lookout.

So Brand put down no roots, told no one his last name and didn't get close to others. Not even beautiful women like Miss Sybil. Especially not a woman like her.

Dawg had trotted toward him as he reached the clearing. Brand bent and scrubbed his fingers through the dog's silky fur now. This was all he could allow himself in the way of friendship.

He had no hope of a life full of peace and serenity. Nor did he intend to disturb Sybil's sweet world.

It took a lot of kicking clumps of dirt and throwing wood on the fire for him to persuade himself he didn't mind dealing with the truth of his life. Finally, he looked about, determined to find reasons to be grateful. Fall was in the air, filling it with deep-throated scents. Sure, it meant winter would soon be upon them, but he liked the color of the changing leaves, the cool night air and the migrating animals. He glanced up, hearing the honking of a V of geese overhead.

After a bit, his emotions back in order, Brand hunkered down beside the blazing fire, forced to sit a good distance away to avoid being scorched.

Dawg stretched out at his side.

For a time Brand stared into the flames.

"Dawg, you should have seen the commotion." He didn't know if he meant the runaway horses or the reaction to his rescue of Sybil.

"Miss Sybil just stood there as if frozen." He'd seen her eyes. Expected the fear he saw. But there was something more—a watchfulness that surprised him. There was something intriguing about the golden miss.

He dug his fingers into Dawg's fur. "Could be it's because she's such a fine looking woman that I can hardly keep my eyes off her." But his gut said it was more than that. Something that made him consider turning his back on the facts of his life and living recklessly free for a few days, just so he could enjoy spending time with her.

He reminded his gut that to do so would put her in danger. Association with a Duggan—even one not involved in the unsavory exploits of the gang—would sully her name.

Trouble with his gut was it never listened to reason.

How mortifying to be pressed so intimately close to a complete stranger. A big, strong, deep-voiced stranger. Sybil had struggled with trying to decide if she should swoon or fight, when in truth she didn't care to do either. What she'd been tempted to do was so strange, so foreign, she wondered if she'd momentarily taken leave of her senses. She wanted to look into his face and memorize every detail.

Surely her reactions were confused because of the thudding stampede of horses she felt certain would run over her.

She and Mercy had joined the cowboys crowded against the heavy rail fence cheering for the man riding the wild horse. She hadn't felt like cheering. Instead, she'd shuddered as the animal bucked and twisted and snorted in an attempt to dislodge the man on his back. How did he stay glued to the saddle? And didn't all that jolting hurt every bone in his body? Here was a man who thrived on danger. Yet, as she watched him clinging to the back of the wild horse, something tickled her insides. Excitement? Fear? Admiration? She couldn't find words to describe it. And she fancied herself a writer!

The horse had stopped bucking and stood quivering as the big man brushed his hand along its neck and murmured words she couldn't hear, but that stirred her deep inside.

Then a crack as loud as a gunshot had jolted through the air.

A dozen horses had crowded against a split gate. It swayed and then crashed to the ground. The sound of hoofbeats thundered. Frightened horses squealed. The animals were a blur of wild eyes and flying manes.

Sybil had taken a step back, her mouth dry. The noise boomed inside her chest. Dust clogged her nostrils. Uncertain which way to flee, she'd frozen in fear at the melee.

And then she'd been swept off her feet. Rescued from the screaming horses.

No wonder her heart thudded as if she'd run a mile, and she couldn't look away from his face.

But she could not avoid the truth about how unusual her reaction had been, nor could she face the others until she had herself under control. As soon as she reached the big ranch house she excused herself to go to the room down the hall from the kitchen.

Life in the West was certainly different from the one she'd known back in England.

At the thought of where she'd come from, her tension returned. She sat on the edge of her bed and pressed cool fingers to her hot cheeks. Of course she was upset. Her fear had immobilized her. She would have been trampled to death if the bronc buster hadn't swept her off her feet and pressed her to his chest.

A very broad, comforting chest.

*Sybil, stop it. It doesn't matter if the chest was broad or fat or sweaty or...*

But it wasn't. He smelled of leather and horses and wild grass. A very pleasing blend of aromas.

*That doesn't matter. He means nothing to you and will mean nothing to you. Besides, didn't Eddie say the man would stay only long enough to break some horses? And hadn't Eddie further said the man gave no last name?*

Quite the sort of fellow any woman would do well to avoid.

Not that Sybil Bannerman had any intention of doing otherwise. In her twenty years, she'd had her fill of people being snatched from her life or simply leaving of their own will, breaking off pieces of her heart in the process.

She bent over her knees as painful memories assailed her.

At only twelve years of age, Suzette, her dearest friend in the whole world, had drowned, leaving Sybil, also twelve at the time, lost, afraid and missing a very large portion of her heart.

She'd recovered enough at age sixteen to give her heart to Colin, the preacher's son. They'd spent hours talking of their hopes and plans, and dreaming of a future together. She'd finally found a soul mate to replace Suzette. She had opened her heart to Colin, expecting his attention to grow into a formal courtship. She even dreamed of the frothy white dress she'd wear at their wedding, and considered where they might live. For the first time since Suzette's death she'd felt whole and eager to share her thoughts and dreams.

No one had warned her it was temporary. Colin had never hinted that he'd changed his mind about how he felt about her, but a year after they met he left without a word of explanation. He never wrote or made any effort to keep in touch.

Another slice of her heart was cut off.

Losing her parents to fever a year and a half ago, within a few weeks of each other, had been the final blow.

From now on, she vowed, she would guard her heart, though she had very little of it left.

She sat up. Why was she having this argument with herself? It wasn't as if being rescued by Brand meant anything. As he said, he was simply in the right place at the right time. It made sense that she would feel some type of bond with a man who saved her life. But that's all it was.

Intending to calm herself, she pulled a notebook to her lap, just as Mercy rapped on the door and entered, without waiting for an invitation to do so.

Mercy nodded at the journal. "I'm guessing you're writing all about that handsome cowboy."

Her friends knew she made short notes about each day in her diary. They would never believe she wrote for publication. She'd never told them. Most people she knew didn't think a young woman should have her name mentioned in such a public way.

She didn't mind that as much as knowing most people didn't think a young woman would have anything of value or interest to say. That had been the comment of the only editor she'd been brave enough to speak to, a couple years back.

But surely Mercy would understand. She didn't share the same sense of outrage at women doing different things.

Sybil retrieved papers she'd secreted away earlier. "I'm writing a story."

"Uh-huh."

"Do you remember reading that article written by Ellis West? You know. The one that described the ship's captain from our journey here."

Mercy laughed. "He really made us see the pompous man."

"I'm Ellis West."

Mercy snorted. "Ellis West is a man."

"No. It's a pseudonym I use."

Her friend's eyes widened, then narrowed. "Are you sure?"

Sybil laughed. "Of course I'm sure. Why do you find it so hard to accept?" Was she wrong in thinking Mercy would understand?

"You?" Mercy shook her head. "It just seems so out of character."

"Look at this if you don't believe me." She held out her notes for an article about the life of a cowboy.

Mercy read them through. "You wrote this?"

Sybil sighed. "What does it take to convince you? Remember Mrs. Page on the boat? She's secretary to the editor of a newspaper back East. She saw me writing and asked about it. I showed her what I'd written about the captain. She asked if I had more. I gave her four stories I'd composed, mostly for the fun of it." Though even after the rude rejection by the one editor Sybil had seen, the desire to write just wouldn't leave her. "She took them immediately to the editor, who offered to publish them. I gave him half a dozen stories before I left the ship." They'd been published and she'd sent several more describing the West and the inhabitants of the territory. She expected they might have already appeared in the Toronto paper. The newspapers didn't reach Edendale for several weeks after they appeared back East.

Mercy hugged her. "How exciting."

"The editor has asked me to find a bigger-than-life cowboy and write his story." He'd offered a nice sum of money for such an article.

An idea flared through her head. She'd had recent experience with a bigger-than-life cowboy, a hero, as she'd said. "Brand—best bronc breaker in the country—fits the bill to perfection."

Mercy bounced up and down on the bed. "He's exactly what you need. I say write his story."

"But how am I to get the details of his life?" Sure, Sybil could ask others what they knew. Certainly make her own observations. But the best source was the man himself.

Her skin burned. Her lungs refused to do their job. There was no way she could ever approach this man and ask personal questions. There was something about him that threatened the locks on her heart.

*You're being silly. He is just a man. Observe. Ask questions. That's all you need to do. He doesn't have to know that you're writing something about him.* Besides, she'd learned people were more honest, their answers more raw, if they weren't aware they were being interviewed. And who would suspect a woman of interviewing them for a story, anyway?

She could not let this opportunity pass. Or let her natural reticence—or as Mercy insisted, her fear—get in the way of this story.

"All you have to do is ask him questions. You're very good at that. People seem to trust you." Mercy flung herself back on Sybil's bed. "With good reason. You are a good person."

"It's very kind of you to say so." Sybil listened distractedly as her friend chattered on about whom she'd seen and talked to, and how she meant to pursue certain activities, until Sybil caught the words, *"learn to trick ride."*

She spun around to confront her. "Tell me I didn't hear you say you mean to learn to trick ride."

"Okay. You didn't hear me say that." Mercy grinned.

"Good. Honestly, sometimes you scare me with your rash words and even rasher actions."

Mercy regarded her with a teasing grin. "No more than you worry me with your careful way of living. Sybil, my friend, if you're not cautious you'll end up living a barren life, when there is so much to know and enjoy out here." She waved her arms in a wide circle as if encompassing the world.

"I'd sooner be safe." Sybil hoped Mercy would never learn that barrenness felt better than having your heart shredded. Besides, she experienced lots of adventures through the stories others told her. All without the risk to herself.

Mercy laughed. "And I'd sooner have fun." She draped an arm about Sybil's shoulders and rested her forehead against hers. "We are an odd pair and yet you are my best friend."

"What about Jayne?" Jayne Gardiner Collins had been good friends with her and Mercy for several years…since they'd met at a tea party given by a dowager of London society. Despite their differences in nature, they got along well, and the three of them had crossed the ocean and traveled across most of Canada together. Sybil had allowed herself these friendships, knowing from the start they wouldn't last forever. The three of them would go their separate ways. Some to marriage. Likely they would lose touch. Truth was, Sybil simply kept most of her heart safely protected from the pain she knew she'd experience by allowing any friendship to grow.

"Pshaw." Mercy waved her hand dismissively. "She's no longer any fun. She's only interested in Seth. Honestly, I get tired of 'Seth said this, Seth did that, Seth likes such and such.'"

Sybil giggled. "They're in love. What do you expect?"

Mercy laughed, too. "I'm never going to let her forget she had to shoot him to catch him."

"It was an accident," Sybil protested.

They fell back against the bed, laughing at the memory. "I tried to warn the pair of you that no good would come of shooting a gun."

"And she proved you wrong."

"I guess she did."

"Goes to show you should live a little dangerously once in a while. It's worth the risks."

Mercy left a few minutes later.

Sybil stared at the wall. Could she write Brand's story? Yes, of course she could. The bigger question was could she do it without endangering the carefully constructed walls about her already damaged heart? The man held inherent risks for her, as she'd already discovered by her reaction to being rescued by him.

*Oh, stop fretting about that. You were frightened. Snatched into the arms of a tall, dark stranger. It was an unusual experience. Of course you had an unusual reaction.*

She made up her mind. She'd write the story, keeping her eyes wide-open to both her initial, surprising response and her prior knowledge that he didn't mean to stay. Eddie said the man never did. He was a born wanderer. Forewarned was forearmed. This time, unlike her unfortunate experience with Colin, she knew what to expect.

She pulled out pen and paper and wrote a letter to the publisher.

I have exactly the man for the assignment you've offered. He is a bronc rider, a quiet loner, a strong and mysterious man. Certainly bigger than life in a world that is full of strong, bold men.

She would find ways to get information about him without letting her silly reaction to being rescued cloud her good sense.

# Chapter Two

Her resolve to pursue a story about this man firmly in place, Sybil went to the kitchen.

"Are you sure you weren't hurt?" Linette asked as she bustled about the large room. A big wooden table filled one corner; cupboards and shelves occupied the opposite corner. East windows on either side of the outer door allowed them to enjoy the sunrise as they ate breakfast. Another door opened to a spacious, well-stocked pantry, and a third doorway opened to the hall that led to the rest of the house. Another door, always closed, hid the formal dining room, which Linette refused to use.

Even though she expected a baby in a few months, it didn't slow her down. She never seemed to stop working.

"Frightened is all, but I'm fine now. What can I do to help?"

Mercy sliced carrots into a pot.

Roasting meat filled the room with enough aroma to make Sybil's mouth water. Food certainly tasted better when it came fresh from the garden and when she had a hand in preparing it. Something she'd never done before her arrival at the ranch.

Meeting a man like Brand—big, strong, bold—would

have never happened back in England, either. The men she'd been acquainted with would pale in comparison.

Mercy paused. "That bronc buster is a fine-looking man." She gave Sybil a glance that demanded a response.

"Can't say I really noticed."

Mercy laughed. "Hard to see much with your face smashed against his shirtfront."

"He was fast enough and brave enough to rescue me. I thank God for that." Except she'd forgotten to thank Him and she made up for it on the spot, uttering silent thanks.

"I join in thanking God," Linette said as she poured water from the boiled potatoes, saving it in a jar to use later, when she made bread.

Sybil watched everything Linette did. She'd found so much satisfaction in learning to cook meals, bake bread and cookies, and even preserve garden produce for the approaching winter months. She'd only meant the trip to western Canada as a chance to start over, to rebuild her heart and strengthen the barriers around it, but she'd found so much more. She'd found purpose in doing useful things.

"I regret Mr. Brand refused to come for supper," Linette said. "But I've decided to send supper to him. Eddie said he'd be an hour yet. Would you two take a meal to Mr. Brand?"

"Of course," Mercy said.

Sybil wanted to refuse, because her heart still beat a little too fast as she remembered being held so firmly. But it provided a chance to meet him in a less emotionally packed way and learn about him, so she could write a fine story. "Certainly we'll take a meal to him." No need for her silly reaction to repeat itself. She knew how to control her emotions.

Linette piled a plate high with what looked to Sybil

like enough food to feed a family. She couldn't get used to the amount a working cowboy ate. Linette must have noticed her surprise. She chuckled. "I'm guessing a man who makes his own meals around a campfire would enjoy a home-cooked meal." She wrapped the plate in a cloth and handed the bundle to Sybil.

Sybil and Mercy left the house. They paused at the corrals, where the gate had been repaired and the wild horses had settled down. They asked where they could find Brand, and Eddie directed them to the east. They crossed the yard, the grass beaten down and brown after a summer of wear. What must it be like for Brand to eat and sleep outside as the nights grew colder? Sybil wondered. Any cowboy, not just him.

"You be sure and have a good look at him this time," Mercy said as they climbed the hill and made their way through some trees.

Sybil didn't need to give him a good look. She'd already done that and it had caused her heart to quiver. Instead, she concentrated on their surroundings. Dark pines stood like silent sentries. The golden leaves of the aspens swung to and fro, catching the sunlight in flashing brightness.

A dog growled and Mercy grabbed her arm.

"I don't fancy being torn up by a cross dog," Sybil whispered. "Maybe we should go back."

Mercy looked at the plate of food, then back down the trail.

Maybe she was doing the same as Sybil...measuring how fast they could run and considering if an angry dog would stop for the food if she dropped the plate.

"I know you're there. Come out and make yourself known," Brand called out.

Her fingers clutching the plate so hard the china

would certainly crack at any moment, Sybil ventured forward. "I'll throw the food at the dog if I have to," she murmured to Mercy.

"Good idea."

They stepped into a clearing. Wood smoke shimmered in the air. The smell pinched her nose.

A dog lunged toward them. Quite the ugliest dog she'd ever seen. Dirty brown with snapping black eyes and bared yellowed teeth. Not a big animal, but still a threat to life and limb. Only Brand's hand at the animal's neck restrained him.

Sybil squeaked. At the same time, she considered what sort of man kept such a dog.

"Quiet, Dawg," Brand murmured, his voice so deep it seemed to echo the canine's growl. The animal settled into watchfulness that did nothing to ease Sybil's mind.

She swallowed hard and shifted her attention to the man. His cowboy hat was pulled low so all she saw of his face was a strong jaw and expressionless mouth.

She turned. "Come on, Mercy. No one is going to bite." She faced Brand again. "I assume I am correct in saying that." She indicated his dog, though maybe she meant more. Not that she expected Brand to bite, but he certainly filled the air with danger.

Or maybe it was her own heart calling out the silent warning.

"He won't bother you unless he thinks you're threatening me."

The dog settled back on his haunches and watched them.

Mercy laughed nervously. "And how could we do that? We're two unarmed women." She stepped closer, hesitated when Dawg growled louder, and turned her attention to the animal. "Nice doggie. I won't hurt you."

She put out a hand to touch the ugly dog. It lunged with a growl.

Mercy jerked back and Sybil almost dropped the plate of food.

Brand's large hand gripped the dog by the ruff. "Stay!" He gave a tug and the dog settled.

Sybil's heartbeat hammered erratically.

"Why do you keep such a cross creature?" Mercy asked.

Brand looked at Sybil as he answered, though she could not see his eyes beneath the brim of his hat. "He's my kind of friend."

Again Mercy laughed. "I wonder what that says about you."

Sybil thought the same thing. Judging by his quick, selfless actions that day, Brand deserved better company than a cross dog. But considering how he'd declined Linette's dinner invitation, maybe he preferred it that way. That would make an interesting twist to her story.

"Read it any way you want."

Sybil narrowed her eyes and watched his face for clues.

He met her gaze. Something flickered in his eyes. An emotion she couldn't name. Perhaps he gave consideration to his chosen solitary state.

*Having held a woman in his arms so recently, he longed—*

No. That wasn't what she'd write.

*His isolation had been momentarily disturbed by his quick actions in saving a young woman, but he quickly reverted to his usual state. He and his dog...*

Her thoughts abandoned her as she tried to free herself from his gaze. The way he hid behind his hat, the set of his jaw, even eating at a campfire when he'd been

invited to share a meal said he either welcomed loneliness or it had been imposed upon him for some reason. She studied him as if she might be able to discern
which it was.

He dipped his head.

She drew in a sharp breath. She'd been staring. But
only because she wondered about the reason for his self-
imposed solitary state.

She realized she still held the plate of food. "We
brought you supper. Linette decided if you wouldn't
come to the house for a meal, she'd send you one."

After a moment's consideration of the offer, he nodded toward a stump. "Leave it there."

Despite his dismissive words, his solitary state called
out to Sybil. She stepped past the dog to put the plate
on the stump he indicated. "Do you mind if we visit a
few minutes?" Would she be able to discover the reason for his loneliness? Or perhaps something about his
background?

"Suit yourself. Have a seat. Lots of grass to choose
from, or pull up a log." A smile flitted across his face
so fast she almost missed it.

Sybil's curiosity about the man grew. She sank to
the ground. Mercy sat a few feet away, her gaze never
leaving the dog.

Sybil smiled. At least her friend wouldn't be taking
an inventory of Brand's looks and itemizing them for
her later.

He snatched off his hat as if recalling his manners.

She stared, darted her gaze away. Against her better
judgment, she brought it slowly back. Mercy was right.
He was a fine-looking man, dark and mysterious. Black
curly hair that was over long, deep brown eyes, a slightly
crooked nose…

He met her look for a second. She saw a soul-deep sorrow that sucked at her resolve, diluted it and poured it out on the ground. She sought for reason. Perhaps she was taking her study of him too seriously…imagining how lonely it must be for him. But then, she wasn't him, so how would she know until she asked?

Before she could glance away, he shifted his attention to his dog, which was lying at his side, watching Mercy.

Sybil almost laughed aloud at the way her friend and the canine eyed each other. She'd never before seen this side of Mercy, who was usually adventuresome to the point of recklessness. At least that's how Sybil saw it, although she'd be the first to admit she was conservative in the extreme by comparison.

Still unsettled by what she'd seen in Brand's eyes, she shifted her attention back to him, wondering if she'd imagined it.

He stared at something on the ground at his feet. She looked toward the same spot. All she saw were blades of grass.

"They say you never get bucked off a horse. Is that right?" The question had sprung from her mouth unbidden…but not unwelcome.

He chuckled, cut it off abruptly. Was he not comfortable laughing? "I guess you could say that practice makes perfect."

She smiled at how his answer said so much with so few words. "So you took a lot of spills before you got good at it?" Dawg stopped having a staring contest with Mercy and inched toward Sybil, his head between his paws. Poor thing meant no harm. He was likely as lonesome as his owner.

*There you go again. Jumping to conclusions. You*

*have no way of knowing if he's lonely or just likes to be alone.*

That was part of what she hoped to discover.

"I got tossed off many times."

Remembering how she'd held her breath as he rode a bucking horse, and wondering how he could stand it, Sybil shuddered. Getting tossed off sounded even worse than riding. "Did you ever get hurt?"

Mercy leaned closer, earning her a growl from Dawg. She edged back. "It must be so exciting. I think I'll give it a try."

Sybil gasped. "Mercy, you can't be serious." She fixed a demanding, pleading look on Brand. "Tell her she could get hurt. Tell her it's foolish to think of riding a wild horse." Why did Mercy think she must do something crazy and reckless all the time?

Brand choked slightly, as if keeping back another chuckle. "Ma'am, she's right. It takes a lot of practice and lots of good fortune to survive some of the wild horses. Sure would hate to see your neck all busted up."

Mercy grinned widely. "Still, I just might see how I fare."

"Have you ever been hurt?" The words squeaked from Sybil's throat. A man with a dangerous job. Likely that explained why he was alone. A woman or a friend would face the constant risk of seeing him hurt or killed by one of those angry horses. How many women would accept that kind of life? She certainly wouldn't. She'd marry at some point, because she wanted a home and family, but she'd want security and safety when she did.

And she didn't intend to involve what was left of her heart. Colin had made her see the folly of that.

Brand answered her question. "Nothing serious, seeing as I'm still here and still riding horses."

"But you have been injured?" *Sybil, you don't need to know the particulars to see that this man should wear a big danger sign around his neck.*

Details for her story. That was the only reason she wanted to know.

"A time or two. Once when I was ten."

"Ten! You were hardly out of short pants."

"Ma'am. I never wore short pants. And it was my older brother who thought it was a lark to throw me on a horse he was trying to break. I stuck until the ornery critter stopped bucking."

Another chuckle that he made no attempt to hide. Interesting observation. It would make a nice addition to her story.

*A loner of a man with a deep-throated laugh that broke out unexpectedly from time to time, surprising the cowboy as much as it did those who heard it.*

"I felt so high and mighty about riding a horse my brother couldn't that I climbed to the loft and jumped out the open door."

Mercy laughed as if it was the funniest thing ever.

Sybil gasped. "Why on earth would you do that?"

"I was ten. I didn't need a reason. But I guess I thought riding a wild horse made me invincible."

Sybil laughed softly. "Let me guess. That's when you were injured."

"My brother broke my fall, but I still busted my arm." He held it out and had a good look at it.

Mercy leaned back on her hands, her gaze darting frequently to Dawg.

Sybil's mind raced with questions. How many could she ask before he refused to answer? "What happens when you get bucked off?"

"If I did get bucked off—" he made it sound like a

far-fetched possibility "—I'd just get right back on and finish the job."

His answer pleased her. She liked the idea of a man finishing what he'd begun. Except, she reminded herself firmly, in this case, it meant he would break horses and move on. That's the job he'd begun.

Not that she cared one way or the other.

*You're not telling yourself the truth here, Sybil.*

Oh, hush. Her inner voice could be so annoying at times.

*Annoyingly right, maybe? Because you wish that he'd stay around.*

I do not. How could I wish for anything so foolish? A dangerous man. A leaving man. I'm paying attention only because he saved my life and I want to write a good story.

*You're hiding from the truth.*

Sybil wasn't interested in whatever so-called truth that annoying inner voice meant.

## Chapter Three

Brand had almost forgotten about breaking his arm. But only because he hadn't seen Cyrus in a long time. Cyrus never missed a chance to remind him that he likely owed his life to his big brother, and as a result, his big brother deserved a few favors in return. Trouble was, Brand wasn't prepared to dish out the sort of favors Cyrus had in mind. A sour taste filled his mouth. Because of Cyrus and Pa, Brand could never hope for anything but a nomadic lifestyle.

"Have you ever been hurt riding a horse?" Sybil asked, her voice a melody of calm and sweetness…a marked contrast to his thoughts and the raw sounds he normally heard on a ranch. Her gaze riveted him like velvet nails, compelling him to answer.

"A few bumps and bruises. Nothing to take note of."

Dawg wriggled closer to Sybil. Well, if that didn't beat all. Brand couldn't remember when the animal had shown the least sign of interest in another human being. Dawg could spot a sly fox a mile away. Brand could only assume he could equally well spot a sweet, innocent, woodland miss. Maybe this woman warranted further interest. It wasn't like he would be around long enough to put her in danger. He eyed the plate of food. It would have to wait until the ladies left. If he dug in now, they might see it as time to leave.

"I was about to have coffee. Care to join me?" He had only two cups, but he would drink from a tin can. He filled the cups and passed one to each of the ladies.

Sybil's blue eyes held his.

He couldn't remember how to fill his lungs.

Mercy leaned forward, her expression eager. "You must have seen most of North America."

The question, posed as a comment, broke his momentary lapse and he settled back with his coffee. "Been around some."

"Have you been to the Pacific Ocean?"

"Nope. Never had no mind to see it."

She sighed. "I'd love to see it."

Sybil made a scolding noise. "Mercy is restless. Always looking for the next big adventure."

"Uh-huh." He had little interest in the excitement-craving woman. He picked up a piece of kindling and kept his attention on the rough edges of the wood. "And what are you looking for?" He meant the question for Sybil.

It was only conversation. Words to pass the time. But he raised his eyes enough to watch her from under the protection of his lashes.

Her own eyes darkened to the color of the evening sky and her lips pressed together. A very telling gesture. She wanted something she couldn't have. A man, perhaps? But what foolish man would refuse such a woman anything, including his heart and love? Unless he had the kind of life Brand did. One that didn't allow him to give heart and love to anyone. Sometimes he wondered why God had made him a Duggan. Or more correctly, given him a pa and brother like the ones he had. Seems God could have arranged things just a little better.

"I'm quite happy with my life as it is," she answered after a beat of silence.

She might think it true, but he didn't believe her.

Mercy made an exasperated sound. "Someday, Sybil Bannerman, you'll discover your life is far too safe." She fixed Brand with a daring look. "Sybil lives a very careful life. Never takes risks. Obeys all the rules."

He thought of how his pa and brother lived a lawless life. "Rules have their purpose."

"Thank you." Sybil favored him with a beaming smile. "That's what I'm always telling Mercy."

"Okay. Okay." Mercy tossed her hands in the air. "I agree to a point. But rules should not become chains. There are certain risks and adventures that don't follow rules. It's a crying shame to avoid them."

Brand stared into the fire.

He was a risk. Miss Sybil would do well to avoid him and remember the safety of her rules.

"How much longer will you be here?" Sybil asked, and his heart took off like one of those stampeding horses.

He managed to slow it some. It wasn't as if she asked because she wanted him to stay, he told himself. She was only making polite conversation.

"I'll likely finish up tomorrow, then me and Dawg will move on."

"I enjoyed watching you work today," she said. Did he see admiration in her eyes? And why did it matter? He'd move on before she learned his true identity. Heaven forbid she'd learn it before he left and he'd see the shock and horror in her eyes. Best to change the subject.

"So how long have you ladies been in the country?"

Mercy nudged Sybil and answered his question. "A couple of months. Three of us ventured over. Jayne, the other girl, is Eddie's sister."

"So you've come to visit western Canada? Then you'll go back to your English home?" Unless they had an eye to marriage out here and with the shortage of young women in the country, they wouldn't have any trouble fulfilling such plans.

"Yes," Sybil said.

"No." Mercy shook her head. "Sybil, why would you want to go back? You have nothing left back there." She turned to Brand. "Her parents are dead. She has no other family."

He wanted to stuff a handful of grass in Mercy's mouth at the way her words sent shock waves through her friend's blue eyes.

Sybil tipped up her chin. "It's my home and I have Cousin Celia."

Mercy snorted and lifted a hand in what Brand took as exasperation. "You belong here as much as there. And here is a lot more fun."

Sybil studied her friend, her blue eyes troubled. "Your parents are expecting you to return."

Mercy shrugged. "I doubt they'll miss me."

Sybil shook her head and turned back to Brand. "I'm sorry. We shouldn't argue in front of you. It's none of your concern." Dawg had sidled closer still and she stroked his head in an absentminded way that made Brand wonder if she knew she did it.

Brand expected Dawg to object, growl, move away, slink back to Brand's side. Instead, the dog closed his eyes and looked as content as a baby in a cradle.

Brand realized his mouth had fallen open, and he forced it closed. But his surprise made him stare. Dawg never let anyone but Brand touch him. Not until this moment.

Sybil drained her cup. "Thank you for the coffee and the nice visit. Now we must be on our way." She rose to her feet in a fluid movement that reminded Brand of a deer edging from the forest. "No doubt we'll see you again."

The words were said lightheartedly, but Brand felt the promise and threat of them. Did she want to return and visit? Did she hope he'd extend an invitation? But Sybil didn't meet his eyes, so he couldn't judge her thoughts.

When Mercy scrambled to her feet, Sybil caught her arm and they hurried away.

Dawg whined as they disappeared into the trees.

Brand patted the dog's head. "Never seen you get all sappy about a girl before. Just remember, we aren't staying, so don't get too interested in her."

Words Brand knew he should tattoo on his own brain.

He couldn't stay even if he was tempted. If Pa and Cyrus saw him with Sybil, they wouldn't hesitate to threaten her. Even if they didn't catch up to him, someone would surely remember the wanted poster they'd seen somewhere, and place him as a Duggan. And if she learned his name, she'd be shocked. She'd withdraw. And who could blame her? Might as well move on and save her the trouble of telling him to leave her alone.

People would judge a person as guilty by association.

He'd grown to accept that all he could hope for in this life was to stay ahead of the Duggan gang and avoid the hangman's noose.

Sybil's plans to go immediately to the corrals next morning were cut short when Linette said, "Can you show me how to finish the edges on the baby shawl?"

"Of course." As soon as breakfast was over and the kitchen cleaned, they went to the big room overlooking the ranch.

An hour passed before Sybil could slip away. Mercy had disappeared to some unknown destination, so she was forced to go alone.

Not that she *was* alone. There were cowboys everywhere. Eddie had said they were adequate chaperones anywhere on the ranch.

When she'd first looked out the windows, only two cowboys had been watching Brand work, but now several more gathered round the pen, and another jogged over in a rolling, awkward gait that said riding a horse was more his style.

Sybil found a place along the fence next to a cowboy whose name she couldn't recall. "Is he as good as everyone says?"

"A couple of years ago, I worked on a ranch down in Montana." The man barely glanced at Sybil as he talked, his attention fixed on the activities in the corral. "I heard stories about a dark, nameless man who could break the rankest animal to be found. I wondered at the time if it was a tall tale. One of those stories told around the campfire for entertainment. But I'm beginning to think the story held a lot of truth."

A campfire legend. Sybil liked that and would certainly include it in her story.

Already she chose words to describe it to the readers.

*A man with no name, but a reputation from which legends are born. A man whose strength of character made one instinctively trust him. Whose arms—*

No. She would not say that his arms made one feel safe and secure. She wouldn't even let herself believe it. This man spelled danger to her fragile heart.

But he wasn't staying around, so she didn't have to be concerned. All she had to do was write the story.

She glanced about. Strange that all the hands seemed to have gathered at the corrals this morning. Or perhaps not. Brand would finish up before long and no doubt they all wanted one last glimpse of this legend.

"That's his last horse," one of the men murmured.

"Or so he thinks," replied another, with a soft chuckle accompanying his words.

Sybil's attention kicked into full alert. "What does that mean?" she asked the second man.

He gave a wicked grin. "We found another unbroken horse."

Several of the men snickered and nudged each other.

Something about the way they acted warned her they were up to no good. Her nerves twitched with a mixture of anticipation and concern.

Brand rode the horse he was on to a standstill, then spent several minutes riding the animal around the pen, teaching it to obey the reins and the instructions signaled by the rider's legs.

"That does it." He swung from the saddle and hung a rope over the nearest post. His eyes touched her, making her forget momentarily that they were surrounded by a horde of cowboys.

He shifted his gaze around the circle.

"Where can I find Eddie?" he asked.

Sybil glanced at the assembled crew. Odd that Eddie wasn't with them. Nor the foreman or any of the other cowboys she was familiar with.

Cal answered Brand. "Boss got called away to tend a bull."

"When he returns, tell him he can find me at my campsite." Brand headed for the gate.

"Hang on. There's one more horse to go."

Sybil felt the tension radiating from the cowboys. It trickled up her spine, caused her to curl her fingers until the nails bit into her palm.

Brand stopped, studied the circle of cowboys. "There wasn't another this morning."

Cal chortled. "We found this one 'specially for you."

Only because she watched so carefully did Sybil see the way Brand's shoulders tensed and his breathing paused for a second. Then he emptied his lungs in a slow sigh.

"Special for me, you say? Let me guess. This horse is meaner than a twister, ain't never been rode, and has been known to bite, kick and generally let people know he don't intend to be."

Cal's laugh seemed a little strained despite his obvious glee. "Let's see if you can live up to your reputation. Or are ya scared to get on this horse?"

Brand tipped his hat back and slowly shifted his gaze from cowboy to cowboy. Several of them squirmed.

Then his gaze fell on her. His eyes—the color of warm chocolate—filled with resignation and a loneliness he would no doubt deny, but she felt it clear through to the bottom of her heart. "You don't have to do this," she whispered.

Acknowledgment flickered through his eyes, though he couldn't have heard her. Something shifted in his demeanor. It was as if her inaudible words encouraged him, let him know that not everyone shared Cal's wish to see him tossed into the dust.

"Bring him on." Brand jerked his hat down low, widened his stance and waited.

Three men pulled on ropes to drag in a black horse with white-rimmed eyes. The animal snorted and kicked.

Sybil held her breath.

Again, she whispered, "You don't have to do this."

But Brand never noticed.

Every eye was on that wild stallion. Every man held his breath.

"Throw on a saddle if you can." Brand's voice dared them to fail.

It took an additional two men to get a saddle blanket on the horse and then the saddle. One of them came away limping after a kick from the angry animal.

"Hold him while I get seated." Brand spoke calmly, as if the only uncertainty was the ability of the struggling cowboys to do so.

Sybil's chest hurt from holding her breath as she watched him gingerly arrange himself in the saddle.

"Let him go."

The cowboys released their ropes and raced away, throwing themselves over the fence, then scrambling around to watch the show.

Sybil could not tear her gaze from the big man on the horse. He sat poised and ready. At first the horse simply stood quivering, then it erupted into frenzied movement. It seemed to jerk every which way at the same time. She'd watched Brand buck out a number of horses over the past two days, but nothing like this. Hooves flying toward the sky. Back twisting two different directions at the same time. Head down. Snorting. Blowing. But Brand clung to the gyrating animal.

"He's good," said the cowboy on Sybil's right.

"He ain't done yet," Cal answered, disappointment in his tone.

Then the horse stopped. It stood there quivering.

A murmur of approval circled the crowd.

"He did it," Sybil said.

"Don't think so, not yet."

And then the animal turned and tried to bite its rider. As Brand kicked away from the teeth, the horse suddenly started to buck again.

Brand fought to stay in the saddle.

The horse ran for the fence, ramming him against the boards.

Several cowboys groaned. "That's got to hurt," said one. "Be a wonder if his leg ain't broke."

The horse stampeded along the fence, several times banging Brand's leg into the boards. It bucked. It snorted.

Still he stayed on board.

And Sybil's heart swelled with pride in the man's accomplishments. Brand was far more than a campfire legend. He was the real deal. He could ride. He was a man who stuck to his decisions.

Now, where did that last thought come from? She knew nothing of his actions outside this corral.

*And the feel of his arms about you as he swept you off your feet.*

Nonsense. It didn't mean that much. Just that he'd saved her life and now she felt a special bond, as if she mattered to him.

*Huh. I wonder if he even remembers your name.*

She silenced the inner voice.

The animal trying to toss Brand to the ground finally wearied and stopped bucking.

"I'd say his reputation is well earned," Sybil said, loudly enough for several of the cowboys to hear. This story would be the best one she'd ever written.

*Never once did he reveal a hint of fear as he swung into the saddle. Those watching caught a collective breath and held it, wondering who would win this contest between man and beast.*

Two men jumped forward and took the horse.

Brand slipped off, leaning against the fence.

The cowboys clapped and cheered as he limped away, none louder than Sybil. Without turning, Brand waved his hand in acknowledgment. "Tell the boss he knows where to find me." He made his way across the yard and into the trees toward his campsite.

Sybil watched him leave. He had been hurt, though he hid it admirably.

At that moment, Eddie rode into the midst of the men. "I didn't find any bull needing help."

"Must have been mistaken," Cal murmured.

Eddie glanced around the group, studied the horse now turned into the bigger corral. Several of the men tried to slip away unnoticed. "Wait up."

They ground to a halt.

"Anyone care to tell me what's going on?" Eddie leaned over the saddle horn, looking casual and relaxed. But Sybil certainly wasn't fooled by his posture, and she guessed from the shuffling of booted feet that the cowboys weren't, either.

Slim sat on a horse at the boss's side and looked about ready to give them all a good chewing out.

Eddie's gaze settled on Cal. "You sent me on a wild-goose chase. I'd like to know why. And why is that stallion in the corrals? Haven't I told you all to leave him alone? He's a man killer."

Eddie's answer confirmed her suspicion that the cowboys were all involved in this potentially dangerous challenge. She glanced to where she'd last seen Brand. How badly had he been hurt?

Cal stepped forward. "We just wanted to see how good a rider he was. After all," he said, growing bold, "you can't just take his word for it."

Eddie studied Cal long enough that the younger man squirmed. "Did he ride the stallion?"

"To a standstill," one of the others answered, when Cal hesitated.

"Then he deserves his reputation."

A murmur of agreement came from the group.

Eddie continued to study Cal. "You can shovel manure for the next month. With no help."

Without another word, the boss reined away and rode to the big house.

Sybil hid a grin at the disgruntled look on Cal's face.

*Not even a wicked man killer of a horse could unseat this big, bold bronc buster. The cowboy rode the rank horse to a standstill...*

Her gaze found the path where Brand had disappeared. He'd done his best to hide his pain, but she knew he'd been hurt. Did anyone care?


Brand waited at the campfire for Eddie to appear with the money he'd earned. Then he'd be on his way.

He sucked in a deep blast of air and rubbed his leg. That mean sucker of a horse had had murder in mind. Seeing as he hadn't succeeded in bucking Brand off so he could trample him, he'd meant to try and knock him off. Had banged his leg good and hard against the fence. It hurt some, but it wasn't anything he couldn't live with.

He gingerly stretched out his leg and leaned back, smiling up at the brilliant sky. He kind of enjoyed the way Sybil had watched him and clapped when he rode the horse. He snorted and pulled his hat over his eyes. No point in looking at blue skies and dreaming of possibilities.

He could never be anything more than Brand, the bronc buster.

Enough staring into nothing. Time to get something to eat. From his meager supplies he chose a can of beans and opened it. Opened a second can for Dawg.

He downed the beans cold, chasing them with hot coffee.

His thoughts wandered again to a golden gal whose blue eyes smiled so gently at him he could almost believe she cared. But how could she? She knew nothing of him. Certainly not who he really was. A Duggan. Part of an outlaw family. Even if for some reason he stayed, he could never tell her, and lose the memory of that smile.

What would it be like to return home every day to a smiling welcome like that?

Brand Duggan would never know.

His leg pained him. It wasn't broken, but bruised enough to remind him with every move that a horse had almost got the better of him. But the pain paled in light of a deeper pain that never left. Oh, sure, he sometimes managed to ignore it, push it away, pretend it didn't exist, but all his efforts were but a thin scab that could be easily dislodged.

Something about Sybil had done more than dislodge it. Her gentle manner had scrapped away the protective layer, exposing the rawness beneath.

So many things contributed to the wound. Too many to count. Besides, what was the point?

He missed Ma. He missed conversations. Heart-to-heart talks. Teasing and laughing. He missed a warm bed and a hot meal at the end of the day. He missed having a home.

*Home.* The word reverberated through his head, his heart and his soul. A trumpet sound of despair that he couldn't deny.

Something Ma had often said to him sprang into his

mind. *God will always be with us. Always guide us to a safe place. Always. We have to trust Him.*

He'd long ago dismissed the words. He didn't see how God being with them had made any difference. Pa always ended up finding them. Yes, Ma and Brand had always slipped away, hoping to find a place where no one knew who they were. At first, Ma had urged Brand along, helping him hide, taking care of finding a place for them. Then Brand had needed no more urging. He'd helped Ma carry their meager possessions. Had sometimes been the one to find them a safe place. He'd often been the first one to hear rumors of robberies, and know Pa and Cyrus were close by and it was time to move on.

Just as he must leave here to stay ahead of the Duggan gang. But what would happen if he stayed a few more days? Not with any idea of putting down roots. No. He knew better than that. Sooner or later, Pa and Cyrus would show up.

But a few hours. A few days. What could it hurt? He wouldn't do anything rash, like attempt to court Sybil, simply enjoy a moment of her company here and there. Shoot, he'd be content to watch her from a distance. Then he'd leave, with his heart full of memories to last him a lifetime.

Memories. Nothing but memories. The word screamed through his brain, tearing a wide, aching, oozing path.

"Isn't like I have any reason to stay," he muttered to Dawg, who replied with a yawn. "Don't see anyone throwing out the welcome mat."

Brand rubbed his aching leg. At least this pain would abate and he'd soon forget it. Unlike the emotional pain.

Dawg bolted to his feet, hackles up, growling.

"I hear it." Hoofbeats thudded. Someone approaching

the camp. Brand's skin prickled as it always did when he knew someone watched him. His hand crept toward his gun belt and rested on the grip of his pistol. Had his identity been discovered? Did someone seek the five-hundred-dollar reward for the capture, dead or alive, of any of the Duggan gang?

Friend or foe. He'd give his last nickel to never again have to wonder which it was every time a stranger approached. At least he didn't have to worry about whether or not he could trust a friend. He hadn't allowed himself one in a very long time.

Eddie rode into sight and air eased from Brand's lungs.

He pushed to his feet. His leg protested the change in position, but he straightened it and waited as the rancher swung from his horse.

He'd get his wages and be on his way. And if his insides twisted at the thought, he wouldn't acknowledge it. Nope. He'd move on. Forget those he left.

This time would prove more challenging than simply waving goodbye to a bunch of cowboys who spoke no more words than necessary, and would forget him as quickly as he forgot them. This time he would turn his back on a pretty young lady who had momentarily—and not of her choosing—rested in his arms.

Eddie stood before him, a grin on his face. "Got some good news for you."

Brand nodded. Only good news he could think of was the Duggan gang had disappeared into Mexico. As if it would really make a difference.

"I ran into Sam Stone today."

"Uh-huh." Whoever Sam Stone was.

"He runs the OK Ranch to the north of us."

"Oh, yeah." Still didn't make any difference to Brand.

"I finished breaking the horses. Some will need a bit more handling, but they're all fit to ride. So I'll be moving on."

"Wait until you hear what I have to offer."

He waited. As if he had any choice. Eddie seemed set to drag his news out as long as possible.

"Sam sold me a herd of wild horses. Said he didn't have time or a man to deal with them." The rancher rolled back on his heels, as pleased with his announcement as any man Brand had seen. "I want you to stay on and break them for me."

Brand's shoulders jerked up. His spine pressed against his skin. Stay? Wasn't it exactly what he'd wanted? A few more days of watching Sybil. Of storing up memories. His muscles tensed at the risks it involved.

How long had it been since he'd last seen Pa and Cyrus? Longer than usual. Come to think of it, he hadn't heard mention of the Duggan gang since he'd crossed the border into Canada.

A grin crept around his heart and eased toward his mouth. Could it be that the Duggan gang didn't care to meet up with the Mounties? No doubt they'd heard the tales of how tenacious the mounted police were. How they always got their man. The grin grabbed his mouth and Brand allowed his lips to curl just a little. Maybe he could be free of them if he stayed in Canada. Even as he allowed the hope, he knew he couldn't trust it. At least not for long.

"I could stay around a few more days, I guess." His casual words disguised his eagerness.

"You're welcome to bunk with the others and eat at the cookhouse. Cookie makes a fine meal."

"I don't doubt it." He'd breathed in the rich aromas

every day from the cookhouse's open windows. "But Dawg here ain't very friendly."

Right on cue, Dawg snarled at Eddie.

"He sure isn't. I wouldn't tolerate him biting anyone at the ranch."

"Never known him to bite. Mostly he threatens." Brand must make sure Eddie didn't encourage anyone to challenge Dawg. "Figure he'd only bite if he thought someone meant to harm me."

The rancher nodded. "Good enough. I'll expect you in the morning then. You want your wages for what you've already done?"

"I'll pick them up when I'm finished." No need to get them now. When he was done he'd go to town and buy some supplies and a warm winter coat. He'd plumb wore out his last one and given it to Dawg to use for a bed. Dawg had chewed it to pieces and they'd left the remnants behind a few months ago.

Eddie mounted up and rode away. And Brand allowed the waiting smile to claim his mouth. "Well, don't that beat all?"

Dawg whined, studied him with head tilted to one side.

"It's only for a short time. Then we'll be gone." A few more days wouldn't compromise their safety or Sybil's, but no point in explaining that to Dawg.

Brand settled back on the ground and smiled up at the sky. Ma's words seeped into his soul. God had led him to a safe place. Though he understood it was only temporary.

His leg twitched and he rubbed it.

How long would this place be safe?

Not long enough.

## Chapter Four

Sybil's heart bucked and twisted like one of those wild horses. As if Brand meant to tame her heart, too. She shook her head. How silly. She lived a careful life that didn't need any taming. Brand filled the qualifications of a larger-than-life cowboy for her story. That was all. But she failed to still the furious pounding of her heart at having just seen him ride a rank horse, stand up to the challenge of the cowboys, and walk away as if he felt no pain. She knew otherwise and it concerned her. Would his pride and isolation cause him to neglect an injury?

She crossed to Jayne's house and knocked on the door.

"Did you see that?" she asked when Jayne called for her to enter.

"I've been busy making a shirt for Seth." Her friend held up the brown fabric. "It's proving a bit of a challenge." She let the cloth fall to her lap, and turned her attention to Sybil. "What's going on?"

"Brand rode a horse Eddie had forbidden any of them to ride." She filled in the details.

Jayne's eyes widened in horror. "Was he injured?"

"He was limping."

"Don't you think someone should check on him and make sure he's okay?" She narrowed her eyes at Sybil.

"Me?" She wanted to know he was okay, but surely someone else could take care of that. Her boundaries already felt threatened. She pulled the gates to her heart closed so she would be safe.

"Seems to me you're the one who should. Mercy says he likes you."

Why would Jayne say such a thing? Had Mercy been dreaming up stuff again? Brand had certainly never given any indication that he even noticed her. Oh, he might have let his gaze linger a bit long on her while he'd considered riding that awful horse. Simply because she was the only one to offer any sympathy at the challenge thrown before him.

"His dog might like me," she finally said. She'd petted Dawg without any growling from the animal. "It's hardly the same thing." Sybil pretended a great interest in the view from the window as her cheeks burned with—

What? It wasn't embarrassment. She had done nothing for which she should be embarrassed, except grow overly curious about a man who did not belong in her world.

Which, she reasoned, made him a perfect candidate as the hero in her story. Just not the perfect man to fill her head with all sorts of unfamiliar feelings and a thirsty longing to experience firsthand the kind of strength she'd felt when he swept her out of harm's way. She knew a deep sense of emptiness when she watched him, when she thought of him.

Surely, only because she knew a man who allowed himself no last name must be very lonely.

But, she realized, in the awareness of his loneliness

there was an answering echo of loneliness in her own heart.

Of course she was lonely. Her parents were gone. She had no family except elderly Aunt Celia, who cared not whether Sybil was there. Nor did she allow anyone to fill that hollowness.

Certainly Brand couldn't be allowed to intrude into that loneliness. Only God could, and she tried to focus her thoughts on Him alone. *He is my strength and shield. A present help in time of trouble.*

The empty feeling in her heart refused to abate.

But she didn't have to let her confusion get in the way of her common sense. Someone needed to make sure Brand was okay, and if she had to be that person, so be it. She turned to face her watching and waiting friend. "You're right. Someone should check on him. Not because Mercy thinks he might like me. She is always dreaming up mad notions. But because he is alone with no one to care." She'd go with gifts, so she wouldn't wound his pride if he thought revealing an injury was a sign of weakness. "I'll beg some cinnamon buns from Cookie and take Grady with me."

"That's the spirit. Show some spunk. Take life by the horns and hang on. Just like Brand on that horse."

Sybil chuckled even as the words slapped her on the side of the head. Wasn't that exactly what she'd been thinking only moments ago? Only it had been Brand taming her heart. "I could never be like that. I don't want to be." Writing her stories was enough danger for her.

Jayne laughed. "Someday, my dear cautious friend, you will find some reason to step outside your careful boundaries."

Little did Jayne know how wobbly her boundaries were proving to be when she watched Brand and took mental notes. "Not me." She hurried across to the cook-house and explained her request.

"I keep hearing tall tales about the man," Cookie said. "Wish he would come and visit me, but I understand he prefers his own company. He saved your life, though, and for that he has my gratitude." The big woman wrapped some fresh cinnamon rolls in a piece of brown store paper. "You tell him thanks from me and Bertie." Bertie, her husband, helped run the cookhouse.

Sybil took the buns and headed up the hill to the big house to ask Linette to let Grady accompany her.

Linette readily agreed and a few minutes later Sybil and the boy made their way toward the clearing.

Dawg's growl greeted them before they stepped from the trees.

Grady clutched Sybil's hand. "Mercy says he's got a mean dog."

"He won't hurt you." Though he certainly managed to keep most people at bay, she felt no threat from the dog.

Grady refused to take another step even when Dawg's growl became a whine of greeting.

"Come on in," Brand called.

Sybil struggled forward, her progress impeded by having to practically drag a reluctant Grady. Perhaps that was a sign she should stay away from Brand and his campsite. But now that she was here she couldn't retreat, even if she wanted to. Of course she didn't; she wanted to make sure he wasn't injured. She could do that without stepping across any invisible lines she'd drawn for herself.

She entered the clearing.

Brand lounged back on his saddlebags. He made no attempt to rise at her presence.

That alone caused concern. "Are you okay?" she asked.

"Just resting." He tried to hide it, but she heard the strain in his voice.

"Your leg must be injured."

"It's fine."

She studied him a moment, noting how the lines in his face had deepened. Why couldn't he admit he had pain? "I know you're not."

He shrugged. "It's not as if I jumped out of the loft door."

"I saw how the horse rammed you into the fence. I'm certain your leg has been bruised or worse."

"Only a bump. Nothing to be concerned about."

There seemed no point in arguing. "Grady came to say hi." She turned to the boy, who darted a look from Brand to Dawg and back again.

Sybil nudged him.

"Will your dog bite me?"

"I don't know. Let's ask him. Dawg, you gonna bite this boy?"

Dawg gave a wag of his crooked tail.

"Nope. But he's not exactly the friendly sort."

Grady carefully kept Sybil between them as Dawg wriggled closer. The nearer he got, the tighter Grady tucked himself into her other side, as if he hoped to disappear into the fabric of her skirts. She bent to pet the dog, but couldn't with her hands full, so held the brown-paper-wrapped gift out to Brand. "Cookie sent some cinnamon rolls. The best in the country. She says she regrets you never stopped in to see her."

Brand took the package. His long fingers grazed Sybil's knuckles, making her heart buck three times in quick succession.

He sniffed deeply of the aroma. "If they taste half as good as they smell…" He waved for his visitors to sit down.

Grady kept close to Sybil as they settled on a log.

The dog slunk closer to Sybil. She hesitated a second. Was Dawg as cross as Brand led everyone to believe? She had no wish to have her hand torn off. Then she saw the welcome in the animal's eyes and knew she was safe. She stroked the brown head, finding his fur surprisingly silky.

She felt Brand's gaze on her and met it. "He's a nice dog."

Brand's eyes filled with something she could only take as regret.

Did he mind that Dawg accepted her attention? She almost withdrew her hand, but couldn't deny either herself or the dog this comfort. "Eddie wasn't happy about the cowboys bringing in that wild horse."

Brand shrugged. "It happens a lot."

His words burned through her. Did he face this kind of challenge wherever he went? "Young Cal got put on manure shoveling for a month." She laughed softly. "He didn't look too happy about it."

"It's a smelly job."

"You ever had to do it?"

"Shoveled my share of the stuff."

"When? Where?"

"Here and there. Every cowboy has to do it."

She'd hoped for more explanation but he didn't offer any.

"What's the hardest job you've ever had?"

He stared into the distance. "Burying my ma."

Sybil's thoughts stalled as pain and regret clawed up her limbs. She'd expected him to talk about horses. Instead, he reminded her of her own loss and loneliness, and her chin sank forward. "I'm sorry. It's hard to be without parents."

He didn't answer.

She sucked in air to fill her tight lungs. Was he all alone? Did that explain why he drifted from place to place? Perhaps he sought for belonging. Family. Or home. "Brand, who are you?" The words sprang forth unbidden, but she ached to know.

He grunted and any welcome she might have imagined in his eyes disappeared into a stone-hard look. "Exactly what you see. A cowboy with a horse and a dog."

"But you must have a name besides Brand. You must be more than that."

His eyes grew harder, colder, if that was possible, and she shivered.

He might well have said, "Goodbye, this conversation is over."

She had enough for her story.

*He was known only as Cowboy. He never did give a last name before he rode into the sunset. He didn't welcome any questions about his true identity. But he was the best bronc buster in the territory. A reputation well earned.*

*It began when he was ten...*

But she wasn't satisfied.

He interrupted her thoughts. "You best get the boy back before his folks start looking for him."

She wanted to know what caused the pain she glimpsed before Brand pulled his hat lower. It wasn't from his leg, but a tenacious wound that she suspected went deep and needed tending.

A wound left to fester was dangerous.

She patted Dawg one last time and rose to her feet. "Goodbye. Perhaps we'll meet again."

She took Grady's hand, but faced Brand another moment. "Be sure and take care of your leg." Brand would have to find his own way of healing the deeper wound in his soul. "May God go with you and keep and protect you."

She and Grady left.

Brand would be gone in the morning. She'd never see him again. She wished she'd been able to get more information, but that did not explain the sense of loss she felt.

She had no explanation for that and forbade herself to dwell on it.

Sybil took her time returning to the ranch site. She didn't know whether to kick herself for being so direct with him, or put it down to an honest question that deserved an honest answer.

Grady ran ahead and joined his friend Billy near the foreman's house.

As Sybil passed the cookhouse, Mercy sprang to her side, causing her to jump and press her palm to her chest to calm her heart. "Where did you come from?"

Mercy tucked her hand around Sybil's arm. "Jayne told me what happened and said you'd gone to check on Brand. How is he?"

As evasive as a turtle. But of course, Mercy meant his leg. "Said it hurt some but he'd live."

"You sound disappointed. Did you want to see him hurt?"

The words stung. "Of course not. But I had hoped he'd reveal a bit more about himself."

"Ahh. So it's all about your story?"

"Certainly. What else would it be?"

Mercy drew back and held her hands up. "I thought it might be about the man."

She *had* been thinking of the man, not the story. Not that she'd ever admit so to her friend.

"Did you get up the nerve to ask him questions?"

She had. But it wasn't nerve that prompted her question. Nor was it curiosity. She really wanted to know more about him. As a man. Best if Mercy didn't know that, however. "As soon as I asked him who he was he got all cold and distant."

Mercy grew thoughtful. "He must be running from something or maybe hiding something. Maybe he killed a man and is running from the law." She shrugged. "Or maybe he just doesn't like human company."

Sybil shrugged. "Who knows? And I guess it doesn't matter. He's leaving as soon as Eddie pays him. I'll write a story based on what I have, and that's the end of it."

"I'm sorry."

Sybil had no idea what her friend was sorry about and didn't intend to ask. No doubt Mercy would have more to say than she cared to hear.

*Who are you?* The question ricocheted around the inside of Brand's head.

The words that had pressed against his lips were not the words he could allow himself to utter. He was a man who longed for female company. Even more than that, for someone with whom he could share the ordinary events of his life…even his thoughts.

He shook his head at the crazy notion.

Brand stared at the cold fire. If he meant to stay here he should get some more supplies. But he didn't want to spend too much time in town. He could survive on cold beans. Had done so on more than one occasion, usually because he was trying to make time and not reveal his whereabouts with a fire.

He unwrapped Cookie's cinnamon buns and took a bite of one. It was really good. He ate all three of them.

He should have told Sybil who he was. Who he had to be. A Duggan on the run, hiding his name, hiding from his pa and brother, hiding who he really was on the inside. He couldn't change that fact. All he could do was accept it and be grateful he had been able to stay ahead of the gang.

Once Pa and Cyrus found him they became unstoppable.

How many times had Cyrus slammed him against a wall saying, "You been friends with those uppity people. Guess they must have money hidden in their house. Where is it?"

No matter how many times, or how hard Brand denied such knowledge, Cyrus would not accept it.

"Go back there and find out where they keep their money. We'll be waiting and watching until you do," he would press his face close and growl.

"Cyrus, be nice to your brother," Pa would say. He said the right thing, but he didn't intend to let Brand go, any more than Cyrus did.

"I can't believe you're my brother." Brand had once spat the words at him.

Pa didn't intervene when Cyrus punched Brand in the gut.

Brand had learned to wrap rags around his horse's hooves and find his way out of town in midnight darkness.

The lonesome call of a coyote echoed across the dusky plains, breaking into his memories. Another call came from the opposite direction.

Brand shuffled about. Most days he enjoyed the way the coyotes called to each other, and the yip-yip-yi of their singing, but tonight the sound ached through his insides like an untreated sore, filled with painful loneliness.

Was it loneliness that had driven him to court May? He'd thought her so sweet, a real lady. He tried to recall her face, but saw only blue eyes. No, May's eyes had been brown, like her hair.

They'd met five years ago, when she came into the store where he was buying supplies, in one of the many towns he'd stayed in only long enough to keep ahead of Pa. Brand could barely recall the names of most. This one had been Lost River, Wyoming. She'd asked a few questions and got vague answers, just enough for her to guess he was alone and unsure of the future. She'd invited him to join her and her family for church and then dinner afterward, shared with her parents, a widowed aunt and a sullen younger brother. Following the meal, they'd played board games.

It was the best Sunday Brand had known since his mother died.

Sundays with May's family became a regular occurrence, as did Saturday afternoon outings. He and May spent time with her family. Sometimes they walked along the edge of town on their own.

He hadn't seen Pa and Cyrus since Ma's death, and let his guard down, thinking now Ma was gone they had no use for him.

Then he saw their names in a newspaper story. They'd robbed a bank, shot an innocent woman in the ensuing gunfight. A half-page poster accompanied the story. Duggan Gang Wanted. $500 Reward. Dead or Alive.

The ink had smudged, so it was impossible to see

their likeness clearly, and no one looked at Brand with suspicion.

But he decided to tell May the truth. He planned the moment carefully. Saturday afternoon they walked to a secluded spot just out of town, where he could hope for privacy.

"That's my pa and brother," he said, knowing no other way to say it.

"Who?"

"The Duggan gang."

She'd laughed. "Don't be silly."

He laughed, too, though out of nervousness, not mirth. "I've never been part of the gang."

"Of course you haven't." She'd given him a playful push.

"How do you feel about being associated with a Duggan?" He waited, unable to pull in a satisfying breath. Then, overcome with a need to make her see it could be okay, he poured out a gush of words. "Ma and me always ran from them, but they've forgotten about me since my ma died. They'd never harm you. I wouldn't let them." He had no idea how he planned to protect her. In hindsight he knew he had deluded himself into believing they wouldn't come after him.

She'd stared at him, her eyes wide as she accepted the truth. "A Duggan. An outlaw gang."

"Not me. I've never robbed a soul." Surely she couldn't believe otherwise.

She backed away.

When he followed, she held up her hands. Her face twisted. "How dare you? What will happen if people associate my name with yours? A Duggan." She spat the word out as if it burned her tongue.

She flung about and returned to the road.

He went after her. "May, wait." He had to make her understand.

She kept walking. "Go away. I never want to see you again."

He ground to a halt. Again his life had been shattered by the Duggan name. It was a curse.

He'd returned to his job, but three days later knew he had to move on. As he saddled up, a bunch of rowdies rode into town. He'd glanced up in time to see Pa and Cyrus leading a half dozen hard-looking men.

They had come. They would always come. They would find him. Even in Canada. Brand had no doubt of it. And if he had a lick of sense he would leave now. Before they showed up. Before they put Sybil in danger. Before he had to face the same cold dismissal he'd seen in May's face.

Dawg lifted his head and growled.

Brand calmed him with a touch.

Hard voices murmured through the aspen. Hoofbeats thudded. Two horses, if he didn't miss his guess. Had the reward money brought someone to his camp? He reached for his pistol.

The sounds grew closer. He got a glimpse of two horses and riders through the leaves.

His fingers tensed on his gun. Dead or alive meant bounty hunters would just as soon shoot him as tie him up. Less trouble that way.

The trail turned. So did the riders. Not until he could no longer hear them did his grip on the gun relax.

His heartbeat slowed to normal.

How long could he stay without putting himself in danger? Worse, putting Sybil and the others in danger from the Duggan gang?

But he'd told Eddie he would break the horses, and he

meant to keep his word, though it wasn't horses, Eddie or his honor that made him ignore his common sense.

It was the hope of seeing a golden-haired girl again that made him ignore all the reasons for leaving that normally proved enough to spur him on his way.

Dare he allow himself to hope Pa and Cyrus had forgotten about him?

He laughed at such high hopes.

# *Chapter Five*

The next morning, Sybil made her customary notes in her journal, then tucked her writing pad and pencil into the deep pocket of her dress designed expressly to hide them, and left the house. She meant to walk a little distance from the buildings and find a quiet, secluded place to work on the story of the nameless cowboy. Only he wasn't exactly that. He was Brand.

But who else was he?

Her thoughts darted back and forth among the bits and pieces of information she'd gleaned. How much could she embellish to give the impression of strength and honor she sensed in him before her story grew more fanciful than actual?

So lost was she in her contemplations, she didn't realize a man worked with a horse in the corral until she reached the bunkhouse, where she had an unobstructed view.

Her feet stuttered to a stop, matching her stuttering heartbeat.

Was that Brand? She knew the answer even before the bucking horse brought him around to face her.

His head jerked back. Their gazes collided with such

force she gasped and pressed both palms to her chest as if she could stop the frantic surging of her heart.

Why had he come back?

Her mind raced with a thousand possibilities, all of which ended in one question. Had he come back to tell her who he was?

The horse bucked again and Brand turned away.

She blinked back her surprise. She must move on before anyone wondered why she stood in the middle of the yard staring in Brand's direction.

Sybil hurried onward until she found a private spot and sat down, pressing her back to the sunlit poplar. She lifted the backs of her hands to her overheated cheeks and slowed her breathing to normal. Why did she feel such a peculiar leap in the depths of her heart at his return?

She shook away her stumbling confusion. Time to forget uncertainties and get to work. She pulled out her notebook and pencil and turned to the page where she had been arranging notes on Brand's story. "Who are you, Brand?" she wrote.

After thirty minutes or so all she'd put on the page besides that question were a series of doodles—circles that went round and round. Exactly how she felt as her thoughts returned again and again to the cowboy in the corrals. Why had he returned?

*And why does it matter to you?*

Only because I feel like it's an answer to a prayer if he changed his mind about being a nameless, rootless cowboy.

*And why would that matter to you?*

Annoying, persistent voice.

Because.

*Yes?*

She closed the notebook and put it in her pocket before she answered. Because it gives me a chance to learn more about him for my story.

*Oh yes. The story. The one you haven't added a word to in half an hour of sitting here.*

"I will." She silenced the inner voice by speaking aloud. "I just have to learn more about him."

She pushed herself to her feet and dusted off her skirts. She didn't know how long Brand would stay around, but she would find an excuse to visit him and talk to him and get the information she needed to flesh out her story.

Right then she returned to the house to help Linette with kitchen chores. The afternoon sped by as they made pickled beets and filled dozens of jars. The kitchen grew hot and steamy. Sybil's nose stung with the smell of vinegar.

Finally, the bottles of burgundy beets sat in neat rows on the cupboard shelves and Linette rubbed her hands together. "These will be so tasty during the winter months."

Sybil was about to excuse herself when her friend pulled out potatoes for the evening meal. She couldn't leave Linette to prepare supper on her own. They finished just as Eddie and Grady came in. Mercy followed, and they gathered around the big wooden table in the kitchen.

Sybil joined the others for the meal. Would Brand be gone by the time she got a chance to leave the house?

After supper there were dishes. Finally, she dried the last pot and hung the towels to dry. She looked around the kitchen. "I thought I'd go see if Brand is still breaking horses if you don't need me for anything more." She hoped her words sounded casual. As if it didn't matter one way or the other.

Mercy winked at Sybil. "I'll help Linette if she needs anything. You run along."

Sybil ignored her and waited for Linette's reply. "Yes, you run along." And if Linette grinned at Mercy as if they shared a secret, Sybil pretended not to notice.

As she left the house, her gaze went immediately to the corrals. No bucking horses. Was he done, and gone already? She hurried, but not enough to make anyone think she was desperate.

Brand was still there, talking to Buster, the youngest cowboy on the ranch.

Sybil moved to the fence.

"Mister," Buster said, "you know a lot about horses. Maybe you can help me with mine."

"Certainly will if I can." His words were gentle, his tone kind.

Just as she thought—a good man. A good man on the run? She shook her head. She moved closer to catch every word. Listening to this conversation might provide valuable information for her story.

"What seems to be the problem?" Brand asked the young man.

"He always backs away when I try and mount him." Buster hung his head. "Makes me look stupid in front of the others."

Brand clapped a hand to the younger man's shoulder. "Anything else?"

Sybil's throat tightened at the comfort that gesture offered. She'd certainly include that detail.

*Although a loner, perhaps an outcast*—she liked the word for her story, but cringed at using it to describe Brand—*the cowboy never turned his back on those who were weaker, younger, more vulnerable. Whatever had sent him on this lonesome journey, it hadn't destroyed the cowboy's compassion for others.*

Buster pushed his shoulders back at Brand's touch, then continued. "Yeah. When I try and lead him anywhere, he walks too fast, as if he's gonna run over me. Sometimes I get a little nervous."

"Sounds to me like he's trying to find out if you're the boss or not. Bring your horse here and I'll show you what to do."

Buster trotted into the barn and led out a shaggy-haired horse that indeed seemed to be pushing him rather than following.

Brand took the rope from Buster. "You can teach him to follow you by doing this."

He swung the rope in a circle in front of him as he led the horse about. Every time the animal tried to get by him, it encountered the twirling rope.

Sybil stared, mesmerized by the ease with which Brand swung the rope in a lazy loop...the poetry of motion in his limbs.

"Here, you try it." He handed the rope to Buster and let the young cowboy lead the horse.

Brand looked in Sybil's direction, his gaze direct, unblinking.

She'd wondered if he knew she watched, and now wondered if he liked having her there or—she swallowed hard—if he wished she'd leave him be.

Well, that wasn't going to happen. She had a story to write. She girded up her heart with that excuse.

Buster led his horse around the pen and soon the animal decided it was safer behind him than facing the swinging rope.

Brand slowly took his attention from Sybil and she sucked in air to relieve her starving lungs.

"Let's see you get on."

Buster saddled his horse, but when he tried to mount it backed away just as he'd said.

Brand nodded. "Let's try making it so he doesn't want to do that. Grab under his chin and make him back up. When he gets to the fence, bring him forward and do it again. Soon enough he'll decide it's easier to let you get up than to be pushed around."

As Buster followed those instructions, Brand sauntered toward Sybil. He leaned against the fence not four feet away from her.

She took it as invitation to talk. "I was surprised to find you here today."

"Eddie bought some more horses."

"I see." She scratched at a splinter on the fence and pretended her throat hadn't tightened. He'd mentioned only the horses. Of course she wasn't surprised, and certainly not disappointed.

"Look," Buster called. "He didn't back up." The young cowboy sat in his saddle, as pleased as could be. Then he jumped off and led his horse toward Brand. "Mister, you're pretty good with horses. How'd you learn that?"

The question brought Sybil's thoughts back to her purpose for being there—to get information. She watched Brand. He continued to lounge casually against the fence. Only a tightening around his eyes indicated the question struck a nerve.

"My pa was good with horses."

She caught the past tense of the question. "So your pa is dead?"

He hesitated a beat. Two. "Not that I know of."

"That's good." Buster's sad tone was a contrast to his positive words.

Sybil shifted her attention to the young man. "Buster, how old are you?"

"Sixteen, ma'am. Or I will be pretty soon."

He was barely more than a child. "Where are your parents? Why aren't you with them?"

He looked beyond her into the distance. "I left them on a farm in the Dakotas."

"You seem young to be on your own. Why did you leave?"

"They were dead, ma'am. All of them. My ma and pa and two sisters." The words were barely audible, though Sybil caught no hint of self-pity. And he certainly had every right to feel such.

Her heart twisted with knowing how alone he must feel. "I'm so sorry." She looked at Brand. His eyes darkened. His jaw muscles twitched. Compassion filled his gaze. Surely if he chose to be a recluse it wasn't because he hated people. Or even because his dog came first.

What was his secret?

She couldn't believe he was a wanted criminal, as Mercy had suggested. He simply didn't seem the type.

*What do you know about the type? Have you ever met any wanted criminals?*

No, but surely their hearts would be cruel.

*You think him helping Buster means he's got a good heart?*

Yes, of course it does. Besides, I've other evidence, such as his friendship with a dog and how he rescued me.

*Aha. That kind of makes you see him with stars in your eyes, doesn't it?*

Not with stars, but with certainty.

*You're certain to have your heart dashed to pieces if you think it meant anything more than a man in the right place at the right time.*

And willing to do the right thing. That makes him noble, if nothing else.

*But are you ready to risk your heart on that?*

No. She would be detached. A gatherer of information. Nothing more. She'd discover who he was. Criminal or otherwise.

*Everything he did revealed an honorable heart. Those around him wondered how such a decent man had ended up being such a loner. It wasn't because he had no family. Although his mother's death had ripped away a portion of his heart, he talked affectionately of playing with an older brother, and pride filled his deep voice when he told how his father had taught him about breaking horses.*

"You're doing just fine," he said to Buster, and the boy lifted his head and smiled.

"Good evening, ma'am." Buster led his horse away, swinging the rope to keep the animal behind him. Proud and sure of himself now, thanks to Brand's kindness.

Again the question raced through Sybil's mind. Who was this man?

"Did you have supper yet?" Seems he might have eaten with the others at the cookhouse.

"No, ma'am," he said, imitating Buster's formal politeness. "Me and Dawg were about to go to camp and make our supper."

"Why don't I bring you a plate of food instead? Unless you prefer your own cooking."

His laugh sent ripples of joy through her veins.

"About all I got in my pantry is beans."

"Fine. I'll be along shortly with a plate of food." She paused. Maybe she'd misunderstood. "Unless you plan to ask Cookie for a late meal."

"No, ma'am. No such plans." He watched her from under the brim of his cowboy hat.

She tried to read his expression. He revealed nothing. "You could come with me and eat in the kitchen."

He lifted his head. His face remained expressionless. His eyes darted past her to the big house, then to the woods, and finally to her. She saw a world of sorrow and regret that jarred her. Was this the look of a man who had committed a dreadful crime?

No, she couldn't believe it. Any more than she could explain the ache clenching her heart, squeezing out sorrowful tears. She gave herself a mental shake. All this talk about parents had simply reminded her of her loss.

And loneliness.

*You have no reason to make so many assumptions. Sorrow, guilt or innocence all based on the way his eyes darted about and grew dark. The way he and Buster make you think of your parents.*

No reason, she argued, but the witness of my heart to his. I know sorrow when I see it. I recognize it as different than guilt.

Then he blinked. "Me and Dawg will go to our camp, if it's all the same to you." He whistled for the dog, which rose from the shadows of the barn and trotted after his owner.

"I'll bring you a meal," she called.

He didn't turn, but it sounded as if he said, "Suit yourself."

God had given her a second chance with Brand and she didn't intend to waste it.

She dashed up the hill, her feet light. Just before the door, she drew to a halt. What chance did she mean—to learn more about Brand for her story or for her own sake?

Her story, she silently insisted. That's all that mattered.

That and keeping her heart safe. She knew all too well the sorrow of a leaving kind of man.

He should have told her he didn't want a meal brought to him, but he couldn't deny himself a visit from Sybil. He lifted his head as she stepped from the trees, bearing a covered plate, and thankfully saving him from having to analyze why he allowed himself to enjoy her company and ignore the warning of his gut.

Dawg bent his tail to one side—the closest thing to a wag Dawg ever managed.

"I hope there's enough food for you." She handed Brand the plate and removed the cloth.

He bent over and filled his nose with the aroma of hot beef and rich gravy. The mashed potatoes were a small mountain. "Reminds me of the meals my ma used to make." Now where had that come from? Except something more than the food reminded him of Ma. Sharing mealtime with a woman, listening to her talk, were sweet moments he'd tuck next to his heart to warm him throughout the long winter months.

"She sounds like a good woman."

"She was."

"Do you mean because she made good meals?"

He sensed Sybil's probing. It surprised him some to realize he didn't mind. It would be good to talk to someone besides Dawg for a change. Dawg might be a good enough friend but he wasn't much for carrying on a conversation. Brand would simply have to choose his words carefully and not reveal anything that would identify him as a Duggan.

"She was a good cook, all right. Sometimes there

wasn't much in the pantry, but she always managed to find something and make me feel like I was privileged to have it. I guess I was. But she was so much more than that. Do you mind if I go ahead and eat?"

"By all means."

He took three bites and savored the flavors. The break gave him a chance to consider his words. "Ma never let life get her down. She used to say, 'God sends the rains that bring on the flowers.'" He fell silent. The words might sound silly to someone else.

"I like that. So your mother was a believer?"

"To her dying day." She would be disappointed to know Brand had let his faith lag.

"Are you also?"

"A believer? I am, but I don't think about it much anymore."

Sybil turned to consider him with probing blue eyes. The look went deep, knocking at closed doors, examining forbidden corners. "Why have you let it slide?"

He couldn't tell her, and shifted away from her intensity, directing his attention to the plate of food.

She turned, releasing him from her intense study, and he filled his lungs with relief.

"My parents were older when I was born," she said, her voice low as if she was lost in her memories. "They said I was a special gift from heaven, and treated me that way. They taught me my life was precious and I shouldn't waste it on foolishness." She let out a long sigh. "Mercy says I am controlled by rules, but I don't see it that way. I simply realize that life is full of dangers and risks, and yet we can do much to avoid them."

He watched her out of the corner of his eyes. She again seemed lost in thought. If she knew how much danger he posed to her and the others at the ranch, she would run back to the shelter of Eddie's home as fast as her legs would carry her. Likely she'd tell him about Brand, and Eddie would run him off the place.

Not that Brand would blame them. He already felt guilty at putting them in peril.

She nodded once as if she'd made up her mind about something. "I expected to have my parents around for a long time yet. They were only in their sixties when they died, within weeks of each other." She glanced at him, her eyes dark with sorrow. "A fever. I nursed them to the end."

Was she aware that a shiver ran up her body? "I guess it just goes to show we can't count on anyone staying around," she added.

His fingers knotted as he considered his actions, but he went ahead and pressed his hand to her forearm. "I'm sorry. It must have been very difficult."

She nodded again, slowly turning to look into his face. Her eyes glistened with tears. "It was the hardest thing I've ever dealt with." One tear slipped from each eye. "So I understand when you say burying your mother was the hardest thing you've done."

If only he had the right to pull Sybil into his arms and comfort her. If only he could ever have the right. But being a Duggan made it impossible for eternity...a thought that scalded his insides.

She gave him a watery smile. "It's almost two years ago. You'd think I would be past the crying stage."

He lowered his hands to his knees and shifted his attention to Dawg. "Maybe there are things we should never get over." Like being a Duggan.

"Over and over my father and mother instructed me on the importance of obedience to God and living a wise life. I simply can't imagine leaving the faith of my parents." She blinked back her tears and squinted hard at him. "I can't envision what would cause anyone to neglect their faith. Was it something really awful? Was it because your mother died?"

He shifted his attention to Dawg again, unable to reply to her question because he didn't know the answer. It was a thousand little things and two major things—his brother and father. Finally, he shrugged. "Just happens, I guess."

"Then I shall pray it unhappens." She practically glowed, as if she imagined it had already occurred.

He allowed her words and her faith to warm him for two heartbeats before he gave himself a mental shake. What she thought or wanted or believed would not change the facts of his life.

He cleaned the plate and handed it back to her. "Thanks for the meal." He couldn't bring himself to tell her she'd best be going, but she must have sensed his unspoken words. Her expression flattened and she pushed herself to her feet.

"I'll be getting along." She paused to pat Dawg on the head. "Good night." She sucked back a gust of air and turned to face him. "Brand, I don't know who you are or what you're running from, but remember wherever you go, God goes with you. He loves you and protects you."

Before he could pull a word from his stunned brain, she was gone.

*God loves and protects you.*

Words Ma had said over and over. When had he quit believing them? He sat back and stared into the darkening sky. About the time Ma died. Or maybe when the Duggan gang—in the hopes of getting Brand to find out when the payroll was being delivered—had beat up a young man he had befriended.

Brand had learned two valuable lessons that day. Don't make friends and don't let Cyrus and Pa catch up to him.

So why was he still here?

Only a few more days and he would ride out as fast as his horse could go.

He hadn't prayed much in many years, but tonight he asked one favor of God. *Please don't let them find me while I'm here, where my presence could put Sybil in danger.*

Did God love him enough to hear the prayer?

## Chapter Six

Sybil had gone to the corrals twice the following day, but Brand barely glanced her way. She told herself she wasn't disappointed. Of course he was busy. She knew that and appreciated his dedication to his job.

When he disappeared at suppertime, she prepared a plate of food again. At least he'd never refused to eat.

Yesterday she had learned wonderful things about him. He'd had a faithful Christian mother. The way he talked about her revealed a tender side. Something or someone had wounded that tender spot.

Sybil slowed her steps to savor the memory of the previous evening. She couldn't explain why she'd told him about losing her parents, but she didn't regret it. Not for a moment, because he'd touched her arm in comfort. His eyes had softened as she shed a few tears. She had almost expected him to pull her close and pat her back.

Maybe *expected* was too strong a word. She'd wished for it.

Now she could hardly wait to learn more about him.

He stood as she stepped into the clearing and handed him the plate.

"Go ahead and eat. You must be starving."

"I shouldn't be. I've eaten better the last few days than I have in months."

She waited until he sat and then chose a spot beside him, careful not to touch him lest he think her too bold.

"You worked hard today."

"Lots of horses to break," he said.

"Guess you're in a hurry to finish up and move on."

He seemed preoccupied with his food, but after a moment said, "It's what I do."

She didn't detect so much as a whiff of regret. Not that she was surprised. She'd known from the start he meant to leave. She expected it. People left. One way or another. Suzette by death. Colin by choice. Afterward Sybil could only do her best to put the pieces of her heart back together. It had never quite been whole again, so she hardened the fences around her heart now, not intending to let anyone hurt her.

"My parents weren't the only ones I lost." She didn't mean to talk about it, but the words escaped and once started, she couldn't stop. "I had a dear friend, Suzette. I knew her from as early as I can remember. We were so close." Sybil held up two fingers pressed together to indicate what she meant. Her breath jerked out and in again before she continued. "We liked to play in the bushes, making playrooms in little spaces beneath the branches." She tipped her head back as sweet memories filled her thoughts. "We had all sorts of babies. Real dolls but also pretend babies we made out of knots of wood." A tiny laugh escaped her lips. "The gardener made a swing for us at the bottom of the yard. My, we spent many happy hours on that swing. The seat was wide enough that we could sit side by side and swing together."

"Sounds nice."

She had stopped talking as she recalled the warmth

and joy of those days. "It was real nice, but it ended so fast. I wish I could have stopped time before that dreadful day."

He waited, not rushing her to tell what had happened, as if he understood she could hardly bring herself to say the words.

"One day she didn't come to play as usual and Mother took me to my room. She pulled me down beside her and held me close as she told me Suzette had drowned while on an outing with her family." Sybil shook her head. "To this day I can hardly believe it."

Brand squeezed her hand gently.

She held on for dear life.

"How old was she?"

"We were both twelve."

His hand clasped hers, warm, solid, reassuring. "So young. I'm sorry for your loss."

The tension in her body slowly dissolved. "I haven't let myself think of her or talk about her since she died."

"Aren't you robbing yourself of happy memories by doing that?"

Sybil turned to look into his face.

His eyes were filled with warmth. "It seems a shame to throw out the good with the sad."

She looked deep into them, finding nothing but kindness. Something inside her shifted…a sense of being released. She sat back, stared at Dawg lying at her feet. A truth hit. "All this time I was so afraid of the pain I felt at her loss that I've buried my memories." A smile filled her heart. "I miss her terribly and always will, but my childhood was rich because of Suzette. She was full of life." Sybil told him many stories of two little girls with vivid imaginations. The games they'd played and adventures they'd had without leaving home.

Brand didn't say much, but she didn't need a lot of encouragement to continue.

Dawg stretched, turned around and settled at Sybil's feet.

She grew quiet. She'd talked for so long. How could she be so selfish and thoughtless? She'd never learn anything about him if she did all the talking. And she still held his hand, as if her life depended on it. She slipped it to her lap. "I'm sorry. I've talked about me this whole time."

"I don't mind. I'm sure your life is more interesting than mine."

"What makes you say that?"

"You lived a privileged life with all sorts of advantages."

She turned to look at him. "You make that sound like it somehow makes me different."

"It is different than my upbringing." His eyes were curtained, letting her see nothing of what he thought. "It allowed you to cross the ocean in the company of other fine women."

"Humph. Since my parents' death I've been living with my elderly aunt Celia. She's old and set in her ways. She doesn't like the curtains opened, so I spent last winter in gloom." Sybil jerked about to see his reaction. "Do you think that was a joy and privilege?"

His grin was lopsided. "Not when you put it that way."

"How did you spend last winter?" There were so many things she wanted to know about him.

"Holed up in a remote cabin on my own with Dawg."

"Sounds lonely. What did you do to pass the days?"

"I hunted game to feed us, chopped wood to keep us warm and twice ventured out to the nearest town for supplies. A man gets to crave coffee when he's been out of it for almost two weeks."

She laughed. "What I miss most about life in the West is having a grocer close enough to go every day. I could hardly believe it when I first came. But between the big gardens and generous storerooms, the ranch has its own grocer."

He joined her in laughing. "From the little I've seen this is one of the best run ranches in the territory."

"Eddie is determined it will be the best."

They sank into silence again.

"Tell me about your dog."

Brand chuckled, the sound filling her insides with pleasure at getting him to laugh. "Found him beside a trail a couple years back. Don't know if he was lost or forgotten, but his paws were raw from walking."

Dawg lifted his head and looked toward Brand as if knowing the man talked about him. His tail bent in one direction.

"I suppose he was glad to see you."

Brand laughed again. "You'd think he might be, but even then Dawg had a bad attitude. He tried to bite me."

Sybil wanted to know more. "What did you do?"

His eyebrows lifted in silent question.

"To befriend him," she added.

"Nothing. I just made camp and cooked a meal. Guess Dawg was hungry because he soon sidled toward me. Eventually he decided it was okay to be friends. Of a sort."

Sybil studied the dog. "He's not as ugly as I first judged him, but he certainly isn't a thing of beauty, either."

They sat in peaceful contentment for a moment. She'd learned much about him.

*Cowboy understood how to approach wounded and frightened people and animals alike. He never pushed, never expected anything in return for the help he offered.*

She realized the same patient technique that caused Dawg to judge Brand a safe friend had worked on Sybil, too. When had she ever talked so much about herself? About Suzette? But perhaps her openness would make it easier for him to speak honestly.

"Brand, tell me more about your mother."

"Why?"

She shrugged. "I heard pride and affection in your voice when you spoke of her."

"I was proud of her. Still am. She lived by high standards despite our circumstances. She did sewing to support us. I went to bed many nights with her sitting by the table, the lamp close as she sewed."

"And your pa?"

"Nothing to say about my pa."

Before she could ask the question on her lips, Brand added, "Or my brother."

She didn't press. She squeezed his hand gently and quickly withdrew before he could think her inappropriate. "I'm sorry. Whatever happened, it has hurt you deeply."

He neither acknowledged nor denied it.

She sought for something to bring back the peace she'd felt talking to him about Suzette, something to offer the same understanding he'd offered her.

"Nothing can separate us from God's love." She waited, hoping he would acknowledge her words. When he didn't, she added, "Unless we let it."

"I guess that's so."

"You make it sound like it doesn't matter. But it does."

"My ma would agree." He hung his hands over his knees and stared at them.

Sybil couldn't bring herself to say anything more for fear of adding to his dejection. Besides, it was time she returned to the house. She rose to her feet. Dawg stood, too, as if expecting to go with her. She patted him on the head, then brushed her hand across Brand's shoulder. "God is our refuge and strength, a very present help in trouble. Therefore will we not fear, though the earth be removed and though the mountains be carried into the midst of the sea." She hadn't meant to preach to him, but the words had come of their own accord. She would pray they would comfort him, whatever the cause of his discouragement.

Brand left his camp early the next day, and made his way toward the ranch. Why had Eddie bought so many wild horses? Could be he meant to sell them at a profit. But even putting in long hours, Brand wouldn't be able to leave for several more days.

A fact that should make him nervous, but failed to do so. And why shouldn't he enjoy a few days of visiting with Sybil? He'd succeeded in revealing nothing that put either of them at risk. She'd never know his pa and brother were wanted men.

Brand might not be a praying man, but his heart murmured one prayer over and over. *Please don't let Pa and Cyrus find me here. Let me get done and leave before that can happen.*

The tree before him made him think of Sybil's story of two little girls playing on a swing. It would be a perfect tree for a swing.

He reached the corrals and roped the first horse of the day. Of necessity, he must keep his mind on his task or end up facedown in the dirt. Ruining not only his clothes, but also his reputation as the bronc rider who never got thrown off. But he still found space in his thoughts to replay every word Sybil had spoken the night before. As the day progressed a plan evolved.

Partway through the morning, Sybil stepped to the fence and watched him. He nodded once in her direction, then forced himself to concentrate. Although he tried to ignore her, he knew the moment she stepped away. She and the other ladies went to the garden with baskets that they soon filled with vegetables. Then they returned to their various houses.

Only one other time did he see her, on the hill beside the ranch house, throwing out a bucket of water.

It was late afternoon when he turned loose the horse he'd finished working on. But rather than catch another, he went to the barn. With Eddie's permission, he cut a board the size he wanted and chose a length of rope, then made his way to the tree he'd noticed in the morning. In a few minutes, he had a swing hanging from a branch.

He returned to where he could see the ranch house, and waited, hoping Sybil would come down to the corrals before suppertime. He halter broke a horse as he waited. Fifteen minutes later, she trotted down the hill.

He slipped the halter from the horse and turned it loose. This one time he would think about something besides work. Though he could never stop thinking about the Duggan gang. During the passing hours he'd convinced himself he would surely hear rumors of them long before they could reach this area of western Canada. Their reputation had a way of preceding them. He'd have time to ride away before they found him.

He was hanging the halter over a post to take care

of later when he saw her approach the fence. "Howdy," he said.

"Hello." She glanced about the pen. "Are you done for the day?"

Did she sound surprised or pleased? It didn't matter. "I have something to show you."

Her eyes lit up, bright blue. "Really?"

"Yup." He vaulted over the fence. "Come and see." She kept close to his side as they crossed the yard. His grin grew to rival the sky for size.

"Where are we going?"

"You'll see." He slowed, smiled even wider when she matched his steps. How was he going to surprise her when she'd be able to see the swing as soon as they passed Seth's cabin? Only one way. Would she agree? "I need you to close your eyes."

"Why?"

"It's a surprise."

"All right." She closed her eyes.

He swallowed hard. She looked as if she waited for a kiss. Every nerve in his body sent up a red flare. She was very kissable, but not by him. She was out of his class. She deserved better than he could ever offer her—a life on the run. Most importantly, if she discovered his identity, her eyes would snap open and fill with fear and loathing.

Nope. He'd sooner leave with memories kept sweet by hiding the truth.

"What direction am I to go?"

Her question brought him back to his purpose. "Straight ahead."

She took one step and stopped, her hands before her. "I might stumble."

He wiped his palms against his trousers and ignored

the red flares of warning as he took her hand. "I'll show you the way. Trust me." His heart slammed against his ribs. Ironic assurance from a man hiding the truth.

But she rested her hand in his, following his lead without hesitation until they were within ten feet of the swing.

"Open your eyes."

She did, looking at him, her gaze so full of sweet expectation that something within him wrenched, a fierce sensation of both pleasure and pain.

He forced himself to break away from her look, and nodded toward the swing.

She looked and gasped. "Where did that come from?"

"I made it for you." He sounded too keen. "I thought of how you enjoyed swinging with Suzette, and thought you might still enjoy swinging even if your friend can't be with you." Did his explanation make him seem less eager? He didn't think so.

She clasped her hands to her chest and laughed. "A swing." Her eyes were awash with tears.

Had he made her cry? The thought slammed into him. "I thought you'd like it. I can take it down if you want."

She caught his hand. "No. It's perfect. I'm surprised and pleased that you would think to do this." She rose on tiptoe and kissed his chin. "Thank you."

Pink stained her cheeks and she rushed away to try out the swing.

Heat flooded up his neck and stung his ears. If he'd known she'd be this grateful, he might have thought twice about putting the swing up. Shoot. Who was he kidding? He didn't mind in the least. One more stolen memory. Based on hiding the truth.

What would she say if he told her he was a Duggan?

Would she laugh and say it didn't matter? Or would she look shocked and refuse to speak to him?

He couldn't risk it.

Sybil laughed, a sound of pure joy to rival the sweetest of the bird songs he often enjoyed on lonely evenings.

"I'd forgotten how much I like this." She swung back and forth. Each time she did, their gazes collided.

Every lonely night, every cold morning alone, every goodbye rolled and twisted at the bottom of his stomach. Each glance from her tempted the feelings upward, as if they wanted release. He fought them back. He fought his own longings and wishes. He almost lost when she tipped her head back and let her laughter roll out in time with the movement of the swing.

A soft laugh came from his lips. He leaned back on his heels and savored the moment. The memory of this evening would have to suffice for the rest of his life.

Thor, the fawn that hung around the place, trotted toward him. Dawg growled, but at Brand's command backed away and sat down.

The fawn saw Sybil swinging and jumped away in playful surprise, then chased her back and forth.

Soon Sybil laughed so hard she had to stop swinging.

The sound of their play attracted Billy and Grady, the two young boys who spent time together.

"A swing," Grady said. "Who built it?"

"I did," Brand replied.

Billy looked him up and down. "I thought you broke horses."

Sybil chortled. "I guess a man can do more than one thing." The look she gave him slid right past his brain and oozed into his heart like warm syrup.

Billy nodded. "I guess so. We used to have a swing."

Sybil sobered. Her eyes dipped downward.

Brand tried to think why, but couldn't.

She got off the swing. "Do you boys want to have a turn?"

Grady hurried to get on.

For the next half hour, Brand and Sybil took turns pushing each boy on the swing, at the same time teaching them how to pump so they could make themselves go high.

As the boys grew more confident, Sybil and Brand sat nearby to watch.

"Did you wonder why Billy said he used to have a swing?" She told him how Billy and his brother and two sisters had been left orphaned. "Roper and Cassie found them and cared for them and later adopted them." The foreman and his wife lived in a new house on the Eden Valley Ranch.

"It's nice to know things work out well for some children." Brand managed to keep his voice from showing any regret that he had not been so fortunate. But it hadn't been so bad. He'd had a mother who cared for him, prayed for him and protected him to the best of her ability.

"Supper!" The call came from up the hill on one side and within seconds echoed from Roper's house.

"Coming," the children called, and scampered away.

"I have to go, too." Sybil smiled at Brand. "You're welcome to join us for a meal."

He hesitated a heartbeat, then shook his head. He had already crossed too many of his boundaries. "I'll be going."

Her smile lingered. "I can't thank you enough for the swing. It will provide hours of pleasure not only for me but for the others." She brushed her hand over his arm. "Brand, you're a good man." Then she turned and skipped toward the ranch house.

He stared after her, his heart swelling until it crowded against his ribs. She'd said he was a good man. Then he snorted. *Brand, it don't matter whether or not you're a good man. You are a Duggan.*

Five hundred dollars. Dead or alive.

Sooner or later someone around here would see a wanted poster. Then what?

Someone would come gunning for him. But worse, far worse, he'd put Sybil in the way of danger simply by allowing a friendship between them. Danger from the Duggans. Danger from bounty hunters.

Would she believe him guilty?

Perhaps he would come right out and tell her who he was. How would she react?

He slapped his forehead. It was bad enough that he sat about expecting a woman to feed him. But now he'd crossed a line, thinking he could get away with admitting he was a Duggan. No one would believe him innocent, and just being associated with him put Sybil at risk. Cyrus wouldn't hesitate to harass or threaten her simply to get at Brand.

He knew what he must do. He returned to his campsite, saddled his horse, threw his saddlebags on the back and swung up. "Come on, Dawg." He clamped his teeth together so hard his whole head hurt. But a man must do what a man must do.

This time he didn't leave solely to protect himself from the noose. He left to protect Sybil from the Duggan gang.

## Chapter Seven

Sybil did her best to hide her pleasure throughout the meal. If she gave it free rein she would smile from ear to ear and doubtless bring probing questions from her friends.

She stilled her impatience as they lingered over the meal and then did dishes at what seemed a leisurely pace.

All the while, her heart danced. Brand had made a swing for her. A sweet gesture that healed a deep fracture in her heart. As he'd said, she had been robbing herself of sweet memories because of the sadness when they came to an end. Every time she sat on the swing she would remember the joy of her friendship with Suzette.

And something more—a growing friendship with Brand.

*What about your vow to never get close to someone again?*

I haven't forgotten.

*Seems you might be getting a little too fond of a certain cowboy. Have you forgotten Colin?*

Of course not. I don't plan to be hurt again.

But she couldn't stop the smile that wrapped around her heart.

"I'll take a plate of food to Brand if you like," she told Linette, keeping her voice flat, as if it didn't matter if someone else took it.

"I do wish that man would either join us or go to the cookhouse," Linette said. "It bothers me to think of him spending every meal by himself."

Mercy snorted. "He's had company every evening since he got here. Sybil sees to that."

Sybil couldn't take offense at her friend's comment, because it was true. "Do you want to take the food to him tonight? I have no objection." After all, as her inner voice had reminded her, she didn't intend to get too fond of the man.

"I'll let you do it."

Mercy waited as Sybil filled a plate and covered it, then accompanied her down the hill. Seems Brand would have two women visiting him tonight.

Not that Sybil had any objection. Only she didn't quite convince herself of the truth of those words.

"I suppose you've been learning lots about our mysterious cowboy," Mercy said. "Where's he from? Where does he plan to go? What's his name? I can hardly wait to read your story. Will you let me read it before you send it?"

"I'm still working on it. He isn't too eager to reveal details." And yet she felt she'd learned so much about him. His caring mother, his Christian upbringing, his tenderness and consideration. "He built a swing." She pointed to it.

Mercy gave a low whistle. "The children are going to enjoy that." She shook her head. "Seems a strange thing for him to do. Kind of out of character."

"I guess it depends on how you judge his character."

"I see him as a tough loner, likely with a dark secret

that drives him." She turned to squint at Sybil. "Are you softening the man?"

Sybil widened her eyes. "I don't know what you mean." But the idea pleased her.

Mercy laughed and patted Sybil's hand. "You go soften him up some more. Maybe you can convince him to settle down. I'll see you later." She turned toward Jayne's cabin and Sybil continued onward.

She stepped into the clearing and looked to where he usually sat. "Brand?"

She swept her gaze around the clearing. No dishes. No Dawg. No Brand. Nothing. She bent over the ashes. Cold as creek rocks. She straightened. "Brand?"

His name echoed

"Brand, where are you?" She crossed the clearing and pushed through the trees to another opening that allowed her a good view to the north and west. Nothing moved except the leaves, the birds and the grass.

She retraced her steps. Surely she'd missed something to indicate where he was. She poked through the flattened grass and parted the nearby branches.

Finally she sank to the ground and faced the truth.

He was gone.

Her heart shuddered.

Not a word of goodbye.

How could it be? Less than two hours ago they had shared a special moment. Why, she'd even dared kiss his cheek.

Was that it? Did he find her too bold? Did he not want affection?

A calming thought intruded into her shock. Maybe he'd decided to join the others at the bunkhouse.

Maybe—a grin exploded on her face—maybe her

sign of affection had persuaded him to abandon his re-
clusive ways.

She jumped to her feet, grabbed the plate, which she'd
momentarily forgotten, and raced toward the ranch.

She passed Jayne's cabin and skidded to halt. Sybil
could hardly rush up to the bunkhouse and ask if Brand
was there. She spied Eddie talking to Slim by the corrals. She shifted direction and went toward them, standing back and waiting for a chance to talk to Eddie alone.

"Okay, boss." Slim tipped his hat toward Sybil as
he left.

"Do you need something?" Eddie said.

"I took a plate of food out to Brand."

Eddie studied the still full plate. "I take it he wasn't
hungry."

"Uh…" Wasn't this where Eddie said Brand had eaten
at the cookhouse? "He wasn't there. I thought—" She
glanced toward the bunkhouse. "Maybe he joined the
others."

"No. I'm sure Slim would have said so if he did. However, he can't have gone far. He still has horses to break
and he hasn't picked up his pay. Maybe he's gone hunting."

"I suppose." But she didn't believe it. Why would he
take every belonging if he'd only gone hunting?

She scraped the food off the plate into the cat dish
outside the barn, and half a dozen cats raced over to
enjoy the meal Brand had missed. Mercy was likely still
visiting Jayne, but Sybil didn't want to talk to anyone,
and she slipped into the big house. She tiptoed past the
living room so as not to attract Linette's attention. She
passed the library full of books, a big desk and several
reading chairs without even glancing in, and crossed the
kitchen to her room, where she wilted at the edge of the

bed. Despite all her fine talk to the contrary, she had let herself care too much.

When would she ever learn to guard her heart?

Dawg followed Brand, but as they put distance between them and the ranch, the dog stopped, turned back and whined.

"Yeah, I hear ya. She made me want to stay longer, too, but we just can't." He faced forward. *Gotta keep moving. Gotta keep ahead of the Duggans.*

As he rode into the afternoon sun he repeated the same words over and over. But every few minutes, other thoughts intruded.

Thoughts of a golden-haired miss whose blue eyes smiled so gently at him he could almost believe she cared. But how could she? She knew nothing of him. Certainly not who he really was. Even if for some reason he stayed, he could never tell her and lose the memory of that smile.

What would it be like to return home every day to a smiling welcome?

Brand Duggan would never know.

He found a spot with a rock cliff at his back. It wasn't a bad place as far as campsites went. He'd had worse. Tomorrow he would ride to the west, find a place deep in the mountains to hole up for the winter.

But tonight his bones ached for something more comfortable than a campsite. He ached for a place of warmth and welcome and belonging.

He shot two rabbits and dressed them, burying the entrails a few feet away, then put the rabbits on a spit to roast. A little later, he ate one and gave the other to Dawg.

He missed Ma.

*Home.* He dare not dream of a home of his own, shared with—

He hadn't cried for a home since the first week after he'd buried his ma. And he never let himself look back and wish for things that couldn't be his.

But tonight the ache would not leave.

Ma's oft spoken words sprang into his mind. *God will always be with us. Always guide us to a safe place. Always. We have to trust Him.*

Tonight the words wouldn't be dismissed.

He finally fell into a troubled sleep in which Pa and Cyrus chased cowboys from the ranch, while Brand tried to ride his horse through the crowd to someone beyond them. He couldn't see who it was, but terror filled him at the thought of being unable to get to the person.

He yelled at his pa to get out of the way, and his voice jerked him awake. He sat up and rubbed his face. Sweat beaded his forehead even in the cool night air.

He reached for Dawg. Found the spot empty. "Dawg?"

His senses kicked into full alert and he grabbed for his pistol. A scream rent the air and raised the hair on the back of his neck. A cougar.

"Dawg!" he bellowed. Had the fool dog gone after the animal? Dawg loved to torment cats of every size.

Brand scrambled to his feet and jammed on his boots. He grabbed up a smoldering log and trotted toward the sound, his gun ready.

A deep growl came from the dark. "Dawg, you dumb dog. Get back here."

Brand rushed onward, struggling to see with the help of the glowing hunk of wood. Despite his hurry he didn't take any chances. He didn't want to feel the sharp claws of a mountain lion tearing him apart.

Then Dawg yelped. An awful sound that tore at Brand's heart.

He fired into the air overhead, hoping to scare off the wildcat. "Dawg, where are you?"

A whimper drew him in the right direction. In three more steps he saw the dog lying in a heap, his side torn by the mountain lion. Brand held his gun at the ready, shone his light in every direction, but saw no sign of the animal. He rushed to Dawg's side and bent over him. He was torn up bad. "How many times have I told you not to chase animals bigger than you?" Had the smell of the rabbits drawn the animal? Brand should have been more careful about disposing of the remains, but thoughts of Sybil and home had made him careless. Now Dawg had paid for it.

The dog whined and tried to lick Brand's hand.

"You just lie still. I'll take care of you." He gingerly picked up his pet and carried him back to the campsite. He threw more wood on the fire until flames licked upward. Surely it would be enough to scare off any wild beasts that might be attracted to the smell of blood, and there was blood everywhere. "You got yourself tore up real good, didn't you?"

He warmed water and tried to clean the dog. "You're going to need stitching back together." He couldn't do it alone. Dawg might be smart and cooperative and lots of other thing, but he'd react to being sewed up. He'd likely fight or bite or both.

"Don't ya dare die on me." He studied the sky. How long until morning? It was impossible to tell.

He made some strong coffee, drank two cupfuls so hot it burned his tongue. Tried to get Dawg to lap a bit of water, and waited for morning.

Then he would do what he must do.

\* \* \*

Sunday morning arrived with late summer warmth, which did nothing to ease the cold tension wrapping about Sybil's heart. She slipped out of the house just as the eastern sky flared with pink and orange and purple. She caught her breath at the beauty, then turned her steps toward Brand's campsite. No, she didn't hope he had returned. She wasn't foolish enough to harbor empty dreams. But she needed time to adjust her thinking. She'd made a mistake by opening her heart to another man. Hadn't she learned from Colin to be more cautious?

She certainly had learned this time. This lesson would not have to be repeated for it to sink into her heart.

She sat with her back against a tree and stared at the cold ashes of Brand's campfire. Eddie expected him back to finish breaking horses and get his pay, but she didn't think he'd return. No, she thought he meant to ride away and never look back. She'd known it all along and expected it, so she had no reason to feel torn and empty inside.

It was for the best. Now she could write his story and then forget him.

She wouldn't ever forget him. Despite the knowledge that he was a man without a home who lived a life of danger—someone she would do well to avoid—she had only to close her eyes to see him. His strong features, his strong hands, his—

Oh. What was wrong with her? She knew nothing about him. Not even his name. He was only a hero in a story she continued to work on. She'd brought a copy of her notes with her and bent over the pages. Soon she'd have the story ready to send to the editor.

It didn't matter that there were so many unanswered

questions in her mind. The story was good without those answers, even though she ached for more.

A sound of horse hooves startled her from her thoughts. She glanced to the right.

"Brand!" She bolted to her feet. "You've come back." Her heart threatened to explode. Her feet wanted to dance. So much for all her fine thoughts.

She sucked in a hard breath and pushed a boulder over her errant emotions. Her heart was locked solidly. Nothing would induce her to open it.

Brand didn't even bother with a hello. "It's Dawg."

She strained forward at hearing the agony in his voice.

"He's been hurt." Brand dipped his head toward the animal cradled in his arms.

Sybil tucked her notes in her pocket and rushed forward. Five feet away she saw the matted blood on Dawg's side. "What happened?"

"He figured he could take on a cougar. Dawg ain't too bright at times."

"How can you say that? Poor doggie. You were just being brave, weren't you?" She closed the distance between them and reached to pat the dog's head, then hesitated, not sure where she could touch him without hurting him.

Dawg whined.

"How bad is he?"

"Bad. I need help with him. You're the only person he's ever let touch him except for me. I thought…"

She swallowed hard. "I'll do what I can to help, but I've never done anything with an injured animal."

"You figure Eddie will let me put him in the barn?"

"Of course he will. You go on ahead. Don't wait for me. I'll get there as fast as I can."

But Brand stayed at her side as she turned toward

the ranch buildings. Knowing Dawg needed immediate attention, she lifted her skirts and trotted toward the barn, pushing open the door so Brand could duck his head and ride in.

Slim stood before a workbench in dark pants and a light brown shirt, his hair slicked back, reminding Sybil it was Sunday and people at the ranch were preparing for the church service. "Is Eddie about?" She hadn't seen him on the way toward the barn.

"Last I seen of him he was taking feed to the pigs."

Even on Sunday, a day of rest, the animals had to be fed.

Slim's attention riveted on Brand. "Can I do something for you?"

"Dawg is hurt. If you could let me use a stall to doctor him up, I'd be grateful."

Slim nodded, but didn't make a move toward the dog. Like the others on the ranch, he'd learned to keep his distance. "Far pen is clean and empty. Help yourself. I'll let the boss know."

"Thanks."

Sybil followed the horse and rider down the aisle and swung the gate open. Brand slowly dismounted. Dawg growled a protest. "Sorry, old pal, but I gotta do this." He looked about. "I need the saddle blanket for him." He nodded toward the blanket still on the horse's back, beneath a large saddle.

She assumed he meant for her to get it for him, but she had no idea how. "Tell me what to do and I'll get it."

"Take off the saddle."

"I don't know how." Surely that was the weakest thing she'd ever said.

"Reach under and undo the cinch."

Reach under the horse? "He's big."

"He's used to it."

Ignoring the trembling of her insides, she did as Brand directed. She should have followed Mercy's example and learned to do these things for herself.

Slim moseyed to the pen. "Here. Let me."

Gratefully, she stepped back. She couldn't look at Brand. He'd think her useless. But she'd never ridden a horse unless it had been saddled and brought to her. As she considered the fact now, she vowed she would remedy that as soon as she had a chance.

She grabbed the saddle blanket and arranged it on a mound of hay Slim put out.

Brand gingerly lowered Dawg to the bed and knelt beside him.

Slim shook his head. "That don't look good."

Sybil caught her bottom lip between her teeth. It certainly didn't. Dawg had been torn to pieces. It looked as if clotted blood and matted hair was all that kept him together.

"He'll survive." Brand made it sound like an order. "Most of it is only skin deep."

"I'll get the supplies." Slim stepped out and returned in a moment with a box of veterinarian necessities, which he put at Brand's side.

Dawg bared his teeth and growled.

"Sure ain't discouraged his bad attitude." Slim stalked away.

Sybil knelt at Brand's side, resisted an urge to pat his hand. "What do you need me to do?"

"You want to hold him or stitch him?"

She gasped. "You're going to sew him together?"

"Got to." She felt a shudder race up Brand's body. And this time she followed her instincts and pressed her hand to his arm. Later, she would return to her vow to forget him, to remind herself that he was leaving…that he was the sort of person she should avoid if she didn't want her heart torn asunder again.

"You have to do what you can to save him. I'll help." She edged around to Dawg's head. "I'll hold him." She gave Brand an unblinking look. "We can do this."

He nodded. "He ain't gonna like it much, and as Slim said, Dawg's got a bad attitude toward most people."

"He'll be good for me, won't you, Dawg?" She scooted closer, put the animal's head between her knees. "Dawg, I'm here to help," she murmured softly. "So is Brand, but then you know that. I expect it will hurt some." She drew in a steadying breath. "But it's only because we want to help."

Dawg whined.

She cupped her hands over his head. "We're ready."

Dawg flinched as Brand pushed back the matted hair and dabbed away the blood. Then he threaded the needle and held it poised above the wound.

"He ain't gonna like it."

Sybil leaned over the animal. "Dawg, you can't fight."

"Don't put your face so close. What if he bites?"

She jerked back, her eyes widening in shock.

"I'm just saying he's a dog with an anger problem, and what I'm about to do is gonna hurt." Brand's jaw clenched and he began his task.

Dawg yelped. He snarled. He fought. He tried to free his head so he could stop Brand, but Sybil held him tight.

Brand pressed his knees to Dawg's paws to immobilize them, and continued the job.

"It's okay," Sybil crooned over and over, not certain if the words were meant for Dawg, her or Brand.

Brand paused and wiped his forehead on his shirt-sleeve. He threaded the needle again, clenched his jaw so tight the muscle corded and continued sewing.

Sybil's arms began to ache from restraining the dog. Her vision blurred several times as she saw how much pain it caused the animal. She bit back a cry and had to turn away when she observed the agony on Brand's face.

Finally he finished and put everything away before he fell back on his heels.

Sybil collapsed against the wall as Brand stroked Dawg's head.

"I'm all done, old pal." He raised weary eyes to her. "I just hope it's good enough."

"You did your best."

"Thanks for your help."

She nodded, her heart bursting with so many things she couldn't even name them. Sorrow at the pain Dawg had endured. Admiration and pity at how Brand had done what was necessary. And a feeling that went deeper than any of that. A sense of having been part of something wonderful with a man who continued to earn her respect with his courage and determination.

The warning bells rang inside her head.

He'd won her admiration, even as he had earned her caution. He'd left once without a word. She knew he'd do it again, but she wouldn't let him take her heart with him when he did.

He met and held her gaze. "You asked what was the hardest thing I ever did. I'd like to change my answer. This was."

Dawg whimpered and they both sprang forward.

"Do you think he would take a drink?" she asked.

"Sure would be good if he did."

"I'll find something." She got stiffly to her feet and went in search of a dish. She found a battered tin bowl on the workbench and stepped outside to dip it in the trough, then took it back to Dawg. As she sat again, she placed it at his muzzle, but he showed no interest.

"Guess he's too exhausted at the moment." She set the bowl where he could reach it.

"He's a trooper." Brand sounded weary. "So are you."

She faced him, saw gratitude in his eyes.

His gentle smile curved his mouth and softened the skin around it. "You did real well."

She reached out and squeezed his hand. "You did the hard stuff."

He turned his hand and caught hers. "We did it together."

She couldn't move, couldn't break away from his touch nor end the look between them. It went on and on. Reaching deep corners, touching tender spots, awakening places she'd vowed to guard. She fought to regain control.

Booted footsteps sounded in the aisle and she jerked her hand free and relocked her heart.

Eddie leaned over the gate. "Heard your dog met with some kind of accident."

"A cougar."

"Sorry to hear that." The rancher made it sound like a death sentence.

Sybil immediately sat up taller. "Brand sewed him back together and did a fine job." Her voice carried more assurance than it had a few minutes ago, but Brand wasn't ready to give up on Dawg and neither was she.

"Linette sent me to say it's time for church," Eddie said. He addressed Sybil, then his gaze went to Brand, as if considering the situation. "You're welcome to join us."

He shook his head. "Thanks all the same, but I'll be staying with Dawg, if that's okay."

Eddie nodded.

Sybil rose and brushed off her skirts. She crossed to the gate, which Eddie held open for her. Then she turned back to the man and his dog. "I'll be back." It was a promise.

He flicked a glance at her in acknowledgment.

As she accompanied Eddie to the house, she made a silent vow.

She'd help Brand with Dawg. But she would not let her barriers down again.

## Chapter Eight

Sybil had to hurry to change her clothes, now stained with dirt and blood. It would take a lot of scrubbing and spot removing to make the dress wearable again. She pulled a clean frock on and brushed her hair into submission, then rushed out to join the others as they made their way to the cookhouse, where church was held.

She found a seat beside Mercy and glanced around. The place was crowded. As usual, Ward and Grace and her little sister, Belle, joined them. Ward had once worked for Eden Valley Ranch, but moved to his own place after he married Grace. Ward's mother accompanied them. She had her own house on their ranch.

Jayne and Seth came across the road. Cassie, Roper and their four children joined them from the foreman's house.

Sybil adjusted her skirts and settled into a more comfortable position as Cookie rose to lead the singing. And then her husband, Bertie, spoke. Sybil had learned to appreciate his homespun talks.

After the service, as they left the cookhouse, she glanced toward the barn, but saw no sign of Brand. She couldn't slip away to see him and Dawg as everyone but the cowboys made their way to the big house, where Linette would soon serve a meal. Sybil helped with the preparations. Then she sat through the leisurely lunch and listened to visiting among old friends.

Over and over her mind skittered to the barn, where Brand and Dawg sat alone. She sought to still her thoughts. It wasn't as if Brand needed anything. Cookie had already sent over a plate of food.

Slim or one of the other cowboys would be about if Brand needed something for Dawg.

No, he certainly didn't need her, and she would do well to stay away from him as much as possible if she meant to guard her heart. But she would allow herself a visit to check on Dawg, and because she had promised to return.

However, after the meal, there were dishes to do. And the usual Sunday afternoon activities, which she normally enjoyed. Only today they seemed to go on and on. Would Brand wonder if she meant to keep her promise?

She gave a mental snort. Most likely he hadn't even paid attention to her words nor noted her absence.

Finally, the guests departed. Linette hid a yawn, then announced she'd have a nap, if no one minded.

"We're perfectly capable of entertaining ourselves," Sybil said. Now she'd be able to slip away to check on Brand. And Dawg, she insisted. "I'm going for a walk."

"I'll join you." Mercy fell in at her side. "Unless you prefer I didn't come along." She nudged Sybil.

"Now, why wouldn't I want your company?" Except her friend was right. She'd hoped to be on her own.

"Oh, I don't know. Maybe because you want to spend time with a certain cowboy."

Mercy was far too perceptive, but Sybil wouldn't give her the satisfaction of letting her know it.

"I wonder what Jayne's doing," Sybil said.

"I expect she's enjoying time with Seth. You're stuck with me."

"I don't mind."

"It's nice of you to say so." Mercy directed their steps away from the ranch house and up the hill, until they could view the road to Edendale. "It's been a long while since we went to town. Do you think we could persuade Linette it's time for a trip?"

"What do you need in town? It seems the ranch has everything you could want."

Mercy sighed. "Not everything." But she didn't elaborate. She stared in the direction of Edendale and sighed again.

Sybil recognized her friend's restlessness. But she didn't share it. "Let's go back."

"Why? There's nothing back there. Everyone has someone to spend the afternoon with."

Sybil tucked her arm around Mercy's and pulled her close. "We have each other." She couldn't leave her friend alone in this mood. "Let's walk along the river." That was one of their favorite pastimes.

Mercy shrugged. "We've done that a hundred times."

"So let's do it a hundred and one."

"Oh, very well."

Sybil knew Mercy agreed only because she could think of nothing else to do. They wandered along the river for a bit.

"This is pleasant." Sybil pointed out the birds in the trees nearby. "They sing so nicely, don't they?"

Mercy shrugged. "They're just birds."

They reached the bridge and saw Seth wave as he headed to the barn.

"He's going to do chores," Sybil said. "Let's go visit Jayne."

Mercy let herself be shepherded toward the cabin.

"Come on in and help me arrange these flowers." Jayne had a basket of golden gaillardia, white daisies and branches with clusters of red berries. She handed Sybil a blue pitcher and Mercy a tall red tin. She had a glass vase. "I love to brighten up the place."

Would the Sunday activities never end? But Sybil tucked away her impatience, chose her flowers carefully and cut the stems in various lengths. She envisioned a full, well-shaped bouquet.

Mercy grabbed an assortment of flowers and branches and stuck them in the tin, then stepped back. "I like it wild and free like that." She moved toward the door. "I'm going to practice my roping. I've got to get it down to a fine art if I'm going to catch a man that way." She laughed merrily as she closed the door behind her.

Sybil stared after her. "You don't think she really means it, do you?"

Jayne shrugged. "I can name at least two cowboys who would willingly let her rope them." She chuckled. "Not that she'd need to."

"I hope she doesn't make a foolish mistake and fall in love unwisely." Sybil paused, then added, "I can see her seeking someone wild and untamed. Wouldn't that make for a fine pair?"

Jayne held a branch of red berries and considered Sybil. "You mean like Brand?"

It was exactly what she thought, but she didn't want to admit it to either herself or her friend.

Jayne didn't wait for her to answer. "He's certainly wild and untamed, but I don't sense any spark between him and Mercy. Not like I do with you."

Sybil pushed her thoughts into submission. "What do you mean? I'd never be interested in someone like him. Why, he never stays in one place."

"He might if he had reason enough."

"He's running from something."

"Probably. But sooner or later, don't people have to stop running? I had to stop running from my fears. You need to stop running from yours. So does he. There comes a time when we need to trust God for those things."

"Me? I'm not running. What on earth do you mean?"

Jayne gave a tender smile. "You run—or maybe hide—from change. You think it's the same as danger."

Sybil drew back, her upper lip stiff. "I left home and crossed the continent to get here. That's a lot of change. And a lot of danger. So you are wrong. So very very wrong."

Jayne shrugged, her smile never fading. "Would you ever consider following a man like Brand into the wilds?"

"No." Her lungs clenched so, she couldn't breathe. She couldn't leave the safety of her life. Certainly not to follow a man who would surely ride away one day and leave her on her own.

Her friend nodded, then leaned forward and caught Sybil's arm. "Don't be so careful you rob yourself of the very thing you seek."

"Of course I won't." She said the words automatically, not sure what Jayne thought she sought. Thankfully, Jayne didn't ask, because Sybil couldn't have answered honestly. Nor could she stop her errant heart from seeing Brand as the answer to the question. Brand riding a rank horse. Brand, his leg hurt, but revealing no pain. Brand building a swing to remind her of the sweetness of time with Suzette. Brand with his injured dog cradled gently in his arms. Brand sewing up the same dog, his jaw clenched as he forced himself to do something very difficult.

"I think he's a man a person could count on." Jayne patted Sybil's arm and returned her attention to arranging her flowers.

She had voiced the very thing Sybil knew was impossible. The only thing she could count on from Brand was that he'd leave.

She took her time finishing her own flower display. Rearranged it several times even after she was satisfied. Fussed with a dry leaf, all the while knowing she did it to keep from hurrying back to the barn to check on Dawg. And Brand.

She wouldn't return. It was best if she didn't. But every time the door opened or the floor squeaked, Brand jerked his head up. Eddie came by twice. Slim brought Brand a cup of coffee and plate of food from the cookhouse. A couple other cowboys he didn't recall the names of stopped at the gate and grunted when Dawg growled at them.

Brand waited until they left to scold Dawg. "You gotta stop scaring everyone away." Guess it was Brand's fault the dog did so. He'd kind of encouraged it. Made it easier to move on if he kept everyone ten feet away.

The door opened and he knew it was Sybil even before Dawg whined in anticipation. Brand's heart took off in a wild leap, like a horse bucking. His nerves tingled. All because her quiet entrance informed him of her presence.

In the few seconds it took for her to reach the pen, he gave himself a serious scolding. Letting anyone get

close to him put them in jeopardy. He would disappear
into the wilds before he brought any danger to Miss
Sybil. He needed to—

But before he could decide what it was he ought to do,
Sybil cracked open the gate and stepped inside.

"How's he doing?" She nodded toward Dawg.

Dawg opened his eyes, but didn't lift his head.

Sybil sank down at the dog's side. "Cookie gave me
some beef broth. It will give Dawg strength." She gently lifted his head and held the tin bowl to his muzzle.

Dawg whined a protest.

"Come on, try it. You'll like it. It will help you."

Brand figured Dawg lapped at the liquid simply to
please Sybil. But four laps was all he managed.

Sybil lowered his head. "Good boy." She stroked him.
"You're doing just fine." She leaned back against the
wall next to Brand, where he sat with his knees drawn
up. "How are you doing?"

"Me?" He almost jolted at her question. "I'm not the
one hurt."

"But he's your dog. I know how fond you are of him."

"He'll survive."

"You're right. He's tough."

Brand chuckled, though he felt no mirth. "He's mean.
Too mean to die."

She patted his hand where he pressed it to his knee.
"You're talking like that because it hurts to think of
him injured."

Brand stiffened. Did she have any idea how her touch
flooded his insides with warmth and something sweet
as honey on fresh bread? But he must resist such notions. "Says who?"

She squeezed his hand, an action that likewise
squeezed his heart until he grew light-headed. "If you

didn't care you wouldn't have come back and sewed him up yourself."

"A man has to take care of his beasts." No way would he admit to deeper feelings. He was Brand. A nameless, homeless cowboy who never showed a speck of emotion. He must maintain the illusion.

She laughed, the sound dancing through him. "You're more than you want people to see."

The truth of her words melted his resolve. How he longed to be more than he could allow. But it was impossible. Nothing would change the fact he was a Duggan.

Female voices came down the aisle.

Sybil glanced up. "That's Jayne and Mercy."

When two women peered over the gate of the pen, Sybil introduced Jayne.

"I heard about your misfortune," Jayne said. "So sorry."

"You'd be the other young lady who recently came from England."

"That's correct."

Mercy gave a teasing grin. "She's already married, though she had to shoot Seth to catch him."

"Mercy, at least tell the truth." Sybil's voice held shock. "I can't get over how you make things seem other than what they are."

Brand swallowed the accusation. Wasn't that exactly what he was doing? She'd be just as shocked to learn the truth he hid.

Mercy wrinkled her nose. "It is the truth, isn't it, Jayne?"

"It's sort of true," Jayne confessed. She fixed Brand with her confident smile. "I did shoot him, though it was an accident."

Brand chuckled. "I think the three of you might put all the young men in the area at risk."

Mercy grinned. "I'd never shoot a man to catch him, but I might rope him." She swung her arm to illustrate. "I've been practicing."

Sybil sighed. "Have you got someone in mind?"

Her friend appeared to study the question. "I've got it under consideration," she finally said.

"I would never stoop to such things." Sybil's voice was filled with caution. "I'm content to let God do the work for me."

Well, that left Brand out—if he'd ever considered he was in. God would not be working out anything, not even an accidental shooting, or a roping. He grinned at his foolish thoughts.

"Sometimes God expects us to do a little work ourselves," Mercy replied.

"Well, I've no intention of shooting a man nor of roping him."

Mercy and Jayne both considered Sybil with determination in their eyes. She shifted and studied a board at the bottom of the gate as if it held important information.

The two other women turned to each other.

"There are equally effective, gentler ways, don't you think?" Jayne said.

"Oh, indeed. Some men are best caught by kindness. You know—" Mercy tipped her head toward the dog "—like helping out in a tough situation."

Sybil bolted to her feet, her cheeks red enough to ignite the hay on the floor. "I'm only…" She lifted her skirts and prepared to depart. But she hesitated at the last moment, as if reconsidering. "I'll be back to check on Dawg."

She accompanied the others down the aisle.

Brand chuckled softly. Seems her friends thought she might be a little interested in him.

He let the notion flit about in his head like a sun-struck bird, then shot it down.

Even if he hadn't been a Duggan, he had nothing to offer a fine woman like Sybil.

"You and me will do just fine together," he told Dawg, who fluttered his eyelids in acknowledgment. Or was it in disagreement? Dawg had made it clear he didn't want to leave the ranch. In fact, if it wasn't so far-fetched, Brand might think Dawg had challenged the cougar so they would be forced to return.

His dog wasn't that stupid.

And Brand wasn't dumb enough, nor reckless enough, to consider staying.

## Chapter Nine

The next few days fell into a sort of pattern. Brand stayed at Dawg's side at night. During the day, he worked on the few horses left to break. If not for Dawg, Brand would have joined the other cowboys at the cookhouse for his meals. Or so he told himself. And tried to believe it.

Well, he might have if it wasn't his habit to stay away from human company as much as possible.

And—he tried to ignore the real reason—if Sybil didn't bring him supper most nights.

He was seven kinds of stupid for looking forward to her visits. Ten kinds of reckless. Should Pa or Cyrus learn of his friendship with her—

It didn't bear thinking about.

But how often did he scan the horizon, searching for any sign of them? Or listen in the hours just before dark for a familiar sound?

Each time he saw nothing, and heard nothing, he let his breath out slowly. Maybe this time they had decided to let him go.

He shook his head. He dare not hope.

The other cowboys had eaten and left the cookhouse.

Eddie and Grady had disappeared inside the house some time ago. Brand waited at Dawg's side, hoping against all reason that Sybil would bring him a meal.

The time passed with all the reluctance of a winter sunrise. Maddeningly slow. Twice footsteps thudded toward the barn, but he knew they weren't hers. Too heavy. He pulled in a breath and held it, sucking back disappointment that some cowboy headed his way with a piled-high plate.

But the footsteps retreated without any offerings, and despite the growing pangs, he heaved a sigh that the cowboy didn't make it to the pen where he sat with Dawg.

And then soft footsteps approached and his heart rate picked up like a racing horse.

She stood at the pen with a plate of hot food. "Sorry I took so long. Grady was upset, because he wants a dog of his own and Eddie hasn't been able to find one, so I promised to make up a story for him."

"Wasn't counting the hours." Just the minutes. Brand took the plate. "Thanks." He tried to concentrate on only the food, but how could he when Sybil sat so close, her fingers stroking Dawg's head? And how could he envy the animal? It wasn't as if he wanted to be all tore up and sewn back together. Though he suspected when he left, his heart would feel exactly like it had been ripped by cougar claws.

Not that the knowledge should slow his departure. The sooner he left, the better. Only Dawg's injuries kept him here. If he told himself that often enough, he might actually believe it.

Sure, Dawg needed a few days to heal, but that wasn't the main reason he stayed.

Something else bounced around in his head. A welcome diversion to the insistence of his brain that he should be planning to leave. "You make up stories?"

She studied him, her eyes wide. "Doesn't everyone? Don't you?"

"Can't say I do." Sure, he sometimes thought of how things might be different. But that was as far as he got. "What sort of story did you make up for Grady?"

She looked away, pink staining her cheeks. "Just a silly little boy's story. It was nothing."

"Tell me."

Slowly, her gaze returned to his. "You'll think me foolish."

"I doubt it. Tell me." He longed to hear her story, hear her voice, enter into her imaginations. He'd love to take a story with him to warm his winter nights.

"Promise you won't laugh."

"Not unless it's funny."

"Once upon a time," she began, her eyes darkening to deepest blue as she held him in her unblinking gaze, "there was a little boy, a big dog and a bird. They lived in a world full of flowers and mountains and rivers."

She spun a tale of a boy who did heroic things, a dog with extraordinary powers and a bird who talked. They encountered challenges. The bird insisted they must obey God even when it was hard. They solved their problems, overcame obstacles, all while helping each other and those around them, and never telling a lie.

"And the boy climbed to the dog's back, the bird perched on his shoulder and they rode into the mountains, where they would encounter more adventures. The end."

Brand blinked. "That was wonderful." His food had grown cold as he listened, and he hurriedly cleaned the plate. "Have you ever considered writing the story down for others? Why, you could probably make a children's book."

Her cheeks darkened. "I couldn't do that."

"Why not? This is a story that both entertains and teaches. It's not the first you've told, is it?"

She shook her head. "I guess I have a vivid imagination."

"Why not share it?"

"No one will publish stories written by a woman."

"Really? That doesn't sound right. Who told you that?"

"An editor." She dropped her gaze to her hands, fluttering in her lap like trapped birds. "He laughed me right out of the office. Besides, my parents wouldn't approve. They said a lady's name should not be public." She brought her gaze to Brand's. "Doesn't God command us to honor our parents?"

His throat tightened at the way her eyes filled with darkness. She wanted this so badly it hurt, but she feared rejection. He caught her fluttering hands. "Things aren't always so easy and simple. Yes, we do well to obey God's rules, but when it comes to man-made rules, they aren't always in our best interests." In Brand's case, obeying his father would be to break God's law.

"Obeying is the surest way to a peaceful life."

He withdrew his hands. "I suspect it is, but life isn't always so neat and orderly. Sometimes, even when we do everything in our power to do what is right, bad things happen anyway."

"I don't mean to imply they won't. It's just…" She rolled her head back and forth, then her expression grew fierce. "I can't bear to think of my stories being mocked because they are written by a woman."

He realized they were back to talking about her writing, when his thoughts had shifted to his situation. "Well, all I can say is it's a shame you don't share your stories."

"I share them with Grady."

"He's a fortunate little boy."

"Not because of my stories. But because Linette and Eddie love him like he was their own."

"I thought he was."

She told him how Grady's father had rejected him when Linette rescued him, after his mother died on the trip across the ocean.

The story ripped through Brand. Why couldn't fathers be what God intended them to be?

Sybil squeezed his hand. "God has provided for him just as He's promised to provide for all of us."

Had Brand's expression revealed something that hinted at his distress over his pa? Was that why she offered comfort? He wanted to argue with her. Demand to know how God had provided for him. But of course God had given him an upright ma. That was all he'd needed. "Some are not as fortunate as Grady."

She nodded, her eyes wide with sorrow. "How sad that you are right."

Did she realize she clung to his hand? That her expression beseeched him to make the world better? He touched her cheek. "Don't let it sadden you. People learn to adjust to a lot of things." He trailed his fingertip to the corner of her mouth and leaned closer.

She stiffened, pulled away. "What a tragic statement about mankind. We learn to adjust to bad things." She sighed deeply. "Life should not be that way."

He jerked his hands to his lap. Had he thought to kiss her? He must be losing his mind.

For certain, he was losing his grip on the reality of his situation. He shoved rock-hard determination into his heart. He could no longer act as if he lived in a make-believe world.

He cleaned his plate and held it out to her. "Thank you for bringing it, and thank Linette for me, please."

Sybil took the plate, studied him for a heartbeat. No doubt saw he'd withdrawn, saw his dismissal. Surely she understood this was no place for a lady, and he was certainly not the kind of company a lady should keep.

With a nod, she got to her feet. "I'll tell her."

As she crossed toward the gate, he almost changed his mind and asked her to stay a little longer.

But that would be downright stupid.

She turned before she shut the gate. "Good night, Brand. Good night, Dawg. Sleep well, both of you."

"Good night," he murmured, hoping he managed to keep all regret from his voice.

He should be saying goodbye.

Sybil slipped past the occupied living room, calling out, "I'm going to bed. Good night, all."

She wondered if Mercy would trot after her, demanding to know why she didn't stop to visit, and probing her with questions about Brand, but after a few minutes, it seemed she wouldn't.

Sybil collapsed on her bed, staring at the ceiling. Brand had suggested she publish her stories. He meant the ones she told Grady. Had her heart not burned within her at his words? To be recognized as the author of the stories she published...to feel free to submit more... well, it filled her stomach with fluttering butterflies. And made her want to laugh. She was both thrilled and frightened at the idea.

Why had she not confessed she'd published stories under the Ellis West name?

She sat up and stared at her feet. Why had she not told him she wanted to write a story about him and submit it for publication?

Would he be so encouraging about her stories if she had? Would he still suggest there were times a person should step outside of safe boundaries?

She shivered—again with both fear and excitement. No doubt Brand followed his own rules. But where had that gotten him? Alone. Nameless. His only friend a dog that barely survived his wounds.

Brand was everything she didn't need or want.

What she needed and wanted was safety, security.... She pressed her lips tight and squeezed her eyes to stop the threatening tears. And the freedom to write and publish her stories under her own name.

At least she'd been able to publish as Ellis West. That was enough, she told herself.

She pulled out her notes and glanced over them. But she had very little to add.

Because, she realized with a start, in her visits to the barn she'd revealed more about herself than she'd discovered about Brand.

Tomorrow she would remedy the situation.

Questions she wanted to ask flitted through her brain, chased by the fact that she needed to be honest with him about her intention of writing his story.

*Why bother telling him?*

Because it feels underhanded to pretend I'm interested for any other reason.

Cough. Cough. *Wouldn't that be a lie?*

She closed her mind to the inner voice. Truth or lie, she wouldn't admit there was any other reason.

Not unless she sought for a way to have her heart fractured into a million pieces. She didn't.

*Why not convince him to stay?*

Huh. I never thought of that.

*Well, think about it. Maybe it's time for him to put his past behind him and face the future.*

The next day her plan seemed even more reasonable, and she grinned at the basin of potatoes she was scrubbing for the meal. The grin clung to the lining of her heart and tickled the corners of her mouth later as she took a plate to Brand, leaving Sam Stone from the nearby OK Ranch visiting with Eddie and the others.

Sybil handed Brand the plate of food, then sat with her back against the wall of the pen. Would he guess she meant to have a serious, and perhaps long, talk with him?

He settled down beside her and began to eat.

She shifted to study him. "Can I ask you something?"

"Don't see how I can stop you. But I don't have to answer."

She'd thought carefully about how to approach the subject. If she came at it indirectly, perhaps he wouldn't resist her questions.

"Don't you get lonely?"

His fist curled against his leg. His heart tightened so each beat hurt as if it squeezed out shards of blood. "I got Dawg."

The twitch of her eyebrows informed him she thought the answer less than adequate.

Brand looked at his plate of food. He looked at Dawg, who rested at his feet. *Lonely?* The word didn't half describe the empty hours, the silent days, the cold nights. Any more than it described the constant pressure at the back of his neck as he watched for the sudden appearance of the Duggan gang. Being alone hurt. But it sure beat having Pa and Cyrus for company.

Brand couldn't continue to ignore Sybil. Her gaze bored into him.

"Something really dreadful must have happened in your life to make you constantly run." She waited, an expectant silence in which his heart strained at its seams.

He could deny it, but knew she wouldn't believe him. "Guess you could say that."

"I'm supposing it's why you won't reveal your surname."

*I'm a no-good Duggan.* His nerves twitched. He'd been here longer than was wise. But he couldn't leave. Not because of the horses. Not because of Dawg. Even though he knew he might have cause to wish he wasn't so foolish, he couldn't tear himself away from her company.

Nor could he tear himself away from the look in her eyes offering hope and so much more.

She smiled so gently it loosened the cruel fist around his heart.

"You could stop running. Confront your past."

"If only I could." He touched her cheek. Soft as a dewy rose petal. Pink as an autumn sunrise. The color no doubt heightened by his bold touch. "You almost persuade me." If anything could change his circumstances he would stay. Forever. Content to be in the circle of her smile.

"I wish it could be more than almost. Think about it, won't you?" And she placed her hand over his, pressing it firmly to her cheek.

"Would it matter to you?"

She lowered her lashes to hide her eyes, then met his gaze, her eyelashes fluttering. "It matters," she whispered. "I pray you'll find what you need."

"For what?"

"To trust God with your past, your present and your future."

A present and a future of enjoying her company? Was it possible? Eddie would give him a job. He'd already offered. And then what? What about Brand's past?

Maybe Pa and Cyrus would forget about him. Maybe they already had. He sighed. Yeah, and maybe winter wouldn't come this year. The sun wouldn't rise in the east. And he could be a free man.

Not going to happen. Not with a wanted poster for the Duggans.

But with winter coming on, could he hope to remain here undetected for a few months? Would God give him a chance at a regular life? But then what?

Maybe he could have only a few weeks, a few months, but wouldn't it be worth it?

"I guess I need to let Dawg rest a few more days." It was all Brand could give her. All he could give himself.

Her eyes flickered, acknowledging that his answer wasn't what she sought. "I pray you will discover you don't need to keep running and hiding." She looked at him with such hope and assurance that his resistance disappeared like a wisp of smoke.

"You are determined to give me hope, aren't you?"

"Yes, I am." She leaned closer. "You deserve it."

He wasn't sure what she thought he deserved. More than was possible, for certain. But her sweet face begged to be kissed. And he lowered his head and caught her lips in a gentle caress.

She sat back and stared at him.

But she couldn't be any more surprised by his actions than he. His pulse took off in a wild gallop. What was there about this woman that unsettled him so much he forgot who he was, what he must do?

Brand fully expected she would rise in her dignified way and make some excuse as to why she must leave. But instead she continued to study him.

"Why did you do that?"

"Do you wish I hadn't?" He didn't regret it for one moment.

"No. But I wonder what it means."

"I don't know for sure, except you make me forget everything I should remember."

Her eyes crinkled in gentle laughter. "I'm hoping you mean that as a good thing."

"It feels right and good at the moment."

She nodded. "For me, too."

His grin widened until he thought his face might crack.

They shifted, sat with their backs to the rough wood of the pen, their shoulders touching, as Dawg snored and snorted on his bed, and Brand finished the temporarily forgotten meal.

"Gonna miss all this good cooking."

"You could enjoy Cookie's meals all winter if you wanted."

He put the empty plate aside and smiled at Sybil. "You make me wish I could. But it's not possible."

"So you keep saying. Why isn't it?" She grabbed his arm. "Why?"

"It's not, and that's all I can say." His heart lay heavy in his chest. If only things could be different.

"I don't understand."

"Sybil—" But before he could voice what he meant to say, the barn door creaked open and sunlight flared into the interior.

"Glad you could stop by." It was Eddie, bringing Mr. Stone to get his horse. Brand had been introduced to the owner of the neighboring ranch earlier, when Mr. Stone dropped by and was invited to join them for supper.

"Thanks for the meal." Sam threw the saddle blanket on his horse, then paused. "Have you heard about the recent robberies? The bank at Fort Macleod was robbed and a farmer north of there reported cash and goods had been taken while he was away from the place. Constable Allen says it's the work of the Duggan gang. He says they could be headed this direction."

Brand jolted forward, listening intently.

"I'll be watchful," Eddie said. "Thanks for the warning."

Sam led his horse out, called a goodbye and rode away.

Eddie came to the pen to check on them. "How's he doing?" He tipped his head toward Dawg.

"Almost good as new," Brand replied. Good enough to travel.

He waited for Eddie to leave, and then, his jaw hard, his voice firm, he said, "I'll be on my way in the morning." He'd collect his wages tonight.

"I hoped you would stop running." Her voice quavered.

"I can't."

"Why? Don't we all have the power to make our own choices?"

"Sounds good and noble. Doesn't always work."

"Why not? Brand, what it is you are running from?"

His gaze jerked to hers. He must deny any reason for running. Even more than that, he must deny any reason for wanting to stay. He'd been foolhardy to linger as long as he had.

"Dawg is a very fine animal, but a man needs more

than a dog." Sybil swallowed hard. "Brand, would you stay if I asked you?"

He scrubbed his lips together. Pulled his gaze toward the wall. He dipped into the reservoir of strength and shook his head. "Don't ask. I can't stay."

"Can't? Or won't?"

"Same thing either way. I'll be heading off in the morning."

She sank to the floor beside his dog and petted him. "What will happen to Dawg?"

"He'll come with me. As you pointed out, he's my only companion."

"You could have more. So much more."

Brand couldn't face the pain and disapproval in her eyes. He ached for what she offered. But the Duggan gang was too close.

If only he could stop running.

But as long as he was a Duggan, he might as well dream of finding gold in his pockets.

Sybil reached for the empty plate. He didn't want her to leave, but what was the point in asking her to stay? Every minute in her company made it that much harder to walk away without a backward look.

Brand saddled his horse at first light. Dawg limped after him, whimpering. "It's okay, old boy. I won't make you walk."

Other cowboys went in and out of the barn, ready to start their day's work. Dawg growled halfheartedly and Brand simply ignored them.

Cal grabbed a saddle, shot him a challenging look. Brand let it slide off him. Always some young buck wanting to prove something. Let him go ahead and prove whatever he thought he must. Brand wouldn't be around to dispute Cal's accomplishments.

He led his horse from the barn, lifted Dawg in front of the saddle and swung up behind him. He pulled the dog close, holding him gently.

He cast one last glance up the hill to the big house. A shadow flickered past a window. Was it Sybil? Just in case, he touched the brim of his hat. *Goodbye, sweet girl. Thanks for trying to get me to stay.*

"I'll show you who's boss." Cal's harsh words drew Brand's attention.

Cal rode a little black gelding Brand had green broke the first day. Only he jerked on the reins, sawed the bit in the horse's mouth. Brand would have called out a warning, but it was too late.

With a wild snort that signaled both pain and protest, the horse lowered his head and gave a back-cracking buck that sent Cal over his head into a mud puddle. His mount snorted and raced to the far corner.

Cal scrambled to his feet. Several cowboys watched him, but Cal zeroed in on Brand. "You." He jabbed his finger in his direction. "You got paid good money to have these horses ready to ride. And this is what we get?" He stomped off.

Brand called to him. "You're not handling the horse right. You're too hard on his mouth."

Cal shook a fist at him and stalked away.

Brand felt the study of the half dozen cowboys. Yes, the horses were ready to ride. But only if handled with a little common sense. However, the black gelding would now think he could unseat any rider.

Band watched the horse trotting around the corral, and considered his options. If he left now, he would surely be out of Pa and Cyrus's reach in a few days.

However, he could not, in good conscience, leave Eddie with a horse that couldn't be ridden. Another day. No more, he vowed.

Would Sybil realize he hadn't left, and pay him a visit?

"I'll take care of that horse," he announced, and returned his horse and dog to the barn.

He spent the morning working with the horse, teaching it to obey him. He positioned himself so he could see the big house. But the sun was high overhead before he caught a glimpse of Sybil. She stepped outside, the sun pooling in her hair. She scanned the pens and corrals until her gaze stopped on him. Had she seen him?

She shielded her eyes from the glare of the sun and continued to look in his direction. Then she picked up her skirts and hustled down the hill, not slowing her steps until she reached the rail fence. "Eddie said you were still here." Her voice was breathless.

"Had to finish my job."

"That's what he said." Her gaze went deep into Brand's heart, demanding more than an excuse.

Oh, how he wished he could offer more. But nothing had changed. Except he was still here. Even though it must be temporary, he might as well make the most of it. "Want to help me walk Dawg this afternoon?" It was the weakest invite any woman ever had, but it was the best he could do.

"I would like that. If you think he's up to it."

"I figure he's up to a few steps." Half a dozen, likely, but he might be persuaded to make it as far as the trees overhanging the river, where Brand and Sybil could enjoy a few moments of privacy.

*And what, you crazy man, do you intend to do with such?*

He realized he was grinning like a crazy man, and forced his mouth into a more moderate smile.

She ducked her head. "I'll come back later, shall I?"

Her shyness made him feel ten feet tall. "I'll meet you at the barn." He forced his attention back to the task at hand.

When he deemed the sun was in the right position, he hustled to the barn to duck his head in the water trough, and clean his hands and face well. Then he trotted inside and pulled out a clean shirt. Nothing fancy. Just a brown striped cotton shirt that could have used a woman's touch to iron out the wrinkles. Lacking that, he smoothed the fabric as best he could before he pulled it over his head and buttoned it.

He scrubbed a spot in the window over the workbench and tried to see his reflection. He'd have done better to stare in the water trough, but someone might notice him.

Straightening, he warned himself, as he had done all day, this was only a small treat he was stealing, to carry with him the rest of his life.

A warning thunder filled his thoughts. He was taking an awful chance, with his pa so close. But one afternoon. Only one. Was it too much to ask of life? If he was the praying man his ma had hoped to raise, he would ask God to give him this afternoon, to bless it with sunshine and kisses and make it last forever.

Knowing Sybil would soon join him, Brand stepped outside to wait. Just in time. She sauntered down the hill, her golden curls beneath a bonnet of blue. He strode from the pen and went toward her. As they drew closer, her eyes seemed to gather up the blue of her bonnet and the sky and hold it. His eyes watered at how striking she was.

He reached her side. "You look like a sunny sky."

Pink stained her cheeks. "Thank you…you do mean it as a compliment?"

He'd spoken without thinking, but replied, "Yes, it's a compliment."

She smiled. "It's a fine afternoon, isn't it?"

Finer by the moment, but all he said was, "Very nice."

He whistled for Dawg and they waited as the animal limped toward them. The way his tail tipped to the side in a wag, Brand knew Dawg was eager for this outing.

Not half as eager as his owner.

He turned toward the river, his eyes on the goal of that little copse of trees. Their progress was slow as Dawg limped along, encouraged by both Sybil and Brand.

Finally, they reached the river, and stepped into the shelter of the gold-dappled branches.

Dawg lapped up the cool water and lay down on the leafy carpet.

Brand had waited for this moment all day, but now his tongue lay motionless in his mouth. What could he say? "Trees are pretty." Yeah, that was brilliant.

She nodded. "Mercy, Jayne and I walked along the river yesterday and saw a wonderful display of color."

A bronze leaf fluttered from the tree and landed on her shoulder.

He plucked it off. Felt her start at his touch, and he jerked back, crushing the leaf in his palm. He would never have the right to touch her.

"Shall we sit?" She waved toward a tree and they sat side by side, their backs against the trunk. "Eddie's anxious to get the cows rounded up and moved to lower pastures."

Brand didn't care about Eddie's cows. Not with Sybil at his side. If only he could stop time and stay right here. Build a cabin next to the water. Forget he was a Duggan.

Except he couldn't forget, not with news of the gang nearby. Every day made discovery more possible. Not only possible but impending. If he had any guts he would leave this minute. But he sat in the shade beside a pretty woman and discussed the weather, determinedly ignoring the increasingly loud warning bells.

She patted his hand as it lay on his knee. "If you stayed here, you might find you like it."

Liking it was the problem. It had kept him from doing what he always did and must continue to do. Ride away. Disappear. Don't look back.

Dawg rose and whined, looking toward the barn.

Sybil laughed. "Do you think he's trying to tell us something? As in he'd like to go back home?" She got to her feet. "I guess we better do as he suggests."

Thus ended his stolen afternoon.

As he gained his feet, he heard a quail cooing across the river.

Every nerve in his body fired hot lava. His heart took off at a mad gallop.

It could possibly be a quail, but Cyrus used to make that sound to signal to Brand.

Had Cyrus and Pa had found him?

He had delayed too long.

Sybil didn't seem to notice his hurry to return to the barn, and left them at the gate, saying she must get back and help Linette.

He waited until she was out of earshot before he turned to Dawg. "Dawg, we're leaving."

The dog didn't protest, but Brand's heart pounded against his ribs as if trying to get free.

Freedom was not an option for him. Either he ran or he hanged.

# Chapter Ten

Brand gathered his stuff together. If that was Cyrus and Pa he'd heard, they would be watching the place. He'd slip away under cover of darkness. So he sank back on the hay-covered floor to wait, as Dawg slept. Brand planted his hat on his head, tipped it over his eyes and crossed his arms on his chest. Anyone caring to check on him would assume he slept, though the tension coursing through him made that impossible.

He woke from his pretend sleep for only one thing: Sybil delivering supper.

She sat beside him as he choked down the food.

She would be hurt that he simply disappeared. Several times he opened his mouth, and closed it again without saying the words he longed to speak. He wanted to tell her he must leave that very night. But he couldn't face an argument to stay. Nor could he risk having her try and stop him. He had no choice but to keep his plans secret.

She chattered on about Linette's intended trip to town in a few days. "She's hoping for letters from home and something from Grady's father. She is convinced the boy won't ever be happy unless that relationship is mended."

Brand had removed his hat when she joined him,

and sat back at an angle so he could watch her. He had avoided developing feelings for anyone since May had made him see how dangerous that was. Even before, he'd learned to be guarded in his friendships. It was a lesson hard learned in his youth and one he should have heeded. But he regretted for less than a second the exception he'd made in this case. Yes, he had to leave. Hopefully, he could escape his brother and Pa. He'd hole up someplace for the winter as was his habit. But this winter he'd have a heart full of both regret and pleasure at this memory.

"Oh, goodness. I have talked on and on, haven't I?"

"Not a problem."

"But I must be going." She rose in a graceful move.

He scrambled to his feet and stared down at her, hoping his eyes did not reveal how thoroughly he studied every feature, knowing this would be his last time to drink in the details.

She touched the back of his hand, sending warmth racing to his heart. It took every ounce of his self-control to keep his arms crossed, his hand pressed to himself, when he ached to hold her close. Enjoy one brief moment of joy before taking up his old life again.

Perhaps sensing the hardness he must force into his heart, she stepped back. "Good night. I'll see you in the morning."

"Good night," he murmured. He waited until she left the pen before turning to watch and listen to her leave the barn. Then he hurried to the workbench and watched her through the clean spot in the window.

Not until she reached the house and stepped inside did he return to the stall.

He waited until the last of the sunset faded and stars began to pepper the sky before he led his horse from the barn, keeping carefully to soft bits of ground to muffle the sound of his departure. He carried Dawg. Any direction he took would necessitate passing an occupied building, so he must proceed with caution, but once away from the ranch he meant to ride hard in a westerly direction. He made his way past the foreman's house and up the hill. Not until he deemed he was beyond hearing did he swing into the saddle, let Dawg get comfortable in his arms. Then he galloped down the dark thread that indicated the trail.

Deepening darkness enfolded him and he had to pull the horse to a walk to see his way. He continued on for the better part of an hour. With each passing mile, his lungs filled more easily. He planned to ride through the night as long as he could make out enough of the path before him to prevent his horse from stumbling. With every step, he expected to be stopped by the Duggan gang, but he rode onward without any sign of them. Had he been mistaken in thinking they'd found him? Not that he meant to hang about and wait for that to happen.

He settled into the saddle, prepared for a long ride.

Did he hear a horse whinny? He reined in and strained to listen. It came again. Was someone camped nearby? He waited, straining to hear any sound above the heavy thump of his heart.

Suddenly a horse and rider appeared before him, a dim shadow in the darkness.

Brand's hand stole toward his gun belt and he gripped the handle of his pistol.

"We been waiting for you." Cyrus's low voice broke the fearful silence.

Brand's hand relaxed at the same time his insides clenched.

Cyrus rode closer, reined in to press close to Brand's side. "Pa said I should bring you to visit."

"Like I said before, I ain't interested."

"Now, ain't that downright unforgivin' of you. After all we done."

*Yeah, like make my life unbearable. Force me to be on the run.* But Brand kept his opinion to himself. He'd said it all since he was a kid. His protests had earned him a smack across the head and accusations of being ungrateful. As an adult, he'd tried again to say he wanted nothing to do with the gang. Pa had voiced his displeasure at Brand's lack of loyalty, and Cyrus had threatened to tie a licking on him. Only seeing the anger in Brand's face and his clenched fists had convinced him Brand was no longer a little brother who couldn't or wouldn't defend himself.

Cyrus pushed the horses forward. Brand considered reining away and riding until they couldn't find him. But he knew Cyrus would chase him until both horses collapsed. The man had a stubborn streak as wide as the sky.

So he let his brother edge them along. "Care to tell me where we're going?"

"I think it's time you showed Pa a little respect. I'm plumb tired of your high-and-mighty attitude. Your ma was no better than my ma, despite what she taught you."

"She never taught me anything of the sort. 'Sides, it wasn't either of our mothers who robbed innocent people. It's our pa."

"Don't you think he done it for you and your ma?"

Brand did not think so, but he knew arguing would only add fuel to the fire of Cyrus's bad attitude.

"We leave the trail here," his brother said, grabbing the reins of Brand's horse. "Just to ensure you don't change your mind," he explained, his voice full of sneering mockery.

"I don't plan to change my mind." Ever.

They crashed through the bushes with little regard for the amount of noise they made. And Cyrus certainly had no concern for the branches he pushed aside and released so that they whipped at Brand, stinging his face, bruising his arms, almost unseating him. He did what he could to protect Dawg.

Dawg hated Cyrus, but knew better than to growl at him. Cyrus wouldn't hesitate to kick Dawg, saying the animal needed to learn some respect.

Brand finally saw a campfire ahead. Made out half a dozen men lounging around it. None of them showed any concern at the approach of riders.

Only Pa rose to greet them. "Howdy, son," he said, as Brand and Cyrus rode into the circle of light. "Nice to see you again."

"Hi, Pa. Sure wish we could meet under better circumstances."

Cyrus gave a mocking laugh and ordered him off his horse.

Brand struggled to get down while still holding Dawg.

"See you still got that mangy mutt."

Dawg barred his teeth as Brand set him on the ground at his feet.

The fire flared, throwing grotesque shadows.

Cyrus saw the stitches on Dawg's side and whooped with harsh laughter. "He looks like a crazy quilt." He laughed some more.

Brand wanted nothing more than to silence that laugh with a fist to Cyrus's mouth. But he was outnumbered seven to one, and didn't trust Cyrus not to shoot Dawg out of spite, so he ignored his brother and studied his pa.

"You've lost weight," he said. The man was downright gaunt. "Don't you eat?"

"We eat real good," Cyrus answered. "Pa looks fit as a fiddle and don't you say otherwise."

The men around the fire shuffled and tried to appear disinterested.

Brand figured he didn't need to say anything more about the subject. Anyone with eyes could see how Pa's hide hung from his frame. His skin had a peculiar pale hue to it. Could he be ill? Despite the differences between them, Brand ached to think of his father dying. A man lost and on the run. *Please, God, give me a chance to speak to him.* Perhaps Brand could persuade him to stop running.

A shudder snaked across Brand's shoulders. That would mean Pa turning himself over to the authorities. He'd hang. More than once the Duggan gang had left death in the wake of their activities.

"Got any coffee?" Brand nodded toward the enamel pot hanging near the fire.

"Cyrus, get your brother some." Pa made it sound all loving and familial, even though Cyrus growled a protest as he sloshed steaming coffee into a tin mug.

Brand took it without comment. Experience told him Cyrus would object to anything, from a word of thanks to a kick in the shins. Seems he viewed every word and action with the same yellowed opinion.

One of the men took Brand's horse away, leaving him feeling exposed and helpless. But he would never reveal weakness to this brood, and he hunkered down on his heels to nurse his coffee. Dawg pressed close, keeping Brand between him and the others.

Cyrus perched on a tree stump nearby, his boots swinging back and forth inches from Brand's face.

Brand ignored him. Like Dawg, he knew better than to rise to Cyrus's invitations to trouble.

Pa sank to the ground nearby. "Hear you been doing all right fer yerself lately."

"I've been doing all right by myself most of my life." He kept all rancor from his tone, just as Pa had made his words a simple comment, when Brand knew they held a whole lot more.

"You always was ungrateful," Cyrus growled.

Pa signaled for his elder son to be still. "We been looking about, asking questions and learning lots."

"Uh-huh." Brand knew the sort of things they would be learning—who kept a stash of money in their mattress, who had valuables in the house, when the stagecoach carried a heavy strongbox.

"Some interesting things have come to light." Pa inched closer. "This Eddie Gardiner you been working for is one of the biggest ranchers in the territory." He waited for Brand to say something. When he didn't, Pa continued. "And he comes from a rich family back in England. From what I hear they practically roll in money."

"Do tell." Guess it took a certain amount of backing to get a ranch like Eden Valley going, but from what Brand had seen, Eddie and his family lived simply enough. Why, his sister, Jayne, lived in a tiny, two-room cabin with her new husband. Didn't sound like stinking rich to him.

But he knew the futility of trying to make Pa see reason.

His skin twitched to think of his pa spying on the ranch. Had he watched Sybil? Brand clenched his teeth so hard they creaked. If he'd seen them… Well, family or not, he would have shown his objection.

"You've been there some time. Guess you've learned a lot about the goings on of the ranch."

"I broke a few horses. That's all."

Pa shook his head and wagged a finger. "Ain't how I saw it."

Brand dared not react. He knew from the leer on Pa's face they'd seen him with Sybil. His head threatened to explode. His presence had put her in danger. He had known all along he should move on. But had he listened to the warning inside his head? Nope. Foolish feelings had been allowed to rule.

Cyrus laughed mockingly, his voice jarring across Brand's nerves like loud discordant music.

Pa grinned at Cyrus, sending the jarring feeling deep into Brand's gut. He knew what they would ask next. They always asked the same thing.

Could he hope to delay them? Brand set the empty cup down and yawned widely. "I'm tired."

Cyrus's boot connected to Brand's knee. "Guess that's what happens when you spend your time courting. Don't get 'nough sleep."

Brand's fists curled so tight the knuckles cracked. He saw red spots that did not come from the fire, but from the anger rolling inside him. How dare Cyrus violate an innocent friendship with his crude insinuations? But Brand would not let him know he'd touched a raw nerve. Ignoring both the nudge and the comment, he yawned again.

Cyrus bolted from his post and squatted before him, almost nose to nose. "Little brother, you can stop playing the sweet innocent boy with us. We've been watching you. What's more, we know you and that boss man were friendly." His spit spattered on Brand's face. Brand wiped at it with his sleeve.

"I only broke some horses for the man."

"We saw how you hung about. How the man visited

you in the barn." Cyrus leaned back with a malicious sneer on his face.

Brand noted that the five men around the campfire all sat up and watched. His nerves twanged with tension.

Cyrus rose and loomed above him. "We know you got it figured out where the man keeps his money."

Brand had known what to expect, but it still turned his blood bitter that they figured he was the same as them. "Know nothing about it."

Cyrus's mean laugh carried no mirth. "Ya, I guess you want us to think so. Selfish, you are. Figger to keep it all to yerself." His eyes bored into Brand's. "We aim to make sure you don't."

Brand didn't bother sparing a glance at Pa, knowing he would share Cyrus's opinion.

Brand slowly rose to his feet, leaning forward, forcing Cyrus to take a step backward, which earned him one of his brother's black looks. "I know nothing. Now if you give me my stuff, I'd like to go to sleep."

He and Cyrus continued their staring match until the others began to shuffle nervously.

"Stu, get his bedroll," Pa said. "Brand, Cyrus, we'll finish this conversation in the morning."

Cyrus grunted. "You can count on it." When the whiskered man Pa called Stu tossed Brand his bedroll, he stretched out, hopefully giving the opinion that all he cared about was his slumber.

Dawg curled up against him. Brand closed his eyes and feigned sleep. He lay with every nerve tensed, ready for anything, knowing the battle of wits was not over.

He eventually drifted off, though he twitched awake at every little sound, and with half a dozen men snoring and Dawg's hearty snorts, there were lots of noises to waken him. At one point he sat up and looked around, hoping for a chance to escape, but a man sat near the smoldering coals, a rifle resting across his knees. He touched the brim of his hat in mocking acknowledgment of Brand's stare.

He had expected no less. Pa and Cyrus had their sights on picking off the Eden Valley Ranch.

Could he stop them?

Sleep never came, and hours later he watched dawn break reluctantly, clouds hanging low.

"Could get another storm," he mused aloud when the men stirred. Had the Duggan gang been out in the open when the last one pelted down? He kind of liked the idea of them huddled under inadequate slickers, trying to keep dry.

"A little rain never hurt no one," Cyrus mumbled, his usual cheerful self. "'Course, I know you prefer a nice warm house, with a gentle woman to serve ya meals." His laugh brought twisting tightness to Brand's chest. "Now your ma is dead, guess you'll have to find someone else to do it for ya."

Pa slapped Cyrus's shoulder. "Don't be speaking of Brand's ma like that. She was a good woman. Better'n I deserved, for sure."

"She loved you, Pa," Brand said gently, not bothering to add that it had about killed her to see what he'd become.

Cyrus snorted. "She sure found a funny way of showing how much she cared. How often did we have to track down the pair of 'em?" he asked their pa. Then he fixed Brand with an evil look. "And then you got so's you wouldn't tell us about yer friends."

Brand had learned that lesson well. Once he discovered the interest from Pa and Cyrus was only to get information so they could rob his friends' houses, he'd stopped telling them anything.

"Come on, boys, let's have breakfast." Pa nodded for the two men who hunkered over the fire to pass around the food.

Brand ate heartily, even though he found it hard to swallow past the tension in his throat. He slipped some to Dawg. He'd no sooner scraped his plate clean before Cyrus yanked it away and handed it off.

"Now, little brother, it's time to tell us what you know."

Brand shrugged and gave him a defiant look. "I know where the horses are penned. Where the animal doctoring supplies are kept. And I know the cook who feeds the cowboys makes fine cinnamon rolls. That's about it."

Cyrus yanked on Brand's shirtfront. He would have jerked him to his feet, but Brand outweighed him.

"You always were a selfish son of a gun. Now you think ya can keep all the money to yerself." He released Brand with a shove. "Seems yer gonna take some persuading." He pulled out his pistol and aimed it at Dawg, who didn't move, but gave Cyrus a look of hatred.

"How be I shoot this cur?"

Brand's insides curled, but he simply shrugged. "He's about dead, anyway."

Pa shook his head. "Leave the poor animal alone."

Cyrus snorted and stalked off ten paces. He slowly turned to face Brand, with such a malicious grin that Brand struggled to hide a shudder. Sorrow clawed at his gut. Cyrus had once been a decent big brother. Now look what he'd become.

"Dog don't count. Saddle me a horse." He signaled to one of the men, who did as he instructed. Then Cyrus rode away.

Brand stared after him, his heart beating wild as the hooves of a mustang.

What was Cyrus up to?

Whatever it was, Brand knew it was no good.

Sybil thought longingly of her favorite spot—the place where Brand had camped. But Eddie had warned her not to stray too far. She could have found a bit of solitude in the trees next to the river where she and Brand had spent a few minutes. But her memories prevented her from going there, so she settled for a place on the hill, surrounded by trees, within a few yards of the house.

Brand! Why did she keep thinking of him? He was not what she thought.

He'd left without even saying goodbye. Or explaining his reasons. But after Constable Allen's visit that afternoon she understood why. The Mountie had brought a wanted poster for the Duggan gang.

"Morton Duggan and his son Cyrus," the Mountie said. "They gather up ne'er-do-wells, but they're the head of the gang. Notice anything about them?"

Eddie studied the drawings of the men and groaned. "The family likeness is unmistakable." He handed the poster to Linette. Mercy and Sybil peered over her shoulders. The drawings could have been older versions of Brand.

Sybil's insides turned to ice. A wanted man. Why hadn't she listened to the warning voices in her head? Had the voices not said repeatedly that he was a dangerous man? A man who enjoyed risks?

Linette returned the poster to the Mountie. "He seemed like a decent man. Are you sure he's part of the gang?"

Constable Allen considered the poster with a serious look on his face. "From the information I have, he isn't directly involved in the robberies, but it seems he is on the scene first. It could be he garners information that he passes on to his father and brother." The officer turned to Eddie. "I hope you didn't share any information regarding your money or your valuables with him."

Eddie shook his head. "Of course not. Fact is, I didn't get more than a few words out of him, and he certainly didn't hang around socializing with the others. Except—" His gaze hit Sybil like a blow. "You spent a fair amount of time with him. Did he ask any question that in hindsight might indicate he sought information of this sort?"

Sybil's throat refused to work. She shook her head. If they only knew it was she who'd asked the questions. Questions to which she received few answers. Now she understood why. "He said very little and asked no questions," she finally managed to say.

She'd fled the place as soon as she could, cutting short Mercy's excited rant about having a wanted man in their presence and not even knowing it.

Sybil sat on the ground now, her back pressed to a tree. The larches were bright yellow, like bits of captured sunlight. But the sight gave her no joy. Brand was part of the Duggan gang.

And she'd been silly enough to allow herself to care about him.

She pulled out her notebook. At least it would make a good story. But she stared at the page without putting down a word. How could she write about him now? He wasn't a man bigger than life. He was a common criminal. She closed her eyes and leaned her head back, letting disappointment and sorrow scratch at her insides. So much for her hard-learned lessons on guarding her heart.

But how could it be true? Was she so blind she'd missed every hint?

Her cheeks warmed as she thought of the moments they'd shared under the trees. The kiss in the barn. At least no one had seen them.

Did she hear a movement nearby? The rustle of leaves? She blew her breath out. Of course she did. The breeze made all the yellow and gold leaves move. She was just nervous, because of Eddie's warning. Knowing Linette and Eddie would worry about her, she gathered her feet under her and stood. It was time to get back.

A man stepped from the trees.

Her heart clambered up her throat, which tightened so much she couldn't even scream.

"Yer coming with me."

She thought she shook her head, but perhaps she only wanted to. She managed to stumble back a step, never taking her gaze off the leering man.

His eyes reminded her of Brand, but his expression frightened her. This was Brand's brother. Had Brand sent him?

He lurched forward.

"No." The word wailed inside her head, but came out barely a whisper. She darted to the side.

The man laughed. "Wanna play? I like that." He held out his hands and leaned one way and then the other, silently mocking her, urging her to run so he could chase her.

She lifted her skirts and took off toward the ranch. A thin sound meant to be a scream pushed past her teeth. "Help. Help." Surely someone from the ranch would see her and come to her aid. She reached the crest of the hill. Through the veil of leaves she watched Slim saddle a horse. Another cowboy sauntered toward the cookhouse. The sun glistened off the windows of the big house, making it impossible for her to see if anyone stood beyond the glass, but Linette spent much of her time in that room, often glancing out the window. Despite the bushes that partially obscured her view, Sybil lifted her arms and waved frantically. It was possible Linette would see and send help.

"Sure do like this game, but ya gone far 'nough."

Huge arms encircled her waist, sweeping her off her feet. She kicked her heels, knowing a taste of satisfaction when her captor grunted. She flailed her arms, scratched at the hands holding her. Despite his grunts, he did not loosen his grip. Instead, he carried her away from the ranch to a waiting horse.

She saw his intention and flung her head back, connecting with his chin.

His arms tightened cruelly, making it impossible to draw in a full breath, though her tight lungs had already made breathing difficult.

"Yer a regular little fighter, ain't ya? I bet Brand enjoyed that."

The mention of that name filled her with blinding fury and she fought with all her might, kicking, gouging, head butting, but Brand's brother only laughed.

"I can see yer gonna give us some fine entertainment."

She found her voice. "I'll not be entertaining the likes of you."

"Already are, sister." His laugh shuddered along her spine. His sour breath made her cringe, but only for a heartbeat. Then she fought and screamed.

He threw her facedown over the back of his horse and swung up behind her. He slapped her bottom.

She saw red. Never in her life had a man touched

her in such a familiar, rude way. She would get revenge somehow. Never mind that Father said a lady should never show such emotions. She'd find a way of making him pay for this if she had to track him to her dying day.

With deliberate intent, she kicked the horse, slapped him hard, screamed and squirmed. If she could fall off... She'd sooner be killed by the tumble, trampled to death, than endure the sort of treatment she knew this man and the rest of the gang meant to inflict on her.

The horse snorted and reared. Her head swung back hard, snapping her neck. But her captor held her by the back of her dress. She feared if she struggled any harder the fabric would tear, exposing her undergarments. The man would likely see that as invitation to do worse.

He jerked her back in place. "You can make this easy or you can make it hard. Suits me either way." He gave another of those dirty laughs.

She hung limply, weighing the possibilities. Could she pretend to cooperate and gain his trust? Bile rose in her throat at the idea. She'd sooner be hog-tied and butchered.

Did the man purposely choose a gait that bounced her so hard across the horse's spine that she wondered why she didn't vomit? Her ribs hurt. Her head hurt. Her arms grew numb. After a few minutes all she cared about was getting off that rigid spine, getting her head upright. But still the ride continued.

"Where are we going?" she demanded.

"Thought you might like to see Brand again."

"No thanks."

Another mirthless laugh. "He's gonna be surprised to see you."

She saw the legs of another horse, the boots of another rider. Had help come? She lifted her head and saw the rider. Her heart stalled. Given his expression, this man did not mean to help her.

"Got yerself a toy?"

"Keep yer hands off her. She's mine as soon as she persuades Brand to cooperate."

Sybil studied the words, but they made no sense. Except his claim that she was his. She lay still, hoping she appeared somewhat compliant. But she would not be this man's toy or trophy.

"Hey, Pa," Brand's brother called. "Lookee what I got."

Sybil lifted her head. She saw an older, thinner version of Brand, plus several very tough-looking men. Then she saw Brand and gave him a look full of all the anger that had built over the last hour of indignities.

He nodded a curt greeting, his expression stony.

So that was how it was going to be. No hint of regret or apology. But why should she think there would be? He was part of an outlaw gang. His interest in her had been solely for the purpose of learning what he could about the ranch.

"I see you've met Cyrus, my brother," Brand said. "This here's my pa. Can't remember the names of the others."

Cyrus swung down and lifted her to the ground. Her legs were wobbly, but she'd never let anyone guess. Only good manners kept her from spitting on her captor.

She swung her burning gaze at each and every one of the men, curling her lip as she looked again at Brand.

Cyrus laughed.

She'd never heard a more hateful sound.

"Thought she'd be a bit more pleased to see you, little brother."

Brand shrugged. "Could've told you she don't much care for me."

Sybil gritted her teeth. To think she'd tried to persuade him to stay. Had practically thrown herself into his arms. Thankfully, she had restrained herself.

"That ain't how I saw it." Cyrus pushed her forward. "And I'm goin' by my eyes." He stopped pushing her as they neared the campfire with a pot hanging over it. Steam escaped around the lid.

"I'm hungry." He shoved Sybil down on a log.

She sat, grateful to be off her shaking legs.

The others sat, mostly staring at her. Their looks made her shrink back, feeling soiled and exposed. One of the men filled dishes with heaping helpings of beans. All of them were so unwashed she couldn't imagine eating the food, but when she meant to refuse the plate offered her, the scowl on the cowboy's face made her swallow hard and accept it.

But she didn't say thank you.

Brand's pa edged closer. "We saw you and Brand being friendly. Ain't often a woman warms up to him." His smile was sad, regretful. "Or could be he don't often let anyone get close."

"Wouldn't know. Don't care." She took a spoonful of beans simply to discourage further conversation, and forced herself not to gag.

She felt Brand's disinterested look and shot him one that should have melted the flesh off his bones. "Where's Dawg?"

Brand tipped his head to the side. Dawg sat there with his head on his paws, his eyes alert. His tail tilted to one side at Sybil speaking his name, and he wriggled an inch closer.

"Stay," Brand ordered, and Dawg stayed.

Forks and knives clattered on the tin plates. A utensil screeched and Sybil shivered. Fear and anger and disgust raged through her.

When the men finished and handed their plates to the one who had served the food, they shifted their gaze to her. She thought her heart would leap from her chest at the way they studied her.

"Tie her up," Cyrus ordered one of the men. "Then we'll make plans."

Sybil bolted to her feet, thought to run away, but she was surrounded by hard-faced men. One reached for her and yanked her arms behind her back with no pity for how much it hurt.

Brand! She sent him a silent plea, begging him to help her.

He crossed his arms and looked away.

"To think I thought we might be friends." She spat out each bitter word. She was forced to sit with her back to a tree, trussed up hand and foot.

Cyrus laughed. "Brand don't make friends. Why, he don't even like his family much." He edged up to his brother and gave him an evil grin. He grabbed Brand's arm and dragged him away. The others followed and stood in a tight circle.

She strained to hear what the men said. She could make out only a few words. Enough to know they planned some kind of robbery and that somehow, though she'd done nothing to invite such treatment, she was to be used as a pawn. People hanged for kidnapping. She tried to find pleasure in the idea, but instead quivered so hard her teeth rattled, and she wished for a blanket to warm herself.

*Please, God, rescue me.*

# Chapter Eleven

Brand squeezed his fists so tight he wondered if his fingers would ever straighten. He ached to break Cyrus's nose. The man did not have a decent bone in his body.

Brand knew he must keep his emotions under control. There was nothing Cyrus liked better than seeing Brand get upset about something. And nothing had upset Brand half as much as seeing Sybil dragged into the campsite hung across a horse. She must have suffered a great deal, riding like that. And knowing Cyrus, Brand had no doubt his brother had been inappropriate. The only consolation was that Sybil seemed unharmed and full of spunk. If not for the seriousness of the situation he might have smiled to see how feisty the serious little Sybil had grown.

Cyrus faced him across the tight circle. "Now, little brother, you can help us out or watch us have a little sport with that gal over there."

Brand shrugged. "She's just a young lady." He hoped to convey the impression he didn't care what happened to her. "One of the ranch owner's friends." Maybe that would give them pause.

Cyrus snorted and the others pressed closer. Pa managed to squirm a little at the idea of abusing a young lady, but their father had never stood up to Cyrus and Brand didn't expect he would start now.

"Little brother, you can't fool us. We seen you with her. I never seen you spending time with anyone before."

"You don't know a whole lot about what I do. For instance, who did I spend last winter with?" Let Cyrus mull on that for a while as Brand scrambled to think how to get Sybil away unhurt.

"Who cares? That was then. This is now." Cyrus waited.

So did Brand. Unexpectedly, he thought to ask God for help. *Lord, a good idea would be right handy about now.* But when had God ever sent a way out of his family situation? Suddenly Brand didn't care if he was a Duggan or not. *Lord, help me get Sybil out of this situation.* This prayer mattered more than any he'd ever offered. Would God answer?

"The ranchers will all be after you as soon as they discover Sybil is missing."

"Sybil is it? Now, ain't that a fine name? What do you think, Pa? You like the idea of a Sybil in the family? Sybil and Cyrus has a nice ring to it, don't ya think?"

Brand's whole body quivered with anger. But he held it in check.

"'Course I know little brother here had his sights on her first, but seems me being the oldest I should get first chance. Right, Pa?"

Pa didn't say anything.

"'Course I might just enjoy her without marrying. After all, marriage ties you down."

Brand's anger erupted. He sprang forward and landed a good hard blow to his brother's nose before the others restrained him.

Cyrus wiped his nose on his sleeve and laughed. "Knew you cared about her. Now…" his expression hardened "…let's do some negotiatin'."

Brand had little choice. "What do you want?"

"Show us where the rancher keeps his money."

Brand did some fast thinking. "It's where you'd least expect it."

"Yeah? And where would that be?"

"'Fraid I can't tell you, because then I have nothing to bargain with, do I?"

Cyrus snorted. "You ain't got nothin' anyways."

"Suit yourself." Brand leaned back on his heels and waited.

Cyrus gave him a look fit to curl the toes of a new pair of boots. The others shifted and made impatient noises.

Pa sighed. "Seems you two better work this out. Cyrus, hear what he has in mind."

Cyrus grunted, which Brand knew was as much of a yes as he could expect.

"I'll take you where the money is kept on the condition you release Sybil and see her safely home."

Cyrus shrugged. "Sure. Why not?"

Brand knew Cyrus's promise meant nothing, but Pa believed in keeping his word to his family.

Brand turned to him. "Pa?"

The old man considered for a moment, looked at Sybil straining at her ropes. "You have my word to release her once we get the money. But you better not be up to any funny business."

Brand wished he could think of something clever. But he couldn't. All he could hope for was to lead the men away and wait for a blinding bit of insight before they realized he had no idea what he was doing.

Two of the men saddled the horses and brought them forward.

Seeing Brand about to leave, Dawg whined.

"Come." Brand spoke to the dog and headed toward Sybil.

Cyrus stepped in his way. "What do you think yer gonna do?"

"Leave my dog behind. Last thing we need is him barking and giving away our presence."

"So tell him to stay."

"Sometimes Dawg don't listen too good."

"A bullet between his ears would make him obey."

"Dawg might alert us if anyone approaches the camp."

Cyrus considered the idea, the wheels turning with maddening slowness. "Okay. Leave him here."

"That's what I aim to do. I'll order him to watch Miss Sybil." Dawg, with his injuries, might not provide much protection for Sybil, but it was the most Brand could offer. He called Dawg to follow him across the clearing to her side.

"Stay," he said to Dawg, and the animal lay by Sybil.

She gave him a pleading look. "Don't do this."

"I have to do what I have to do," he whispered in reply.

Cyrus, who had been busy organizing the men, noticed Brand still at Sybil's side and chortled. "Trying to steal a little kiss?"

Brand straightened, his back to his brother, his eyes clinging to Sybil. "This is goodbye." He allowed himself a second of enjoying her face. No doubt it would be the last time he saw her. Once Cyrus and the others figured out he didn't know where there was any money, they'd shoot him on the spot. He could only hope and pray Eddie or someone would rescue Sybil before then.

The best he could hope for was to buy her time.

They left Sybil tied to the tree, Dawg at her side and a grizzle-faced man, Jock, to watch her.

"I ain't gonna stay here and be caught by no posse," he groused.

Cyrus leaped from his horse and grabbed the man's shirt. "You'll be here when we get back or I'll hunt you down and shoot you like a mad dog."

It wasn't until they'd ridden back to the faint trail along the edge of a hill that Brand knew what he must do. It was the only thing that offered any hope of success. He reined toward Edendale, praying as he had never prayed before, likely as his ma had once prayed for her husband and stepson. He prayed for help from any source. He prayed that no one would be hurt. He prayed fervently that Sybil would be released unhurt.

He didn't know the man who had been left to guard her. Jock. Dirty-looking and dirty-smelling. Brand's jaw clenched at the thought of the man going near Sybil.

"Where are we heading, little brother?" Cyrus demanded. "The ranch is that direction." He pointed to the left.

"Told you the money wasn't where you'd expect it."

Cyrus's look dripped warning. "You better not try and fool us."

"Trust me."

Pa rode on his other side. "I'm guessing Brand won't do anything stupid, because if he does, that little gal back there is fair game."

Several of the man laughed in a way that made Brand's fists coil around the reins until his knuckles shone white. He chomped back the bile that burned up his throat. "Pa, remember your promise."

"Son, I ain't forgetting the promise was in exchange for leading us to the money."

"I'm doing the best I can." Unfortunately, his best was not much. He let memories of Sybil fill his mind, giving him determination to do whatever must be done.

Sybil sitting under a tree near the ranch, bent over some book, the sunlight glistening on her golden curls.

Sybil gritting her teeth and holding Dawg while Brand sewed him up.

Sybil telling him stories she'd made up. Would she ever get a chance to get them printed?

Would he succeed in gaining her release?

The trail widened. Dust kicked up from the horses' hooves. In the distance the buildings of Edendale could be seen.

Cyrus grabbed Brand's reins and jerked them to a halt. "What kind of trick is this?"

"No trick. Money is kept in the store." Not Eddie's, but someone's was there.

Cyrus hung on to the reins as he considered the notion. "What do you think, Pa?"

Pa studied the situation. "Don't much care for riding into a town. Too many places people can hide. Maybe it's a trap."

Brand wished it could be. "Pa, how was I to plan a trap? I didn't even know you were around. And I have only been in town twice. Once to ride through and once to get some biscuits. A young couple bakes bread and biscuits for the store, so there are always fresh ones on hand."

Still they didn't move.

Finally Pa sighed. "I keep thinking of that gal back at the camp. We watched Brand with her. Know he's fond of her. My question is would he trick us if he thought she'd suffer for it?"

Brand met his pa's gaze, letting him see the truth. He would risk his own skin before he'd let them hurt Sybil.

Pa nodded. "I don't figure he would. Come on, boys." He signaled for the others to follow. "But keep your eyes peeled."

He and Cyrus pressed close to Brand. He'd never be able to get away, call out a warning. Do anything.

He'd never felt so helpless in his life. This would surely end badly. But if Sybil escaped unharmed, he could live with the fact. Or die with it comforting him.

They rode forward slowly, watching for any sign of danger. The town appeared sleepy in the slanting afternoon sun. One horse stood in front of the store. A whirlwind of dust swept down the street. A screen door slapped in the wind. Smoke rose from the chimney of the stopping house behind the store, and the aroma of fresh bread filled the air.

They rode closer. Every nerve in Brand's body twitched. What lay ahead? He felt the same tension in Pa and Cyrus. Their hands lingered on their guns. Would he escape this day without someone being shot?

They rode up to the store and the seven of them lined up in a row, facing the closed door. Through the window, they saw a barrel, some hardware hanging from the ceiling and the counter holding an assortment of jars and tins. But not a sign of life.

"Could be he's in the back room," Brand said, his neck prickling.

"Let's go see. You can go first." Cyrus ordered two of the men to stay with the horses, then pressed his gun to Brand's back.

Their boots rang in the silence as they climbed the

steps and shoved open the door. Brand paused to let his eyes adjust to the dim interior. Cyrus nudged him with his gun.

"Where's the money?"

Brand didn't know. How was he supposed to, when he was making this up? He'd never ridden a wild horse that filled him with more tension.

"Guess you need to ask the salesclerk."

Cyrus yelled, "Hello?" sending a jolt of alarm up and down Brand's spine.

A noise came from the door to the living quarters. The handle jiggled. Brand recognized the man who stepped through the door. And it wasn't Macpherson. Why was the man in civilian clothes? Brand's nerves skittered madly. Something was amiss.

"Can I help you?" Constable Allen asked.

"Yeah, mister. You can give us all the money hid here."

The Mountie lifted his arms. "Sure thing." He moved toward the counter.

Brand tensed until his bones felt brittle.

"No funny stuff," Cyrus warned.

"I'm no fool," the Mountie said, edging closer, his eyes guarded as he took in the scene before him.

Cyrus moved to keep the counter between himself and the officer, his gun steadily aimed at the Mountie's heart.

Brand wondered how the man could be so cool.

Then the Mountie flung himself out of sight behind the counter. "Now," he called.

Men burst through the doors of the storeroom and the living quarters.

The Mountie came up with a shotgun aimed at the Duggan gang. "Drop your weapons."

Cyrus and the others fired and raced for the outer door. Brand dived for the floor.

In a few minutes the shooting was over. Brand sat up, pain burning his side. He pressed his hand to the spot and looked at the blood staining his palm. He'd been shot.

"You are under arrest," the Mountie said, and Brand got to his feet, his hands out to show he was unarmed.

He looked around. Two men lay on the floor. They'd never rob anyone again. The men who had waited outside were gone. And so were Cyrus and Pa.

"We'll find them," the Mountie said, and Brand knew it was a vow. The Mounties prided themselves on always getting their man.

Brand leaned his head against the rough wood, his hands chained to the iron rings anchored in the wall of the livery stable where Constable Allen had taken him after his arrest. He knew he would either be hanged or sentenced to hard labor for the rest of his life.

His only consolation came from having told the Mountie where to find Sybil.

His side ached.

Someone stepped into the barn. "Hello. The Mountie asked me to bring you food."

Tied hand and foot, Brand could not feed himself. Only the aroma of the meal allowed him to suffer the indignity of being fed by the other man.

"Any news from the Mountie?" Brand asked. His thoughts overflowed with worry about Sybil...worry that was not eased despite his continued prayer.

"I don't expect he'll be back until he catches up with the rest of the gang. Constable Allen is very unwavering in his pursuit of justice."

Brand didn't continue the conversation, unable to bear the idea that the Mountie neglected Sybil's rescue in favor of chasing after Cyrus and Pa. *God, keep her safe. Please, God, hear my prayer and answer it.*

Darkness fell and Brand's spirits nose-dived. Had Sybil been left out there, alone except for old Jock? Afraid? Cold?

He shivered as he thought of how vulnerable she would be.

He fell into a restless sleep and woke to find a figure silhouetted against the door. His heart skittered up his throat. Cyrus? Had he returned, intent on making Brand pay for the botched robbery?

He shuddered.

Then the figure moved. He saw it was Constable Allen and he strained against his chains. "Did you find Sybil?"

"She's safe."

He inhaled without pain for the first time in hours.

"I overtook the rest of the gang."

Something in his voice alerted Brand. "It's good news?" Then he realized good news for the Mountie would be bad news for him.

"Your father was injured. Two men are dead. Two of them escaped."

"Cyrus?" Was he dead or alive?

"He got away. I have a posse after him. He'll not get far." The Mountie's voice promised Cyrus's capture.

Brand tried to decide how he felt about it. On one hand he wanted to see the end of the Duggan gang. On the other, Pa and Cyrus were the only family he had.

The Mountie unlocked Brand's shackles and signaled for a man to bring his horse forward. "Mount up."

Brand obeyed and sat stoically on his horse while

the Mountie tied his wrists together and secured a rope to lead him. He submitted without protest. He saw no point in trying to get away. Sybil was safe. He could go to his death or a jail cell content with that knowledge.

"How bad is Pa?"

"He was bleeding badly. Mrs. Gardiner is nursing him." The officer kept his attention forward, but Brand saw the way his jaw muscles tightened. "I'd like to see him stand trial for his deeds."

"Guess he will whether he lives or dies."

Constable Allen jerked his head around. "You're right. Justice will prevail either way." The Mountie rode at his side, directing him down the trail.

Brand thought of the man's desire for justice. "What if God forgives him?"

The constable considered the question for the better part of half a mile, then sighed. "As a lawman I wish to see man's justice, but I have to accept that God forgives sinners." He paused. "And I willingly confess I am a sinner saved by God's grace. I have no right to resent God extending that same grace to someone like your pa."

"Maybe you should tell him that." Brand knew Pa's salvation had been his ma's dying wish.

When they should have headed south to the fort, the Mountie indicated they should go west. They would soon reach the ranch if they continued this direction.

Perhaps the Mountie meant to let him see Pa one last time. If so he would tell Pa himself that there was forgiveness in repentance.

"No one else was hurt?"

"A cowboy in the posse got a minor flesh wound on his leg. Nothing that will slow him down."

They reached the ranch. Brand held back. Only the tug on the rope by the Mountie made him move on. He didn't want to face Eddie and the others. On the other hand, he'd give his right arm to see Sybil and know she was unharmed.

He heard a bark and looked to see Dawg limping toward him. The ropes made it impossible for Brand to reach down and pick up the animal. "Hi, Dawg."

The dog walked to his side. Seemed the old mutt would live. Guess if Brand went to jail Dawg would need a new owner.

The Mountie forced him to move forward, up the hill toward the big house. Eddie, Mercy, Linette and Sybil waited for them.

Brand and the Mountie drew to a halt in front of them.

Brand stared at his bound hands. Although the ropes were weather stained in spots, the jute strands were firm, the twists ready to defy any hope of escape. He kept his hands still, his head lowered, hiding his face as much as he could. His cheeks stung as if he'd leaned too close to open flames. What must they think of him? A Duggan. Branded with the same condemnation as his pa and brother. He expected no sympathy. No understanding of his situation. He couldn't claim innocence, so he wouldn't try.

He lifted his head a fraction, unable to deprive himself of a glance at Sybil's face. Would she be angry? Disappointed? But he couldn't tell from her expression. Seemed she didn't want him to guess at her feelings, because her face revealed nothing but disinterest. Despite understanding he had no right to speak and would likely be cut short, he let his gaze connect with hers. He schooled himself to reveal none of the regret churning his insides at the thought that this was how she would remember him—bound and headed to jail.

"Glad to see you're okay," he said to her, keeping his

voice low and impersonal, while inside raged a loud pro-test. *I'm innocent.* But he'd made a decision and didn't intend to cry about the consequences. He had agreed to help the gang in exchange for her life. Not for a moment would he regret it. "Would you look after Dawg for me?"

A fleeting emotion flicked across her eyes. Too fast, too uncertain for him to guess what it was.

What did it matter?

She nodded. "Dawg will be safe with me."

Her words whispered across his thoughts. If only all his concerns could be so easily dealt with.

Sybil's heart hurt with every beat. Seeing Brand tied up, on his way to trial… She crossed her arms over her stomach and gripped her elbows with tense fingers. Jail or worse awaited him. She had told herself over and over to forget about those few days they had shared when she felt drawn to him. It had all been deception. Yes, she'd known he ran from something, but never in ten thou-sand guesses would she have suspected he was part of the infamous Duggan gang.

"Get down," Constable Allen said, holding a rope that kept Brand from considering flight.

Sybil averted her eyes, unable to bear the sight of Brand's humiliation.

Dawg leaped to his master, placed his paws on his waist and whined.

From the corner of her eyes, she saw Brand pat Dawg's head with hands bound so tightly she knew they must hurt.

She turned to the Mountie, about to ask him to loosen the ropes holding Brand, but bit back the words before she opened her mouth. Of course he must be secured. He was a common outlaw. She squeezed her hands tighter, knowing she'd have bruises on both arms.

"Down, Dawg," he murmured, and the dog dropped to all fours.

"Your father is upstairs," the Mountie said. "The Gardiners have been generous enough to allow you to visit him."

"Thank you," Brand said, his voice as flat as a thousand acres of prairie.

"Eddie will see that you are guarded until I return to take you to the fort. I intend to find your brother and the man with him."

Sybil noted the slight shudder that twitched Brand's shoulders, but he stood tall, revealing nothing but determination. Guess he'd known this day would come sometime.

But she found no pleasure in the justice that he would face. It was easier to be angry at his deception when she couldn't see him or feel anguish at how he was bound.

The Mountie handed the rope to Eddie. "I'll be back when I'm done with this business."

He'd said Cyrus and another man had escaped. Sybil prayed the constable would find them and bring them to justice. Her face burned at the memory of Cyrus manhandling her. How could Brand and Cyrus be brothers? One so cruel? The other—

She stopped the word that sprang to her mind. He wasn't *gentle;* he was a deceiver. His name should be Jacob.

The Mountie rode away.

Linette stepped aside, indicating they should follow her indoors. "Your father is upstairs."

When Brand hesitated, Eddie tugged the rope. "Come along."

As Sybil recalled how Brand had played the innocent, convinced her that he was a worthy man, she was able to hold back any sympathy at his situation.

Brand stepped over the threshold.

Dawg sat on his haunches and waited.

Sybil hated to shut the door against him. "You wait here. I'll come feed you in a bit." She kept her back to the room, staring out the nearby window as Eddie and Linette led Brand upstairs to his pa.

Mercy grabbed Sybil's arm and dragged her to the sitting room, where she pushed her into a chair and sat facing her. "An outlaw in the house. How exciting is that?"

Sybil shuddered. "Mercy, it's not exciting at all. It's awkward and horrible. His pa is shot and lies in one of Linette's beds." Linette took in anyone in need of care. "How will she manage? Do you think it is safe for her in her condition?"

"Do you think he'd hurt her?"

"I doubt Eddie is going to leave him alone with her." Sybil shook her head. All those hours she'd spent unaccompanied with Brand, feeling safe and—she shuddered—longing to touch him, feel his lips on hers. How could she have been so mistaken about him?

When she let emotions rule, danger followed. She'd known it all the while. Only she'd never imagined this sort of thing.

Linette entered the sitting room. "Eddie said he'd sit with Brand and his father for a bit. Then Slim will spell him off. There'll be someone guarding him day and night so we can feel safe in our beds." She sighed deeply. "I still can't believe I could be so mistaken about a man. Eddie is upset that he was, as well. He prides himself on being a good judge of people." With another sigh, she headed to the kitchen with a basin of blood-stained rags to soak.

Sybil followed. Unlike Mercy, she didn't want to speculate or rejoice in the excitement of having two outlaws upstairs.

"You must be tired," she said to Linette. "Can I help?"

Her friend brushed aside a tendril of hair. "I find it very hard to see the pair of them. And feel the tension in the air. There's something between them that isn't quite right, and I can't put my finger on it."

Sybil wrapped an arm about her. "Could it simply be that they are common criminals and don't like being captured?"

"Maybe."

But she knew Linette wasn't convinced.

"I can't get Mr. Duggan's bleeding to stop."

The worry in her voice caught Sybil's attention. "Do you think some organ has been hit?"

Linette shook her head. "I simply don't know. The man is thin except for a pronounced potbelly, and his skin has a distinct yellowish hue."

"You mean jaundice?"

"I fear so."

Jaundice! She'd heard of it. Always spoken in dark tones. A slow, certain death. Often the sufferer would bleed to death or lose his or her mind, dying in confusion. "Does Brand know?"

"I doubt it."

"I guess it doesn't make much difference, does it?" Sybil forced indifference into her voice. "They'll either hang or rot in jail. Dying in a clean bed might be a mercy. An undeserved one."

Linette dried her hands and turned to her. "Do any of us deserve mercy? From God or man?"

"If we live a good life we don't need mercy from man, and if we seek God's forgiveness He offers His mercy."

"But it's so undeserved. And I fear none of us can claim we have not offended another."

Sybil tried to protest, but then thought of her secret. Wasn't she being untruthful in her own way by hiding behind a pseudonym? In talking to Brand with a view to gleaning information for a story without telling him her intention?

Linette turned to meal preparation, and Sybil helped. A little later, Slim came in to relieve Eddie, and Linette served the meal. They ate in silence, as if each of them was struggling to believe the recent events.

Grady studied the sober faces around him. "Is it true? Is Brand a bad man?"

Linette and Eddie exchanged glances, while Mercy and Sybil waited for their answer.

Silent communication passed between the couple. How Sybil envied their love and security. Would she ever enjoy something similar? To her disgrace, she allowed herself to admit she'd given a few thoughts to Brand being like Eddie. How wrong she'd been.

Eddie took Grady's hands. "It would seem he is part of an outlaw gang."

Grady looked around the table, saw the same message in the nod each person gave him. He shook his head. "You're wrong. He's not a bad man. He can't be. Not when Dawg likes him so much."

No one could argue with that.

Grady's lips quivered. "Why are you all being so mean to him?"

The boy dashed out the back door.

Linette pushed herself to her feet, then looked about at the dishes to be cleaned up. She glanced upward. "They need to be fed."

Sybil made up her mind. "You go after Grady. I'll feed the prisoners and then we'll clean up."

Mercy insisted on accompanying her upstairs, and Sybil didn't mind. She couldn't imagine facing Brand. Yet she knew she must in order to erase the false memories of the Brand she thought she had known.

She stepped into the room, Mercy on her heels. Slim sat at the doorway, leaning back in a wooden chair, a rifle across his knees. Mercy handed him a plate of food.

Slim dropped all four legs of the chair to the floor, snagged another chair and pulled it close.

Mercy sat at his side.

Slowly Sybil shifted her gaze, saw Brand's father. At their campsite she had considered him big and menacing. She hadn't taken note of the condition Linette had pointed out. Now, though, under the gray woolen blanket, he looked thin and sallow. Yellowish, just as Linette said.

"I brought dinner." Sybil held a plate of food in each hand.

Brand took one plate, his wrists still bound with thick ropes, and set it on the nearby table. But he didn't eat.

She felt his awkward waiting, but rather than relieve it, she turned to his father. "I brought you food."

He regarded her unblinkingly. "Don't think I'll be needing food where I'm going."

"I'm sure they'll feed you adequately in jail." She hated the judgmental tone of her voice, but she couldn't help it. Brand had deceived her and this man had ordered her held captive. She had every right to judge him for that.

Mr. Duggan gave a faint laugh. "No doubt the food will be better than we deserve."

She again offered him the plate.

He shifted, moaned. The blood drained from his face, leaving his skin even more yellow. He pulled the plate closer.

She stepped back to wait, and flicked her gaze to Brand. "I don't know who you are." Every word dripped with anger, frustration and a thousand drops of pain, disappointment and shame.

He raised his eyes and lowered them again almost before she could see them. But she got a glimpse, long enough to note the indifference. He didn't even care. That was the bitterest thing of all.

"He's a Duggan." The elder man pushed away the plate, the food barely touched. "I'm done."

"Then I'll see to your dressing." She removed the plate, setting it by the door, where Mercy watched, her eyes flashing with excitement.

Sybil lowered the gray blanket to reveal a wound in the man's left side. His belly was indeed badly swollen. The dressings Linette had placed there a short time ago were blood soaked. Sybil removed them gingerly. Blood oozed from the round hole. She quickly placed pads of clean dressing on it and kept her hand firmly pressed to the area.

But warm moisture soon reached her palm.

"It's not good, is it?" Mr. Duggan said.

Her face must have given away her distress.

When she didn't answer, he asked another question.

"How long do you think I have?" He turned to his son. "Brand?"

For the first time since he'd thanked her for the food she'd brought, Brand spoke. "Pa, you're tough. A little gunshot ain't going to finish you."

Pa's smile was regretful, knowing. "Boy, it ain't the bullet that will do me in. It's the rest." He patted his distended stomach. "Like Cyrus says, we eat well 'nough. But still I lose weight. Haven't hardly got energy enough to spit." He closed his eyes as if too weary to continue.

Brand had been eating his food, both hands holding the fork and going from plate to mouth. Now he shoved away the plate. "Pa, you should stop this life."

"Son, this life is gonna stop me."

Brand leaned forward, ignoring the others in the room. "Pa, repent for your sins. Make your peace with God."

"You figure God would forgive an old outlaw like me?"

"God's no respecter of persons."

Sybil observed the pair while pressing her hand to the wound in the hopes of stopping the bleeding. She didn't want to give Mr. Duggan hope. But she knew God offered hope and mercy and forgiveness. The knowledge twisted through her. Sometimes she didn't understand God's mercy. It was so undeserved.

Then her heart smote her. She might not be an outlaw, but she didn't deserve God's mercy any more than they.

Mr. Duggan shifted his gaze to her. "Is that right, miss? Do you think He'll forgive me after all I done?"

Sybil wanted to say he would burn in hell, but didn't God say He forgives all sins? Even the sinner on the cross beside Him? She had to answer Brand's father honestly despite her reluctance.

"Mr. Duggan, I believe God forgives. Didn't He say, 'Father, forgive them?' about the men who killed him?" Now, why had she added that?

Mr. Duggan closed his eyes. "I'll think on it."

"Pa!" Brand surged to his feet and leaned over the bed, bringing Slim crashing to his feet.

Brand darted a glance at the foreman, then concentrated on his father. "Pa, isn't that what you always told Ma? And then you continued on with your outlawing. Don't do it again."

The older man shifted his gaze to Sybil. "Will God forgive my son, too?"

She allowed her gaze to rest on Brand, whose attention was riveted on his father, then she drew her attention back to his pa. "God is merciful." More than she thought any of them deserved.

"You be sure and tell him." The older man closed his eyes.

"Pa." Brand shook him. "Don't keep putting it off."

But the old man did not open his eyes.

"He's sleeping," Sybil said.

Brand sank back in his chair, his hands hanging between his knees, his head bent. "He's getting weaker. I fear…" He didn't finish.

She applied a fresh dressing to the wound and pulled the blanket over Mr. Duggan, then gathered up the bandages and dishes and headed for the door. Mercy joined her as she left the room.

Sybil had hoped for an excuse from Brand for his behavior, an explanation…something that made sense. She hadn't found it. Perhaps because there wasn't one.

Like his pa said, Brand was a Duggan. The man she'd thought she saw a few days ago was nothing but a figment of her overactive imagination.

Time to face reality and bring herself in line with the rules of conduct she'd lived by all her years.

## Chapter Twelve

Brand watched Sybil and Mercy leave the room, listening to Mercy's voice as they descended the stairs. He gave Slim a silent stare, then settled back in his chair.

It was the first time he'd been in a house in a very long time and it was a fine house. Pa lay on a real mattress, covered with real bedding. Likely he hadn't enjoyed such since before Ma died.

Nor had Brand enjoyed such since Ma's death. He'd been always on the run. Always hoping to stay ahead of Pa and Cyrus. Hoping no one would discover he was a Duggan.

But as Pa said to Sybil, he *was* a Duggan.

Although he'd gone along with the gang only to protect Sybil. He hadn't even held a gun during the attempted robbery. Not that he expected anyone to believe him.

There was only one more thing he wanted before he went to his short future—to see Pa accept God's forgiveness before he died.

Brand would also like to see Sybil believe his innocence. But he'd sacrificed that two days ago.

The patient stirred and Brand leaned forward to touch

his arm. "Pa?" he whispered, ignoring eagle-eyed Slim's watchfulness.

Pa mumbled something Brand couldn't make out.

Brand watched his chest rise and fall, his own breathing matching the movement. So long as Pa drew breath he still had the opportunity to seek forgiveness.

Brand kept a careful vigil, waiting for him to waken.

And praying. That surprised him. His neglected, forgotten faith had been right there all the time. He only had to stop and listen to the call in his heart.

The rise and fall of Pa's chest marked off the passing minutes.

Despite his concentration, Brand knew the exact second Sybil stepped into the room. He felt her with every nerve ending that responded in eager welcome. It took every ounce of self-control to keep his gaze on his father.

She was alone, and Slim rose to accompany her to the bed, guarding her.

"The dressings will need changing again."

Pa stirred as she lifted the covers. He opened his eyes.

Brand would not let Slim and his rifle, nor Sybil and her alluring presence, stop him. He leaned over his father. "Please, Pa, before it's too late."

"Brand, stop fretting." His thin hand patted Brand's. "I done made my peace with God. Like you said, He's forgiven me."

Joy erupted in Brand's heart. He had to share this feeling with someone, and looked up into Sybil's eyes, not caring that she would likely not rejoice as deeply as he was. Why would she? Most people would think the Duggan gang deserved nothing but punishment.

Her mouth curved in a sweet smile.

His heart threatened to jolt from his chest. For one heartbeat, two, and then a thunderous third beat he let himself drown in that look. Then Pa grabbed his hand and mercifully brought him back to his senses.

"Son, I ain't long for this world. Promise me something."

He wanted to argue that Pa would recover, but he couldn't. He'd seen how Linette had earlier applied a paste of something she said an Indian woman had given her, said it would stop bleeding in normal situations.

Pa's was obviously not normal, as his wound continued to bleed. "Anything." If it was in his power to do.

"Promise me you'll tell Cyrus he can be forgiven, too."

Surprised at the request, Brand jerked his gaze toward Sybil.

She shuddered. He felt her anger.

"Brand?" Pa sounded anxious, and Brand brought his gaze back to him.

"Yes, Pa. I promise."

The old man sighed. Brand waited, but Pa had fallen asleep, his chest rising and falling rhythmically.

Brand allowed himself to lift his gaze to Sybil again. "Can God forgive my brother?"

She would not meet his eyes. "Of course."

"Can you?"

She gathered up a basin full of soiled rags. "I don't know." And she left the room.

He understood. Neither brother could expect forgiveness from her. Cyrus didn't merit it and wouldn't care.

Brand could never prove he deserved it, even though he cared so much that his throat was impossibly tight.

Sybil hurried to her room, grateful that Mercy had gone out and Linette was busy elsewhere. Sybil needed to be alone. She didn't want to forgive any of the Duggans. And it bothered her more than she cared to admit.

In an attempt to forget about the whole business, she pulled out her notebook, intending to write something imaginary that had nothing to do with outlaws and cowboys—a story for children that ended happily in victory. But her fingers went instead to the pages she'd written about Brand.

She should send the story away as it was. A nameless cowboy. Only he was more than that—less than that. A cowboy with a shameful name, a shameful life. She jammed the pages back into her drawer and flung herself facedown on her bed, burying her sobs in her pillow.

She deserved every bit of pain she would endure. All along she'd known she should avoid the man.

She and Linette, with Mercy's help, cared for Mr. Duggan the rest of the day and throughout the night, but he died as dawn broke over the horizon on Sunday morning.

Both Sybil and Linette were in the room when he breathed his last.

Brand hovered at his side, knowing the end would be soon.

Linette reached over and touched his shoulder. "He's gone. I'm sorry."

Brand sank to the chair, his face drained of all color.

Eddie, who was guarding him, went to his side and squeezed his shoulder. "I'm sorry."

For all he showed, Brand might not even have heard.

Sybil stood immobile. He'd lost his father and that had to hurt, even for an outlaw. It reminded her of her own pain and sense of loss and loneliness when her parents had died. Even her anger at Brand for his deception could not block out her concern.

She joined Eddie at Brand's side.

He lifted his head enough to see the hem of her dress. She waited, wanting more. So much more. All of which she could never have.

Slowly, his head came up until he met her eyes. She knew he tried to bank his emotions, but his eyes darkened until they were almost black. She sensed his difficulty in breathing. Her own throat constricted and her eyes stung with tears. "I'm sorry for your loss."

He nodded, his eyes narrowing, his breathing deepening. "Thank you." He turned to Linette and then Eddie. "Thank you for your hospitality."

Linette smiled. "It's what we do."

The rancher cleared his throat. "We'll give you a moment to say goodbye to your father."

Linette headed for the door. Sybil hesitated. There was so much more she wanted to say. But it was to the Brand of unknown name. Not Brand, one of the Duggan gang.

For just a moment she let herself believe he was still the former, and touched his shoulder as Eddie had. "You have my deepest sympathy." And then, lest anyone misjudge her actions, she hurried after Linette.

Eddie stayed behind, his back to Brand and his father, out of respect for Brand's loss.

That afternoon they buried Morton Duggan in the little graveyard on top of the hill.

Jayne had questioned it. "He's a criminal. Should he be buried in the same ground as these good people?" Four graves of those who had died passing through the territory stood in the small plot.

"He's a sinner saved by grace," Linette said in her decisive way. "Aren't the angels in heaven rejoicing? How can we be less than charitable?"

And so a little assembly accompanied the body to its final resting place. Most of the cowboys refused to attend on principle. Cookie and Bertie came. Jayne and Seth, Cassie and Roper joined the procession, as did Mercy and Sybil. Linette and Eddie led the way, with Brand following them.

Eddie spoke a few words over the open grave. Sybil was not the only one who wiped away a tear. Perhaps, like herself, they were recalling their own pain. Jayne had seen her fiancé shot dead before her eyes. Cassie had buried a husband and two infants. Sybil didn't know what loss the others remembered, but it seemed each had a share of pain. Her own seemed fresh in her mind—a mother and father who'd died within weeks of each other.

A best friend who had died way too young.

Despite who and what Brand was, she felt his sorrow as if it was her own.

He stood before the grave, head bowed, hat in his hands almost hiding the ropes that bound him. Seth had been appointed to carry a gun to guard him. Out of respect the others had come unarmed.

Eddie said amen. Each of them tossed in a handful of dirt then passed by Brand, uttering condolences. Sybil went last. She ached to be able to forgive his treachery and who he was. But how could she? Yet she must let him know she understood his sorrow. She'd tried earlier, but felt he was too shocked by his father's death to really hear her. "I'm sorry," she said. Such inadequate words for all she felt. "I know what it's like to lose one's father."

His gaze jerked to her, hard, glistening with tears, yet probing.

She jolted as his look rattled against the insides of her heart—an intruder, unwelcome, unsafe.

"Your father was a good man. Mine was an outlaw." His voice grated. "It's not the same."

She patted his arm. "He was your father. It's the same."

She left. Why did she say that? It didn't make sense and yet it was the truth, and somehow, she knew he needed to hear it.

Bertie went to Eddie. "Boss, he needs to be alone with his grief and loss."

"It's not a privilege I can give him."

"Give me the gun. I'll guard him but respect his need for privacy."

Eddie considered the request, then nodded to Seth, who handed the rifle to Bertie. Bertie sat on a rock a few feet away.

Brand watched the proceedings without a flicker of expression.

"Ignore me," Bertie said. "I won't bother you unless you try and escape."

Sybil joined the others as they returned to the house. She lingered at the back door, watching Brand standing over his father's grave. Dawg lay at his feet, his head on his paws, watching his master.

Mercy came to her side. "I guess you can't help feeling sorry for him even though they are outlaws."

Sybil didn't answer. She could never forgive him for being an outlaw and for hiding his identity from her. Nor would she listen to her conscience, which said she must forgive if she wished to be forgiven. Any more than she'd listen to the part of her brain that said he hadn't forced her to enjoy his company the few days he was at the ranch under false pretenses.

She turned away and put her efforts into helping

Linette. Her body was usefully occupied. Too bad her heart wouldn't be diverted.

Brand stared at the hole before him. His father lay in the cold ground. He shivered. The grave would soon be covered with dirt and then a layer of snow. But Pa wasn't there. He was in heaven with Ma.

Brand wasn't sure how to deal with the sorrow that clawed at his insides. How often had he wished both Pa and Cyrus would not bother him anymore? But not like this. Death was too final.

He sighed and shifted his gaze toward the house. Was that Sybil in the shadows? Then the figure was gone. She'd expressed her regrets. Said she understood that he mourned his pa. He wished he could think she cared, that it was more than politeness, but he didn't dare allow such a thought.

He was more than grateful for the kindness shown his pa. That had to be all he could think of. Eddie had informed him he could wait in the barn for the Mountie's return. It was no more than Brand expected. He only wished the Mountie would hurry up so he could leave this place. He fought a constant fight against the sweet memories of the past few days.

"I'm done," he said to Bertie.

Bertie led him past the house, Dawg walking at his side. Brand forced himself not to look at the windows for a glimpse of Sybil. He had enough memories to carry him through his future, which would be short and end abruptly.

They went to the pen he and Dawg had recently shared. He averted his eyes from the place where Sybil had sat, her back to the rough wood as she visited with him and touched him. Silently, he submitted to being tied securely to a sturdy corner post.

"Surely hate to do this, son, but I got me orders."

"Don't worry. It's what I expect."

Bertie finished and squatted in front of him, eye to eye. "Linette says your pa made his peace with God before his death. Glad to hear that. What about you? Are you prepared to meet your maker?"

The man's gentle concern melted Brand's frozen heart and he smiled. "I am indeed. My ma was a strong believer and taught me to be the same, though truth be told, I let my faith slip for many years."

"I, too, had a believing ma and I wandered far from God for a time. My mother's prayers brought me back. Seems your ma's prayers have done the same. Do you care to send her a letter informing her of your pa's death?"

"My ma's dead, though she would have been pleased to hear of his change of heart."

"Son, I have to ask you, what led you into a path of crime?"

"I have my reasons."

"Care to tell me?"

"I wouldn't expect you to believe me."

"I'd believe you if it was true." Bertie held his gaze, demanding truth and confession.

Brand swallowed hard. If only he'd had a man like this for a father. The thought unleashed his usual reserve and loosened his tongue. "It was my brother who kidnapped Miss Sybil. He threatened…" Brand shuddered as he recalled Cyrus's ugly talk. "He said he'd do awful things unless I helped him. I figured if I went along she might be rescued." No point in mentioning Pa's promise. No one would believe Brand had trusted the word of an outlaw.

Bertie didn't even blink. "I see. Have you told Eddie this? Or the Mountie?"

"What difference would it make? I was involved in the robbery of the store. I'm a Duggan." And that said it all as far as people were concerned. It always had.

"Seems to me you're more than a Duggan. You're a good man." Bertie rose.

"I'll thank you not to repeat what I just said." Brand didn't want to be mocked for making up stories so people would think him innocent.

The other man rocked back and forth on his feet. "Are you saying you'd refuse my help?"

"I'm saying I doubt you could help, and I don't care to be considered a whiner."

Bertie patted his shoulder. "You're no whiner. Now try and be comfortable. I'll bring your supper when it's ready. You're in for a treat. My Cookie makes the best meals in the whole territory."

Brand chuckled at the man's pride. Not until Bertie left did he realize he'd not given the promise Brand had asked for. Not that it really mattered. Nothing Bertie said would convince anyone.

Brand hadn't slept at all the night before. He settled back in the straw now, Dawg at his side, and let sleep numb his thoughts. He jerked awake as Bertie entered and bent to loosen the ropes on his wrists.

"I ain't into feeding an able-bodied man."

Brand rubbed his bruised and raw skin, then turned to the food. "You didn't exaggerate," he said after his first mouthful. "I realized that when she sent a plate out to me before." He took another bite of the tender roast beef, mashed potatoes and gravy.

Bertie grinned. Then as Brand ate, he sat and told stories of people he'd met and places he'd been. He even managed to make Brand laugh a time or two.

"Son, I'd like to read from the Bible before I go."

The idea sat well with Brand and he agreed.

Bertie read for a few minutes—stories of the Israelites as they wandered the desert.

The words gave Brand comfort, but his wanderings were soon to end and he would join his ma and pa in heaven. The comfort fled as he choked back the tightness in his throat. Tightness from an imaginary rope about his neck.

## Chapter Thirteen

Sybil tossed and turned all night. She could not shake the uncertainty she felt about Brand. She rose tired and angry at herself. She did not want to think of him. He was an outlaw and would soon face justice. But he'd revealed nothing of that sort of nature while she'd kept him company, helped him sew up Dawg, nor when they'd walked to the river. Her cheeks burned with shame to think she had hoped he'd kiss her again. What was wrong with her? Never before in her life had she struggled to keep her thoughts on what was right and wise.

Realizing she was staring out the window in the direction of the barn, she jerked away and went to the library. She would take each book off the shelves and dust the place thoroughly. She sneezed as she tackled the job.

Two hours later she stood back, satisfied. Then her shoulders sagged. Now what? The job had not kept her from thinking of Brand and reliving every moment they had spent together. As it turned out, for her it was in blissful ignorance. Yet even knowing that couldn't erase those memories.

How was she to move on, with her heart so full of regrets and forbidden wishes?

She hurried from the library. The kitchen was empty. Linette must have taken Grady to visit Cassie's children. And who knew where Mercy disappeared to? The empty house echoed with Sybil's inner turmoil.

"I must forget him. Put him out of my mind," she murmured to the silent walls.

But how could she? Perhaps if she confronted him...

Her decision made, she grabbed a knit shawl and left the house, keeping her steps slow and measured, when she longed to rush down the hill.

She rehearsed what she would say: *Why did you not tell me who you are?* However, the answer was obvious. If he had, there would have been no chance of even a hint of friendship between them. Nor would he have been invited to come to the ranch in the first place.

Strange that his reputation hadn't preceded him. Everyone knew him only as a horse breaker. Why had there been no word of him being part of the Duggan gang? How did he manage to hide that and deceive so many people? Of course, his role in the gang necessitated he do exactly that. Win people's confidence, learn their secrets so the gang could rob them.

But if that was the case, why hadn't he accepted any of the invitations into the big house? Why had he shied away from any contact with others?

She pressed her palms to her temples. None of it made any sense. If she answered the questions truthfully, she couldn't see him as guilty. But was she only trying to make herself feel better about the way she had practically fallen over him?

The cookhouse lay on her left. She slowed her steps. Would Cookie soothe her with tea and cinnamon rolls? Jayne's cabin stood on her right. Would Jayne offer wise words? Tell her she should guard her heart?

Sybil stared straight ahead. She didn't want comfort nor wise words. She wanted answers to the ache in her heart, and only Brand could offer those. Though he likely had nothing to give but more lies, more deceit.

The barn door had been pushed open, letting in the cool afternoon air and bright sunshine. Sybil paused to glance about. Noted the thinning leaves on the trees, the dusty brown piles of them gathering along the edges of the yard as if huddling together against winter. They would soon find how futile it was to try and fight the season.

Was she being equally foolish? Refusing to accept the facts?

She opened the gate of the pen in front of the barn and slipped past the bars, holding her breath lest anyone see her and wonder if she had lost her mind.

A man's voice came from the interior of the barn. Not Brand's. She paused in the doorway to listen.

"You're not so high and mighty now, are you?" Cal. She recognized his voice.

She heard no reply from Brand, and wondered whether he spoke so softly she couldn't hear, or if he didn't even bother to answer the man.

"I've half a mind to drag you outside and let all your admiring fans see who you really are." Cal laughed, a short, bitter sound. "In fact, that's what I'm going to do. The others will be showing up for supper about now."

She caught the sound of grunting and scuffling. And Dawg growling.

"Dawg, quiet." These were the only words she heard Brand speak.

"Get to your feet," Cal said harshly.

Sybil clutched at the rough wood on the door frame. Why was Cal so vindictive? What did he hope to gain by parading Brand before the others? Everyone knew he was in the barn and why. But Cal wanted to further humiliate him.

Brand had dealt with enough already. His capture. His pa's death. Enough was enough.

Ignoring the warning voice in her head that said she should stay out of this, Sybil hurried down the aisle. She reached the open gate.

Dawg whined, alerting Brand. He stood before Cal, his hands bound, a rope around his neck. He shook his head as if warning her away.

But she was beyond paying attention to a warning of any sort. "I wonder what Eddie would think of this. Or have you sent him after an imaginary sick cow again?"

Cal spun about, his eyes wide with surprise, and then they narrowed. "It was a bull and this is none of your concern."

A few minutes ago she might have agreed with him. In fact, she might have been compelled to add her own words of condemnation. But suddenly everything was so clear she wondered how she could have been confused for even a minute.

Cal gave her his back as he turned his attention to Brand. "He's an outlaw. Don't bother wasting your time on him."

She stepped into the pen. Dawg pressed to her side and she patted his head, but kept her attention fixed on Cal. When he continued to ignore her, she grabbed his shoulder. "Who appointed you judge and jury?"

He spared her a look full of disbelief. "I could ask you the same thing."

"Sybil, leave it be." Brand obviously did not thank her for interfering.

"I have no intention of leaving it be. Cal, let him alone."

The cowboy laughed in her face. "Who's going to stop me?"

She grabbed the rope, surprising him enough that it slipped from his grip. She glowered at him. "I am."

Cal growled. "Little Miss London. Too good for the rest of us. You might just consider that you don't belong here and this is none of your business." He lunged for the rope, but Brand jerked away, pushed Sybil aside and faced Cal.

"You can call me an outlaw all you want, but you will treat Miss Bannerman like a lady."

Cal's face darkened. His fists curled.

Dawg's hackles rose and he snarled at the man.

Cal kicked at him. "Your dog is ugly and stupid." He grabbed the rope and yanked it tight.

Brand choked, fought the rope with his bound hands.

Sybil shoved Cal. He shoved back and she fell into the boards.

Dawg erupted into a ball of flying fur. He lunged at Cal, grabbed his arm and bit.

Cal shook his arm, balled his fist and—

Sybil screamed.

"Cal, that's enough." Eddie's voice stopped them mid-motion. He stepped into the pen and loosened the rope around Brand's neck. "Call off your dog."

Brand croaked out two words. "Dawg, down." He clutched at his throat. Dawg released Cal and stood back, his hackles raised, his teeth bared as he growled.

Cal held his arm. "That dog attacked me for no reason. I'm going to get my gun and shoot him." He stomped toward the gate.

"Stop." Eddie spoke the order softly but with no mistake. He meant to be obeyed.

Cal halted, his back to the others.

"You can pack your bag and be off the place immediately. I wouldn't advise you to linger. I might regret letting you off so easy if I have time to think about it."

Cal turned. "I ain't done nothing wrong."

Eddie planted his fists on his hips. "I heard enough, saw enough to disagree. You aren't the sort of man I wish to have on the place." His eyebrows rose. "I'm already having second thoughts about letting you just ride out."

Cal spared Brand one hot look and then tramped out of the barn.

Eddie faced Sybil and Brand. "Are you okay?"

"I'm fine," Sybil said.

Brand nodded and backed up to the corner.

"I'm sorry," Eddie said. "Outlaw or not, you don't deserve to be treated like that. I wish I didn't have to tie you up again, but I do."

Brand simply sat down and let himself be tied to the post.

Sybil bit her lip to keep from protesting. "Eddie, do you mind if I stay here and talk to Brand?"

"I believe you're safe enough." He backed away and left the barn.

Sybil lowered herself to the floor in front of Brand and sat staring at him, uncertain what she wanted to say.

He studied her, his eyes flat, his face expressionless. Then he laughed.

She stared. "What's so funny?"

He shook his head, unable to talk.

She lifted her eyebrows, silently demanding an answer.

"You," he sputtered. "'Little Miss London.' You certainly surprised that cowboy. You looked about ready to bear wrestle him." He laughed some more.

"I don't see what's so funny. He was about to hurt you." A trickle of amusement drowned out her fear and a grin grew on her lips. "I did surprise him, didn't I?" Not half as much as she'd surprised herself. Where had the fight come from? She was normally the most agreeable, most nonaggressive person imaginable. Her actions were totally out of character.

He sobered. "Why are you here?"

Her amusement ended as quickly as it had begun. "I don't know." She studied her fingers as they intertwined in her lap. "I guess I was hoping for some answers." She lifted her head and met his look, searching for truth.

At first his eyes were hard, then she detected a softening. He sighed. "What more do you need to know? I'm a Duggan."

"I don't believe that says it all."

He looked past her. Kept his attention focused on something beyond her shoulder.

"Brand, who are you besides that?"

Slowly his gaze came to her, and she shivered at the pain she saw embedded in them. He blinked as if he hoped to erase it, but failed.

She squeezed her fingers tighter to keep from reaching for him. Her heart could not forget the few days when she'd believed in him. The way they'd laughed together, nursed Dawg together. The way they'd kissed. "Why did you kiss me?"

The pain in his eyes deepened, turning them to black coals. "I'm sorry."

She shook her head. "That's not what I want to hear." When had she become so demanding? So outspoken? She knew the answer. When she began to sort out the pieces of what she knew about Brand. "Things just don't add up. If you were staking out the place, as we're supposed to believe, why did you never visit Eddie's house? Why did you avoid everyone on the ranch except me? Why didn't you ask questions about the place? What kind of front man could you possibly be?" She grew impassioned as she spoke, lifting her hands imploringly.

She knew she wasn't mistaken in judging his attitude shifted. His shoulders relaxed. His breathing came easier.

Then he shrugged. "I'm still a Duggan and that is how I'll be judged."

"Are you saying you'll go the gallows with your only defense being that you're a Duggan? Need I point out that is no defense at all?"

He tipped his head to one side in a dismissive gesture.

"I don't understand." She sorted through the events of the past few days. "Why did Cyrus kidnap me? If you were doing the job of spying out the land, why kidnap me? Wouldn't it just bring more attention to the gang? What purpose did my kidnapping serve?"

"Apart from giving Cyrus some sport, you mean?"

It wasn't meant as a question but an answer. A truly unsatisfactory one, she decided.

"I was very angry at first. I don't like being deceived. But more and more the whole situation simply doesn't make sense."

He studied the shape of his dog's head, visually examined the grain of the wood in the wall beside him and generally pretended a great interest in everything but her demands.

"Brand. Can you not offer an explanation? Don't I deserve at least that much?"

He shifted his gaze back to her, all sign of emotion

gone. "You figure one little kiss gives you the right to know everything about me?"

His harsh words drained the concern from her thoughts. She rose to her feet in a slow, self-controlled manner. "I haven't given the kiss another thought." It was as false as his pretense to be a good, kind man. Or was his falsehood in pretending to be an outlaw? She left the barn without a backward look.

But she could not shake off the feeling that things were not as they appeared, if anyone cared to look beyond the surface.

But was anyone willing to do so?

Brand waited until he knew she was long gone before he let out a low groan. "Sure hate to be mean to her," he explained to Dawg. "But what's the point in her thinking I'm innocent? The Mountie caught me in the act of robbing the store." No one would believe he was there against his will. After all, he was a Duggan. And that said it all. He'd ask for no mercy except from God, who knew the truth and had forgiven more than one Duggan.

*Lord, there's still Cyrus. Give him a chance to repent, too.*

*And thank you that Sybil wonders if I'm guilty.*

Brand could die with joy tucked around his heart to know that. More than that. If he held on to the memory of her facing down Cal, he could die happy.

He sobered instantly. He did not fancy dangling at the end of a rope. But he saw no way of avoiding it.

Because the truth was, he had been involved in a robbery. He had become what he had avoided so hard for years.

He'd become a Duggan in more than name.

Unable to guess at the time except to know the sun

shone in the western window of the barn, he settled down to wait, Dawg at his side.

He was roused by a shout outside. "It's the Mountie."

"Looks like he got the men."

"Nothing I like better'n to see two outlaws draped over the back of a horse."

Draped? As in dead? Cyrus was dead? Shock coursed through Brand's body. Somewhere deep in his brain he'd secretly hoped Cyrus would tell the truth about why Brand had been involved in the robbery. Now that chance was gone. Though all along he'd told himself no one would believe one Duggan over the other.

He strained upward, hoping for a glimpse of the Mountie, trying to catch more words, but he couldn't get high enough to see over the sides of the pen, nor could he hear the men as they rushed past and out of his hearing. "Dawg, I sure wish you could go find out what's going on."

Dawg stood at attention, listening to the commotion outside but choosing to stay at Brand's side.

Brand sank back, knowing he would have to wait until someone came to inform him. And wait he did, the minutes ticking by with maddening slowness.

It was Eddie who finally came. "The Mountie wants to see you." He untied Brand from the post, leaving his hands bound. "Trust you won't try and run."

Brand glanced about. "Would seem futile, seeing as every place I look there are people. 'Spect some of them would be happy enough to shoot another Duggan."

Eddie didn't reply as he led him up the hill.

Brand paused inside the door of the big house, struck once again by the size and beauty of the place. It was the right setting for a girl like Sybil.

She stood inside the room to the left of the big entry-way, her eyes watchful and still begging for the truth.

He managed a flicker of a smile that went no deeper than his lips. But he wanted to somehow assure her she needn't worry about him.

Then Eddie led him down the hall to another room. They stepped inside. The Mountie sat in a big leather chair, before an oak desk. Shelves full of books encircled the room, with chairs placed in three of the corners. Just right for reading. A little table provided a place for writing. He allowed himself one mental picture of Sybil sitting there, writing her stories, before he turned his full attention to Constable Allen.

"Guess you got the others."

"I wouldn't be here if I hadn't," the Mountie replied. "They both came back dead." He indicated a chair in front of the desk, and Brand sat. "Sorry about your brother."

Brand didn't answer for several seconds, still uncertain what he thought of Cyrus's death. Finally, he said the only thing that made sense. "I hoped for a chance to tell him he could find God's mercy. Guess it's too late for that."

"Again, I'm sorry."

*Sorry* was a pitifully inadequate word, but he guessed there was no other.

"Cyrus had lots to say before he died."

"Cyrus always was a talker. Ma used to say his tongue was loose on both ends." Now why had he said that? As if anyone cared.

The Mountie chuckled. "I can see why she'd say that. He had some mighty interesting things to say."

Brand held his counsel. Cyrus wasn't exactly the

truth-telling sort, so he couldn't begin to guess what had been said.

"I think he was afraid you'd get off scot-free, so he warned us that you might concoct a story. Even told us what it was you'd say. I found that a little odd. How would he know the details of your story? I've been asking around. Putting the information together."

"That a fact?" Whom had he been talking to and what information had he gathered?

"The facts are this. You were unarmed at the robbery. Miss Sybil says you never asked any questions that would gain you information of the sort needed for a robbery. Macpherson says you had been in the store only twice and both times hurried in and out. Eddie tells me you wouldn't even accept an invitation to the house. Seems odd if indeed you meant to rob him. Then Bertie comes to me and tells me that you were forced to go along with the robbery in order to protect Miss Bannerman. How am I doing so far?"

Brand couldn't put two words together. All those people had spoken in his defense?

The Mountie continued. "I have one question for you." He waited for a nod from Brand. "Are you guilty or innocent?"

Brand considered his answer carefully. He had no desire to hang, but neither did he want to spend the rest of his life running from the Duggan name. "I was with the gang when they tried to rob Macpherson's store, but I did not wish to be."

The Mountie smiled. "I'll take that as a plea of innocence." He closed his notebook and nodded toward Eddie. "He can go free."

The rancher untied his ropes and clapped Brand on the back. "I have to say, keeping you prisoner went against my judgment. I'm glad to see I was right in my estimation of you. Now come and join us for supper."

Brand stood, rubbing his wrists and feeling as out of place as Dawg would have. "Might be best if I move on. I'm still a Duggan."

"Nonsense. If you leave without giving us a chance to prove we believe you're innocent, you'll forever wonder whether or not we do. You want to carry that with you down the trail?"

"I guess not."

"Then come along." And before Brand could think of a reason to refuse, he found himself drawn into a big kitchen, warm with the feel of family and love, full of the smells of good home-cooked food and the smiling faces of those who lived in the house.

He stared at Sybil. He couldn't help himself. She'd spoken on his behalf. Overwhelmed by how things had changed for the better, he lowered his gaze to the floor. "I'm grateful for—" He couldn't even say what it was, so didn't finish.

Linette sprang forward. "I never did believe you were part of the gang. Now sit here." She indicated a chair at the table, and he sat.

Everyone suddenly found chairs and settled into them. Constable Allen sat beside him, Grady beyond that. Linette and Eddie at each end of the big wooden table, Mercy and Sybil across from each other. All Brand had to do was lift his eyes and he connected with Sybil's steady blue ones. He expected his were full of shock, since he hadn't yet processed the events of the past hour. Hers brimmed with triumph.

If only he could guess what that meant. Was she happy she'd put some of the pieces together even without the Mountie's help?

Was she happy Brand wasn't going to hang?

He ducked his head. His heart raced with impossible possibilities.

## Chapter Fourteen

Sybil could hardly sit through the meal. It went on and on as Eddie and Linette shared all the details of what the Mountie had discovered.

As for Mercy...well, her friend said over and over, "I can't believe you have all the adventures, while I can't find one no matter how hard I look."

Sybil only wanted the meal to end. As soon as it did she would find an opportunity to speak to Brand alone.

Constable Allen broke into the conversation and asked Brand, "Would you like to see your brother?"

"I'd appreciate it."

Eddie and Linette shared one of those secret communicative looks, then the rancher spoke. "Do you want to bury him next to your father?"

Brand did his best to hide his emotions, but Sybil felt his surprise and gratitude just as she'd felt it throughout the meal. It would appear that carrying the Duggan name had brought him nothing but regrets. Well, now he could change that.

"He was an outlaw." Brand's words were strained. "And as far as I know, he never repented."

The Mountie cleared his throat. "I don't think any of

us are able to judge that matter. Cyrus did not die right away. I spoke to him once he could no longer talk non-stop. I told him he could make his peace with God."

Brand clenched his knife and fork so hard they must surely leave permanent impressions in his palm. "I expect he told you he didn't care anything for God."

"At first he did, then he asked if God could indeed forgive an outlaw. Much as I wanted to say otherwise, because I sometimes prefer a human form of justice—a man gets what he deserves for the life he's led—I had to say God accepts everyone who comes to Him in faith, seeking forgiveness."

Sybil watched Brand. Hope dawned in his eyes.

The Mountie continued. "I can't be a hundred percent certain, but I believe Cyrus asked for that forgiveness before he drew his last breath."

Brand's lungs emptied in a long sigh. "I am relieved to hear that. Thank you."

"Then it's agreed," Linette said. "You'll bury him next to his father."

"It's most generous of you," Brand said.

"Nonsense." Linette's mouth drew a firm line. "Even if Constable Allen hadn't given us this bit of assurance the offer would stand. I don't believe in living by man-imposed rules."

"Do you want to wait until tomorrow?" Eddie asked.

Brand again got that distant, half-disinterested look in his eyes as he glanced at the window. "Guess we should. It's already dark out. I'll dig the grave myself."

Eddie considered him a moment, then nodded. "I'll get you a shovel." He rose, signaling the meal was over, and Brand and the Mountie followed him outside.

Linette excused herself to put Grady to bed.

Mercy bounced to her feet. "How romantic."

Sybil turned to her as she gathered up the dishes and carried them to the washbasin. "I fail to see how knowing your family is a bunch of outlaws is the least bit romantic." Had Eddie stayed with Brand? she wondered. Or was he alone in the dark digging a hole for his brother's body?

Eddie and Constable Allen came through the door and went to the library, answering her question. They'd left him alone.

As she moved about the kitchen, she paused to glance out the window. A faint glow of a lantern shone from the little plot. She rubbed at her breastbone. A man should not be alone when dealing with his brother's death.

Mercy came to her side. "Why don't you join him?"

"I don't know if he'd welcome it." Her heart ached for his aloneness in the midst of his loss. Every so often the light dimmed as if a scoop of dirt had been tossed past it.

"I'll come with you if you want."

Sybil shook her head. She didn't want Mercy to be with her. "I'm sure he's okay."

Her friend grabbed her arm and shook her a little. "If you don't go out there, I will. The poor man has lost his father and brother. He's been accused of being part of the gang when he wasn't. Don't you think he deserves a little sympathy?"

"He deserves it, but will he welcome it?"

Linette returned to the kitchen. "What are you two arguing about?"

Mercy flung about to face her. "I think Sybil should go up there and keep Brand company, but she doesn't think it's appropriate."

Linette joined them at the window. "I thought Eddie should have stayed with him, but he said Brand asked to be left alone. I guess we need to give him space if that's what he wants."

They watched in silence for a bit.

"Eddie insisted he spend the night in the bunkhouse. Says with Cal gone no one will give Brand a hard time."

Sybil tried to picture Brand in a bunk, with the others nearby. "Did he agree?"

"Said he'd think on it."

Which meant he'd ignore the invitation and find a place on his own.

The distant light grew brighter. Sybil could make out Brand's shadowy shape as he headed back toward the house. She grabbed her shawl. "I'm going to speak to him." She slipped out the door.

"Feel free to use the chairs by the back step," Linette called, as if knowing she wanted to be alone with him.

Sybil caught up to him in a few moments. He'd slung the shovel over his shoulder. His footsteps were weary, heavy. Digging a hole was hard work. Losing a father and brother was even harder.

She fell in at his side. Neither of them spoke. Dawg whined a greeting and she patted his head.

She couldn't say what the silence meant for Brand, but she felt no need for words. She only wanted to be with him. Let him know he wasn't alone.

"Sit and visit a spell." She indicated the chairs along the wall.

He sank down, dropped the shovel to the ground and stared at it, his hands hanging between his knees. Dawg pressed close to his legs, though Brand didn't seem to notice.

The silence lengthened, but Sybil still could not speak until he sucked in a deep breath and sat up straight. "That's the last of my family."

She squeezed his hand. He seemed not to notice that, either.

"At least he managed to establish your innocence before he died."

"I always hoped both he and Pa would stop their outlawing, even though I knew if they did they would hang."

"Such a waste of both lives. How did your mother cope?"

Brand leaned his head back against the wall. "She prayed every day that they would repent. She tried to stay away from them just as I have. It meant always being ready to leave. Hoping no one would associate us with the Duggan gang."

"Her prayers were answered."

He stared at her. "I guess they were." He sounded both surprised and unconvinced.

"I hear Eddie invited you to stay in the bunkhouse."

"It was kind of him."

"But you aren't going to do it, are you?"

Brand shook his head. "I don't think everyone would welcome me. I'm still a Duggan…."

His fatalism made Sybil want to shake him. "The Duggan gang are dead. Isn't it time you stopped living like you're part of them?"

"I'm not. I don't. I never thought that."

"I think you do. They will never be a threat to you again, but they still have a hold over you. When will you stop looking over your shoulder to see if they've found you? When will you stop expecting others to see you as one of the Duggan gang?" She'd said far more than she should, and none of the things she'd wanted to say, but her insides burned with unnamed emotions. She rose to her feet and strode toward the door, pausing with her hand on the knob. "I'm sorry for your loss."

The others were gone and she slipped to her room and sank to the edge of her bed. What was wrong with her? She'd never been outspoken in her life and yet she couldn't seem to stop speaking her mind around Brand.

Maybe Proverbs would help her regain control. Sybil reached for her Bible and notebook. Just below, hidden by a scarf, were the pages she'd written about Brand. She pulled them out and glanced over the words, then dipped her pen in ink and wrote.

*Cowboy had a name...that of a notorious outlaw gang. All his life he'd tried to distance himself from them. He'd run, he'd remained aloof from others.*

She stopped there. How long would it take for him to stop living like a man on the run? Would he ever?

Despite Eddie's generous invitation, Brand took his horse and his bedroll and returned to the campsite he'd used before. Dawg turned about three times before he settled down and instantly fell asleep.

Brand knew sleep would not come as easily for him, if indeed it came at all.

Sybil had suggested he needed to stop seeing himself as part of the Duggan gang. He'd never been one of them...except in name. But she was right about one thing. It would take a long time for him to feel free of them.

Tomorrow he'd bury Cyrus, and then he'd move on before—

He was doing it again. Running from a now non-existent danger. Perhaps the sense of impending doom would never leave him.

He wouldn't run from *them* this time. When it was time to leave, he'd just leave. Sybil's concerned face came to mind. Her laugh. Her courage in facing Cal...

and him. Maybe he wouldn't be in a hurry to leave. But then he thought of Eddie and Linette's house, a beautiful home full of lovely things. Why, the staircase itself had more wood in it than most of the houses he'd lived in. He looked about. The only wood in his current *home* burned in the fire. Sybil belonged in a house like that, married to a rich landowner.

The night closed in around him and he shivered. The first snowfall would come in the mountains anytime. He'd soon have to find a place to spend the winter.

What better place than Eden Valley Ranch?

But did he have any reason to stay? Would Sybil want him to? Or was he mistaking kindness for something more, looking for hope when there was none?

The questions lingered in his mind through the night.

Next morning, Brand returned to the ranch, Dawg patiently at his side. He asked Bertie to say the final words over Cyrus, and then led the way up the hill. Cyrus's body was wrapped in a gray woolen blanket and draped over the same horse the Mountie had brought him in on. Likely most of the assembled figured it was all the outlaw deserved. Cyrus would have been the first to say it was the kind of burial he wanted.

At the hole he'd dug, Brand stopped. Constable Allen and Eddie helped him lower the body into the grave.

People gathered to one side. He glanced at them. Sybil stood front and center in a black dress and bonnet, as if in mourning.

The idea jolted through him. The only time she'd met Cyrus he'd given her no reason to mourn his death.

Brand met her gaze, felt her blue eyes bore through him, challenging him. What did she want from him? What did she expect?

Bertie cleared his throat and Brand brought his focus back to the reason for being there.

"This is not a happy occasion for us, but it's especially sad for Brand. He's buried his father and his brother in two days. There are no words to erase the sorrow he must feel."

Brand began to wish he hadn't asked Bertie to speak. The man had a way of probing at pain with his words. Pain that Brand would just as soon ignore. He did his best to block out the rest of what Bertie said until the final "amen."

Again those present passed by, tossed a handful of dirt into the yawning hole and spoke condolences. He mumbled appropriate responses, though he couldn't have told anyone what he said.

Then he stood alone at the grave, Dawg at his side.

Time to fill in the hole. He turned to grab the shovel that someone had placed nearby...and came face-to-face with Sybil.

"I thought everyone had gone."

"I couldn't leave you alone with..." She nodded at the shovel in his hand. "It doesn't seem right."

"I've been alone a long time. Every Christmas. Every beautiful spring day. Every time I rode through a town or worked at a new place. Dawg here has been about my only companion." Now why had he said all that? As if he cared. As if he wished it could be different.

"Didn't you ever wish it could be different?"

What? She could read his mind? "Not much point in wishing for stars. Might as well be content with candles." He threw in three shovelfuls of dirt.

She leaned back on her heels and watched. Seems she didn't intend to leave.

He paused to listen as she spoke.

"On the other hand, why would you stick to a flickering candle if someone offered you a handful of stars?"

He stared at her. Did she mean it as it sounded? "Are you offering stars?"

"Would you prefer to hang on to your candle?"

"Do you see a candle in my hand?" He returned to throwing dirt over Cyrus's body, trying to think of it as only filling in a hole, not saying goodbye forever to his brother.

Brand stopped and backed away from the hole. He leaned on the shovel, trying to control the way his breathing came in choked sounds. "We used to be best of friends." His words grated from a dusty throat.

Sybil moved to his side and rested her black-gloved hand on his forearm, warm and gentle. "I always wished I had a brother or sister."

"He taught me how to chop wood, how to build a fire, how to cook a meal over a campfire. He made me run hard to keep up with him. Challenged me to take chances beyond my years, rather than let him think I was afraid." Brand couldn't go on. This was the Cyrus he remembered and missed. Not the angry, hurtful man of later years.

"That's how you should remember him."

Again, she had read his mind, voiced his thoughts. How did she do that?

Brand swiped his arm across his face, hoping she would think he wiped away sweat rather than the tear that escaped the corner of his eye. For a moment it was impossible to speak. Then the words came out slowly, haltingly. "Pa and Cyrus weren't always outlaws. Not until…" He let himself remember those strain-filled days for the first time in years. "Pa bought a little farm. He was so proud of it. We had every sort of animal. I loved them all. And Pa never said no to me bringing another one home." Brand paused, gathering together his memories, sorting through them, trying to understand. "He'd had to borrow to buy the place. We lived there for four years and Pa was so proud that he always made the payments on time. 'No banker will ever take the farm,' he used to brag."

Sybil's hand rubbed up and down Brand's arm, soothing away the anger that usually accompanied the memory of those final normal days.

"Then the wheat crop got hit with hail. Lightning killed half the cows. A fire destroyed the hay crop. Pa couldn't make the payment that year and asked for leniency. He came home so angry. A new banker had come to town. He cared not for missed payments, no matter the reason. He gave Pa two weeks to come up with the money or the bank would take the farm. Pa said he'd get the money by hook or by crook. And he did. He robbed the bank that threatened to take the farm. Paid the entire amount of the loan. I think he meant for that to be the one and only time he turned to crime, but then we needed feed. Cyrus decided he needed a fancy riding horse. Pa thought Ma would enjoy a new buggy." Brand shrugged, though he felt anything but indifference.

Sybil's hand tightened on his arm. "Let me guess. Your pa had discovered he didn't have to wait for things. He thought he'd discovered a ready source of funds."

"'Fraid that's exactly what he thought. They were wanted men. Someone was killed in their third bank heist. After that, they were wanted dead or alive. I wasn't yet twelve and Ma took me and moved. We always tried to distance ourselves from the Duggan name."

"Why didn't you go by a different name?"

"We did for years. Then someone noticed my likeness to members of the Duggan gang. So we moved on. After that I never bothered telling anyone my name. Made it easier."

"Is Brand your real name?"

He smiled for the first time all day. "I have Cyrus to thank for that. When I was born, he wanted to know if Pa was going to brand me like they did the calves. Pa thought it so funny he said they'd settle for calling me Brand."

She laughed. "That's sweet." Her gaze held his, caring and searching, delving deep into his thoughts.

He tried to bank his emotions, but her probing went clear through his defenses. He blinked back the sting of tears. No way would he cry.

She reached up, touched the corner of each eye with her gloved hand. "I'm glad you have good memories to cherish."

He caught her hand and pulled it to his chest, so lost in the depths of her gaze that his head spun. "I will prize this moment."

She didn't blink. Didn't withdraw. "So will I," she whispered. "The moment when I met the real Brand Duggan."

He considered her words. Who was the real Brand Duggan? He wasn't sure he even knew. But one thing was for certain: he hoped reality included more times like this.

"Where do we go from here?" he asked, hoping she didn't think he meant to ask if they should go to the house.

She smiled so sweetly his throat constricted. "Wherever we want, I suppose. How about you finish filling in the grave. Say your final goodbye to a brother you loved, then we'll join the others for church."

He nodded in agreement and filled in the hole, smoothing the dirt into a mound. He stood at the fresh grave, head bent, Sybil at his side. "Goodbye, Cyrus. I like to think of you in heaven, your sins forgiven. You did plenty of bad things, lots of them against me. You even hurt Sybil here, and whether or not she forgives you is up to her, but I'm forgiving you. I'm sorry you ruined your life. But that's over. Goodbye, my brother." He was about to step back when Sybil caught his hand.

"Wait. I want to say something, too." She stood by the fresh dirt, looking down as if speaking to Cyrus. "I vowed I would make you pay for how you treated me. But justice belongs to God. I forgive you. Rest in peace."

She took Brand's hand again and led him down the hill to the cookhouse, where the church service was held.

He didn't realize until he stepped inside that he'd agreed to attend. By then it was too late.

# Chapter Fifteen

She dropped his hand as they entered the cookhouse, but not before she felt him shudder, and guessed the cause. She might be wrong, but she believed it would be the first time he'd darkened the door of a building filled with others, especially for a Sunday service, in many years. How would it feel? Frightening, most certainly, but she hoped it also offered a breath of hope to a man used to being so alone no one even knew his whole name.

Several of the cowboys shuffled their feet as if uncertain how to react to a Duggan in their midst, attending a church service.

Brand hung back. He likely would have retreated except for her hand on his elbow, holding him firmly in place.

Bertie sprang to his feet. "Brand, I'm glad as can be to see you here. I told my wife I hoped you'd come. Darlin'?" He turned to Cookie. "This is Brand. Son, this is my wife. Everyone calls her Cookie and you no doubt know why, since you've tasted her cooking."

Cookie swept forward, grabbed Brand's hand and pumped it up and down. "Glad to meet you. Come on in." She practically dragged him forward to a bench, and he sat because he didn't have much choice.

Sybil perched beside him, her elbow pressed to his arm. Tension vibrated from him. His hands clamped his knees and he stared at Bertie, who had moved to the front of the assembly.

Cookie led the group in two familiar hymns. Sybil sang without considering the words. Her mind was on the man next to her. She had the feeling Brand might spring to his feet and dash from the room at any moment.

Then Bertie stood and smiled at him for several seconds until Brand visibly relaxed. Only then did Bertie begin to speak. "I could tell you many stories about sinners saved by grace. I expect most, if not all of you, could add stories. Perhaps your own. But today I want to tell you a different sort of story."

They sat spellbound as he talked about how he had wandered far and been brought back by the prayers of a faithful mother. Then he closed with a prayer.

"Coffee and cinnamon buns coming right up," Cookie said. She faced Brand. "I would be greatly pleased if you'd stay. In fact, I might be offended if you left."

Eddie and several of the others laughed. "Best you don't offend her," the rancher said.

"Please stay," Sybil whispered. "Let people accept you as Brand Duggan."

He flicked a look at her, then returned his gaze to Cookie. "I've had the pleasure of tasting your cinnamon buns, and I have to say I'm not prepared to pass up a chance to enjoy them again."

She beamed at him.

Mercy sat across the table. Linette and Eddie joined them. Roper brought his family forward and introduced them, as did Ward.

"You'll figure them all out soon enough," Sybil assured Brand.

The conversation turned to general things of mutual concern to those gathered in the cookhouse, and Brand sat back, listening. Sybil wondered how he felt about it all.

As people began to leave, Linette turned to him. "We have a big dinner up at the house. I'd like you to join us."

Brand jerked to his feet. "That's most generous, but I've things to attend to." He hurried for the door.

Sybil hustled after him, catching up as he reached the outdoors. Dawg rose to follow him. "Brand, why are you rushing away?" She knew he had nothing to attend to.

He simply shook his head for an answer.

She fell in step at his side. "Promise me you won't ride away this afternoon."

He stopped, stared at her. "Why?"

She knew then that he'd planned to do so. "Because I'd like to talk to you some more." She lowered her head at her boldness. "If you leave today you will still be running. Don't you need to stop running?"

"And do what?"

He sounded truly dumbfounded, as if it was all he knew and he couldn't think of an alternative. Finally, he nodded. "I'll hang around for the day."

"Good. I'll come and visit you."

"Suit yourself." A grin tugged at his mouth before he strode away, and as he disappeared into the trees, she heard him whistling a little tune.

Brand stared at the fire as he ate cold beans right from the can. Dawg happily licked a second can clean.

Yes, he might have enjoyed a pleasant church service with Sybil at his side, but he needed time to think through this whole business. Who was he? A Duggan still. But what did that mean now? Could he make it mean what he wanted?

"Dawg, I plumb don't know what came over me. I went to church. Can you imagine that?"

Dawg didn't look up. He wasn't real good company.

Then Brand had agreed to hang about waiting for Sybil to visit. "It sure didn't take any persuading." How long before she came? Or would she think better of it? "Why would a fine lady like Sybil come out here to visit me? A Duggan?"

*Stop acting as if the Duggan gang is still a threat.*

Well, even if being a Duggan wasn't a problem, Brand was still just a cowboy with nothing to call his own except a dog, a horse, a saddle and a few items of clothing. Sybil was used to so much more.

He argued with himself for hours while the sun passed to midafternoon.

When Sybil never came, his thoughts went dark. She wasn't coming, he told himself. He knew she wouldn't. He wasn't disappointed. Much.

Only enough for him to jump to his feet and kick a cloud of dirt into the fire. Might just as well move on.

Dawg rose, whined and looked to the trees. Brand's heart took off at a full gallop. He slowly brought his head about, hoping it was her, and shielding his eyes under the brim of his hat lest she see his eagerness.

Against the sky-blue backdrop, Sybil stood there and smiled. She'd changed out of her black dress into something yellow as sunshine. Her head was uncovered, her hair pulled back like a golden crown around her head.

His tongue pressed to his teeth and refused to form a word.

"Hello," she said.

When he continued to stare, she glanced about, saw the two empty bean cans and laughed, a merry sound that danced through the air.

"To think you could have enjoyed roast beef and two kinds of pie, plus all the trimmings and extras you could want. Linette and Eddie always put on a big spread on Sunday. Everyone is invited." Her eyes returned to him, burning through his well-reasoned arguments like lightning.

"Maybe you'll come to dinner next Sunday."

He forgot all about his decision to move on. "Maybe."

"Eddie says he could use you on the ranch."

"Uh-huh." Brand seemed incapable of more than grunts and one-word replies.

"Do you have other plans?"

"For what?"

"For the winter…for the future."

Had she added the last out of politeness or did she care?

He shook his head. Why would she? He looked at her mouth. Had one stolen kiss meant anything to her?

"Do you mind if I sit?" She indicated the butt end of a log.

"Sit. Sit." He snatched off his hat, waited for her to settle and fluff her skirts around her. He abused the rim of his hat.

She smiled sweet enough to melt ice. "It would be easier to talk to you if you sat as well."

He grabbed another hunk of log, placed it firmly and balanced on it.

"That's better." She folded her hands primly. "I think it's time to get to know the real you."

"Me?"

"Yes, you. Who are you, Brand Duggan, when you aren't pretending you're nobody?"

Her question slammed into him and reverberated. "I am nobody. Have been for a long time."

She leaned forward, her gaze intent, demanding. "You've never been nobody. Just running from what you feared you were."

"I've never been afraid." He tried to believe it, but remembered how his heart would leap when he thought Pa and Cyrus had found him. Like a few days ago, when he'd heard a quail call.

"There is no reason to be afraid. So tell me about yourself."

He stared. What on earth did she mean?

Her eyes flickered as if she heard his silent question. "Things like your dreams and hopes. What would people say about you if you ever let them get to know you?"

He shook his head. "There are no answers to those questions." There was one way to stop this interrogation. "What are *your* dreams and hopes?"

She drew back, shifted her gaze and considered her answer. "I guess I hope for a life of safety and security."

He waited, never taking his attention from her, knowing her answer only scratched the surface.

She smoothed her skirt and sighed. "I've always wanted to please my parents."

"They're gone. Shouldn't you do what is right for you without wondering what they would think? Seems to me that would make them proud."

Her eyes widened, filled with protest.

In this far already, he might as well go all the way. "You should listen to your own advice, Miss Sybil Bannerman. If you weren't concerned with what others would say, what would you do?"

She swallowed hard, her gaze riveted on his face. "I would try and publish my stories in my own name."

"Then do it."

"It's not that easy."

"Are you afraid of the risks?" Wasn't *he*? "This is the West. Things can be different." His words accused him. "You can make them different." Did he truly believe it? If he did, wouldn't he act on the knowledge?

Her head snapped up. "That's exactly what I've been trying to tell you. You can make people look at the Duggan name differently."

They stared at each other, her eyes blazing with challenge.

He figured his did, as well. Then the humor of the situation hit him and he laughed. "A Mexican standoff."

Her eyes widened. "What's that?"

"It usually means two gunfighters confront each other and there is no way either can win because they are evenly matched. But it can also refer to something like this, when neither party is willing to back down."

She laughed. "I expect you know a lot of cowboy stories."

He shrugged. Of course he knew a few.

"Have you ever seen a Mexican standoff where guns weren't involved?"

Grinning at the memory that sprang to mind, he said, "I once heard of one between two men on horses. Seems they both headed down a narrow alleyway at the same time, coming from opposite ends. There wasn't room for the horses to pass and neither would give in and back his horse out. They spent most of the day there until a Mountie came along and made them both back up and use a different route."

She laughed, the sound dancing across the strings

of his heart. "What do you call a horse like the one Cal found for you? The one Eddie had forbidden anyone to ride."

"That's easy. An outlaw. He obeys no rules. Accepts no authority."

"Oh, I like that." She smiled as if pleased with his explanation. She studied him intently. "You said you spent last winter in a cabin? Is that how you've spent—what is it? Six winters since your mother died?"

A thousand memories, ten thousand hopes and dreams and twice as many disappointments ambushed him, leaving his lungs too tight to do their job. Outlaw lungs. Then his breath eased with a whistle and he was able to speak.

"It was December when Ma died. She'd already made plans for Christmas. She worked extra hard planning a special day. I worked, too, by cleaning out the livery barn every afternoon. Ma did laundry, took in mending and cleaned houses.

"We hadn't seen Pa and his gang in a long time. Ma said maybe they'd decided to leave us alone. I hoped it was so." He broke off and tried to slow his thoughts. "I don't know why I'm telling you this. I've put it out of my mind."

She held his gaze in a velvet grasp that made it impossible to pull away. "You've tried to forget it but you haven't. What happened to your ma?"

"Pa." One word, but it said everything he felt. "Pa and Cyrus showed up. They brought gifts. A blue taffeta dress for Ma. You should have seen her eyes light up. For me, they brought a brand-new pair of alligator boots and a leather belt. I guess my eyes lit up, too.

"But Ma put the dress back in the paper and handed it to Pa. She said she couldn't benefit from ill-gotten gains.

I handed back the boots and the belt, too, though it hurt me a lot to do so." Brand paused, lost in his memories of that time. "I didn't think life could get any worse. But it did." Hearing the regret and maybe a bit of misery in his voice, he held up his hand. "Not that I'm whining. I've had a good enough life." For a Duggan.

Sybil made a disbelieving sound. Her mouth pulled down.

He didn't want sympathy. So he went on with his story. "Pa and Cyrus stormed out. A little later a neighbor rushed over to say the general store had been robbed. Many of the Christmas presents ordered by the townsfolk had been stolen or broken, and the store owner shot."

Sybil touched his hand, squeezed it. "It was your pa's gang?"

"Of course. Guess he figured to make Ma pay for refusing his gifts."

"That's dreadful."

Brand quirked his eyebrows, hoping she would read the gesture as agreement rather than the pain and shame it indicated. "That's what I've been trying to tell you. The Duggan gang was awful."

A few moments of silence passed, filled with regret and shock, before he continued. "Ma knew it was them. We packed up and escaped into the dark, with no place to go on a bitter cold night. We made camp toward morning, hiding in a stand of fir trees. Ma didn't want me to start a fire, but she was so cold I ignored her. She insisted we move on, but she was weak and grew weaker. Three days later, she could barely walk. An old couple found us and took us to their farm. She died December twentieth. They helped me dig a grave in the frozen ground and we buried her there."

"Oh, Brand. How awful."

He shrugged, though he could not dismiss the pain of those dreadful days.

"The old couple was good to me. I stayed until spring. When I heard news of the Duggan gang at work nearby, I moved on."

"And you've been moving on ever since."

"Sometimes not soon enough."

"You can make things different now." Sybil squeezed his hand.

He didn't remember turning his palm to hers, but her soft and narrow hand lay in his and he squeezed back. She offered so much hope, so much promise, but…

"Will you try?"

How could he refuse such a gentle plea? He let himself drown in her gaze and nodded, ignoring the toll of warning bells. The Duggan gang was dead, he told himself, to silence the discordant sound.

The next morning Sybil watched Brand ride into the yard, Dawg at his horse's heels. He spoke to Eddie. They shook hands and Eddie pointed toward the barn.

Brand glanced up the hill and touched the brim of his hat.

She lifted her hand in a wave before he stepped into the barn. She glanced toward the sky. *Thank you, God.* She couldn't stop smiling. Brand had decided to stay and work for Eddie.

Mercy nudged her, sending a jolt of surprise jolt thought her.

"I didn't know you were there," Sybil declared.

"I caught you mooning over that cowboy."

She knew there was no point in arguing with Mercy, especially when it was true. Still, she wasn't about to give her friend the satisfaction of agreeing. "Just admiring the nice day."

Mercy laughed. "Of course you are. Maybe you'd like to go for a walk."

Sybil longed to go to the barn and see what Brand meant to do. She'd like to ask Eddie if Brand had agreed to live in the bunkhouse. Instead, she turned from the window. "Shouldn't we help Linette with the laundry?" She headed for the kitchen, where Linette had tubs of hot water set out. Soon the three of them were up to their elbows, scrubbing and rinsing clothes.

When Eddie came to the house for dinner the laundry was all out on the line, flapping in the cold breeze.

Linette, well aware of Sybil's interest in Brand even though she'd done her best to hide it, waited until Eddie had filled his plate to ask the questions pressing at Sybil's mind.

"Did Brand say how long he meant to stay?"

Eddie glanced up from his full plate. "Said it seemed a good place to spend the winter."

Sybil barely contained her smile.

Linette beamed at her. "That sounds promising, doesn't it?"

Sybil pretended a great interest in spreading butter on a hot biscuit.

Linette turned back to her husband. "Is he going to live in the bunkhouse?"

Sybil's biscuit stopped halfway to her mouth. She couldn't make her hand go any farther as she waited for the answer.

Eddie nodded. "He asked if Dawg could spend the nights in the barn, and when I said he could, Brand threw his bedroll on an empty bunk. He took the one nearest the door." Eddie sounded as if that choice was significant, and Sybil suspected it was.

Mercy said the words for her. "Guess he wants to be able to run if he wants."

"He has no need to run," Sybil protested, even though she'd thought the same. Winter and then what? Would he move on, leaving her to pick up the pieces of her life?

"And every reason to stay." Mercy chuckled.

Linette and Eddie exchanged one of their private smiles.

Grady, quiet until now, looked up from his plate. "He likes Sybil."

All the adults except Sybil laughed. Her cheeks burned. It was on the tip of her tongue to protest, but knowing it was useless, she kept silent.

It was all she could do to keep her mind on her tasks as the afternoon hours passed. Would he come to the house and ask for her? Would he expect her to go down the hill to meet him? Or was she imagining all sorts of possibilities when there were none?

She was at the window when Eddie headed up the hill for supper, Grady at his side. She lingered despite Mercy's knowing laugh as the cowboys hurried toward the cookhouse. Brand brought up the rear—a good ten feet behind the others. Her heart went out to him. How long would it take for him to feel comfortable around people?

He looked toward the house and again touched the brim of his hat.

Mercy chuckled. "I do believe he saw you."

"Why are you spying on me?" Sybil's voice held no rancor. Mercy was simply being Mercy. She liked adventure, liked to keep things exciting, but she didn't have an unkind bone in her body.

"Because it's so much fun."

Sybil turned from the window. "You've stuck close to the house all day."

Mercy wrapped an arm about Sybil's waist as they turned toward the kitchen. "I didn't want to miss anything."

"That's strange. You usually create your own excitement."

"Usually," Mercy agreed. "But you're much more interesting lately. Are you going to meet Brand later?"

She considered saying no just to prove her friend wrong, but then she'd feel obligated to follow through. "Maybe." *I hope so.*

Mercy laughed. "Oh, how our Sybil has changed."

Sybil jerked them to a halt. "What do you mean? I haven't changed a bit."

"You're letting yourself be friendly with an outlaw cowboy. Not too long ago you would have run from such a man."

"He's not an outlaw and never was."

Mercy just grinned and pulled her toward the kitchen. "An outlaw. A cowboy. Homeless. Likely as poor as a pauper. Sybil, so much for living a safe little life."

Mercy meant to tease, but her words stung deep inside. Sybil didn't care about his possessions or lack of them. A person's value wasn't measured in his material belongings.

By the time the evening meal was finished, dusk had fallen. Her glance went continually to the window. Would Brand come to the house? She was almost certain he wouldn't. He'd be uncomfortable. Disappointment as sharp and stinging as acrid smoke burned her eyes.

Mercy nudged her. "Do you want me to go with you?"

Sybil stalled, wanting to go down the hill and see if

Brand was around, but not wanting her friend to know how desperately she ached to see him and speak to him.

Mercy dragged her to the window overlooking the ranch. Lights glowed from the buildings. A lantern hung outside the barn, and in the shadows, a lean figure lounged against the wall.

"Guess who's down there waiting for you?"

"You don't know that."

Mercy snagged shawls off the hooks in the hall and handed Sybil hers. "We haven't see Jayne all day. Let's go visit her."

Without arguing, Sybil put on her shawl.

Linette and Eddie came into the room. Linette smiled at the pair. "Going out?"

"To visit Jayne." Mercy winked and dragged Sybil to the door.

Trying to stop Mercy was as futile as trying to stop a train racing downhill. So Sybil let herself be hustled toward Jayne's house. All the while her heart pushed against her ribs and her eyes sought out the figure leaning in the shadows.

When they reached the cookhouse, the figure stepped away from the barn and toward them. All along she'd known it was Brand.

Mercy murmured softly, "I'll see Jayne on my own." She slipped away.

Sybil barely noticed her departure as Brand moved closer. "Howdy," he said, narrowing the distance between them.

"Good evening." Was that all they had to say to each other?

He took her elbow and guided her down the moonlit path toward the river. "I decided to stay."

"I'm glad you did." They reached the bridge and

stopped to lean on the handrail. They stared at the flashing silver of the water. "Are you enjoying your work?" she asked.

"Yes. And Cookie's food is great."

She saw his smile as she turned to look at him. Their elbows brushed. She could think of a hundred questions she wanted to ask him.... How had he survived his unsettled childhood? How bad did he hurt after losing his family? But she didn't want to shatter the calm between them.

He shifted, leaned on one elbow and considered her. "I imagine you growing up in England in a big fancy house somewhat like Eddie's. Fancy clothes. Fancy parties. Fine books. Am I right?"

"I was lonely."

"What about Mercy and Jayne?"

"I didn't meet them until I was considered old enough to participate in proper social events." Sybil guessed her voice conveyed her regret over the things she'd missed as a child. "Not that I didn't love my parents and enjoy their company."

"No beaux?"

There'd been Colin, but what she'd felt for him paled to insignificance. "I once fancied myself in love."

"What happened?"

"He left and never looked back." She tried to disguise the hurt in her voice. Wondered if she'd succeeded.

Brand touched her cheek. "And hurt you. And I did the same thing. I'm sorry to have added to your pain."

She couldn't push a word past her tight throat.

"Did your parents give you everything you needed or wanted?"

Her breath eased out and she could answer. "They gave me what they felt was best for me."

"You didn't agree?"

She chuckled. "It never entered my mind to disagree until…" She squelched the unfaithful thought.

He touched her elbow. "Until what?"

"My father did much of his work from his office at home. He was a lawyer and saw many of his clients there. When Mother was ill and resting, he let me stay in his office. I had to be very quiet, so he gave me paper and pencils and I amused myself."

"Let me guess. You made up stories."

"Not at first. I drew little pictures. You know the sort…a round ball with a smaller one on top. Add triangles for ears, whiskers and eyes, and I'd made a cat."

He chuckled, making her want to go on.

"I always showed them to Father. He admired them and said how clever I was. He said I must show them to Mother."

Silence descended between Sybil and Brand. A bird fluttered and chirped as if settling her babies, though the babies would have flown the nest by now. Perhaps mother birds always made comforting good-night sounds. Laughter drifted from the bunkhouse and then the mournful sound of a harmonica.

"I soon learned to read and write, and added words to my pictures," she continued. "More and more words, until finally the words grew into stories. They seemed to come from deep inside, pushing at my heart, my head and my fingers." She felt the familiar rush she did when writing.

"I continued to show them to Mother and Father. They continued to say how clever I was. Until…" She drew in a large breath to steady her voice. "Until I said I wanted to one day write stories for everyone to read. I wanted to be an author. They sat side by side as I told them. I expected they'd say how clever I was, how pleased they would be to see others enjoy my stories." She couldn't go on, feeling again the bottom fall out of her stomach, leaving her airless and slightly nauseated.

Brand caught her shoulder and squeezed gently. The warmth of his touch slowly melted the ice about her heart.

"I was so disappointed when they didn't approve, though I still don't understand why. They should have been so proud."

He pulled her closer, pressed her head to his shoulder. The steady beat of his heart vibrated through her. "And now you disappoint yourself."

She sprang back. "You're wrong." Only he wasn't.

"Really?" He leaned back. "Guess I'll never understand, so let's talk about something else. I told you about my last Christmas. Tell me about yours."

She realized he meant the year his mother had died. He saw it as his last Christmas. Six years ago. Six years of loneliness, shutting himself away from others, fearing the appearance of his pa and brother. Treating Christmas as if it didn't matter any more than any other day. And for him it hadn't, which was even sadder. Had no one ever reached out to him? Or had he turned his back on help? Either way, it was a lonely, barren life he lived. Sybil pushed back the sympathy so she could talk.

"I've been living with an elderly cousin and celebrated Christmas with her two years ago. It was very quiet." She made a sound of amusement. "Everything about her house was very quiet. Last year I spent with Jayne at her house. It's crazy there. So much coming and going I don't know how they kept track of everyone."

"And before your parents died?" Brand's low voice

evaded her defenses and took her back to Christ-mases past.

"We always had such a good time. My parents took me to Piccadilly Circus to look at all the toys in the shops. They bought me dolls and books. They each helped me choose gifts for the other parent. I was always so excited on Christmas morning, when we ate a special breakfast of waffles sprinkled with powdered sugar and covered with clotted cream. Father passed out the gifts and we sat around enjoying them while the cook roasted a goose."

Brand turned to look at the water gurgling under the bridge. "You were a loved and adored child."

Something in his voice made her feel she had pushed him away. She tried to think what she'd done to make him grow distant. It was on the tip of her tongue to ask when he spoke.

"It's getting late." He straightened and turned to indicate they should go back. He escorted her to Jayne's house to meet Mercy. Then he hurried away with a barely murmured goodbye.

Sybil paused before the door to the cabin. Why had he retreated so quickly? Did he think she would look down on him because of the way he'd been forced to live?

As soon as she stepped inside the house, Mercy hurried to her side. "Tell us everything."

Seth bolted to his feet. "I think the horses must need something." He fled outside.

Jayne laughed. "Too many females around for him. Too much *romance*." She clasped her hands together, looking starry-eyed, then took Sybil's other hand. "Do tell us."

She allowed them to lead her to a chair. "There's

nothing to report. I merely told him a few things about my childhood."

Mercy groaned. "Now there's a way to make a man feel insignificant."

"What do you mean?" Sybil had no such intention.

"You adored your father. He could do no wrong. He gave you everything you ever dreamed of. How can a homeless cowboy hope to compete with that?"

Had she made Brand feel insignificant? Perhaps she inadvertently had. Now she must find a way to fix her mistake. To make him see that it was the love of her parents that blessed her, not their gifts.

It was love she wanted. Not things. Could she make him understand that?

## Chapter Sixteen

Brand took his time about returning to the bunkhouse. He needed to think. And he couldn't do it with the other cowboys asking questions or looking as if they'd die if they didn't ask one. Though to be honest, none had done either. For the most part they weren't any more interested in him than he was in them.

Sybil's words tortured his brain.

Raised with privilege and prestige. Given everything. He'd always known that, so why did it now fill him with regret? Even with his name purged of the Duggan gang guilt, he was still a nobody cowboy with nothing to offer to a gal like Sybil Bannerman.

He eased open the bunkhouse door, but it squealed like a pig. Someone ought to oil the hinges. Half a dozen heads swung toward him, then returned to what they'd been doing. He was of no interest to any of them. Just a man doing a job.

He flung himself on his bunk and turned his back to the others. He had no wish to join them in a game of cards, or sing sad songs about lonely cowboys. His own sadness throbbed in his heart. Why sing of it when he lived it?

The truth could not be denied. Sybil was out of the realm of possibility. He should leave. Move on. But her challenge to forget being a Duggan rang in his ears. He was through running from the Duggan gang. Besides, he'd given his word to Eddie, and a man was only as good as his word.

The next day he still considered his options. Perhaps he could ask Eddie to send him to the far corner of the ranch. But Eddie had already dispatched riders to bring down the cows in preparation for the soon-to-be fall roundup.

Besides, somewhere deep inside Brand a happy thought warred with the lingering idea of riding away.

If he stayed around he could hope to see more of Sybil. It was a futile, foolish idea, but what harm could possibly come of it? Her interest in him was surely no more than curiosity or politeness.

He alone would bear the pain of their final goodbye, either when he forced himself to move on or when she returned to England. There would be a pain for every pleasure, but it would be worth it.

He glanced at the house up the hill as he left the cookhouse with Slim to fix the fences of the wintering pens. Did he see someone at the window? Was it Sybil? Just in case, he touched the brim of his hat in a pretense of adjusting its position.

A few hours later he and Slim put down their tools and headed to the cookhouse for dinner.

"You done good," Slim said. "I appreciate a hard worker."

"Just doin' my job."

Slim slapped him on the back. "You'll do just fine here. Glad to have you on the crew."

Crew? As if he belonged? Could it be possible?

Brand and Slim returned to the task after a satisfying meal, and worked throughout the afternoon.

Slim didn't say much, which left Brand lots of time for thinking. Try as he did with every bit of energy he could muster to avoid one topic, his thoughts continually circled back to Sybil.

Would she again traipse down the hill after supper and spend a precious hour or two with him? He grinned in anticipation even as he told himself it was a foolish wish. Then, hoping Slim hadn't noticed his silly grin, he forced it away.

Later, as soon as he'd scraped his plate clean after two helpings of Cookie's mashed potatoes, gravy, roast beef and carrots, he left the cookhouse and parked himself by the barn door. Someone had lit the lantern hanging there and he stood at the edge of the circle of light. Sybil could see him if she cared to check. He told himself he wasn't waiting, even though his gaze was glued to the house up the hill.

When the door opened and the light flashed golden, his breath caught partway down his throat.

Dawg rose and whined eagerly. "Settle down," Brand murmured to the animal, and told himself the same.

A door slammed to his left and children's voices called out.

Both he and Dawg shifted their gaze in that direction. The foreman's three oldest children scampered down the trail toward them.

Dawg whined again.

"You like kids?" It surprised Brand, though they'd never been around children much, so maybe the dog had always been this way.

Dawg, taking Brand's surprise for disapproval, flopped down and put his head on his paws.

"It's okay. Kids are kind of…" He had no idea what word to use. *Friendly. Innocent. Accepting.* Maybe all that and more.

The children drew abreast. Neil, the oldest boy, saw Brand first. "Hi. We're going to get Grady and play tag."

At that moment, Sybil reached the corrals. Although his attention was on the youngsters, he'd been aware of her the whole time. Every step she took closer made his heart beat stronger, until it now thumped against his ribs like a trapped animal trying to escape.

She spoke to the children, who paused long enough to respond to her greeting, then she turned toward Brand, the width of the corral separating them. "Nice evening, isn't it?"

He had paid scant attention, but now realized the full golden moon gave everything a shimmering appearance. The warm kiss of a gentle evening breeze brushed against his cheek. He inhaled the scent of fresh hay and poplar leaves. "Very nice," he murmured.

"It's a perfect evening for a walk." Her words carried warmth and welcome. "Care to join me?"

Brand jolted from the wall. He swallowed hard and forced himself to saunter, when every muscle wanted to gallop. "Sounds like a fine idea." He fumbled with the gate, his fingers stiff, and finally managed to release the latch and slip through. "Where are we going?"

Her merry laugh sang through the air, danced through his veins and vibrated in his heart. "Do we need a destination? Can't we simply enjoy the evening?"

He could have said they wouldn't need to move from this spot and the evening would be special enough to stay in his thoughts the rest of his life. Instead, he managed one word. "Sure." And fell in at her side. His arm brushed hers, sending a rush of tingles up his skin.

They walked west, toward the foreman's house. Lamplight filled the windows. They saw Roper and Cassie in matching rocking chairs talking to each other. Cassie's back was to them, but Roper faced them, a smile of pure contentment filling his expression.

"He looks happy." The words were out before Brand could stop them.

"I expect he is. He's gone from a lonely man raised in an orphanage and never knowing family, to a man loved and adored by a wife and a ready-made family."

They passed the house.

Sybil sighed. "Kind of makes you envy him, doesn't it?"

Brand had thought exactly that, but it seemed weak to say it. And why would she think such a thing? She'd been raised in a loving home. Of course, she was now an orphan. "Do you plan to return to England?"

She hesitated long enough for his lungs to ache for air.

He remembered he had to breathe.

"It's the only home I have."

*You could stay here.* The words hovered on the tip of his tongue, but he bit them back. He had nothing to offer her. No fine house. No abundance of books. Nothing. So he kept silent.

The children ran down the path behind them calling, "Not it." Thor, the fawn, raced after them, darting from one to the other.

They drew closer. Dawg whined and looked back.

"Do you want to play with them?" Brand asked.

The dog gave a little bark.

"Go ahead. Suit yourself." He never would have guessed Dawg would want this.

But Dawg yapped and ran toward the children, his wounds completely forgotten. The youngsters halted and waited, uncertain about Dawg's behavior. Thor bounced a safe distance away and watched the dog with wide eyes.

"He wants to play," Brand said.

Neil crouched down and held out a hand.

Dawg went eagerly, squirming with excitement. Suddenly all the children surrounded him, then backed away, calling him, as Dawg ran from one to the other, barking happily.

Daisy turned toward the adults. "Do you want to play tag?"

Sybil grabbed Brand's arm. Her fingers dug into his muscle. He couldn't tell if it signaled fear or anticipation. Was she afraid of the children? Or did she long to play with them? He was about to say no when Billy tagged Sybil.

"You're it and you can't catch me."

The children closed around them, teasing her to catch them. Brand had instinctively stepped away from her so he became part of the circle.

In the moonlight her eyes were dark and unreadable, but her lips were parted as if surprise held her immobile.

Billy darted toward her. "Catch me if you can."

She scrubbed her lips together, considering the challenge, and then darted toward the boy.

He shrieked and ran away. The other children scattered.

Brand ran, too. He'd played this game many times as a child. Often with Cyrus thudding after him. His heart clenched. He missed Cyrus. Not the man who had become part of the Duggan gang, but the big brother who had played with him. He lost his concentration and turned to look up the hill toward the little graveyard. Even if the sun shone overhead he couldn't see from where he stood, but he knew the exact location of Pa and Cyrus's final resting place. Would he see them both along with Ma in the hereafter?

He realized footsteps raced toward him, and ducked away.

They played a rowdy game of tag with the children, catching and being caught their share of times.

He was it again, having been tagged by Neil. The children raced off, disappearing in the shadows. But Sybil's golden hair caught the moonlight and gave away her position. He knew if he raced toward her, she would run the opposite direction, so he tiptoed in a roundabout way until he came up behind her. She strained forward, listening for his approach, ready to take flight. For a heartbeat, two, three, he didn't move. He simply stood there taking in the fact of his freedom. For the first time in many years he could take part in a simple game of tag without glancing over his shoulder, fearing the Duggan gang.

Grinning for a dozen different reasons, he tiptoed forward.

Sybil must have heard him, for she turned just as he reached forward to tag her. His hand caught her arm. "You're it."

Was that hoarse voice his?

"Oh, you. Sneaking up on a girl like that."

"All's fair." In love and war. He felt suspended between the two. The war of outrunning Pa and Cyrus was over. But he was not ready to believe he could love and be loved. He hadn't felt that way since Ma died. Not that that was the sort of love he ached for. When had his thoughts gotten so muddled? He released her arm and called, "Sybil's it."

The children dashed by her, teasing and tempting her to chase them.

The game continued in the cool, moon-drenched evening until a rectangle of light shone from either end of the ranch and Linette and Cassie called out to their respective children. "Come in now. It's bedtime."

The little ones stopped their play and sighed. Then, calling good-night over their shoulders, they trotted home.

Sybil chuckled. "That was fun. It's the first time I played tag."

He stared at her. "You're joshing."

"No, really."

"That's positively unnatural. Tag is a favorite children's game." They fell in step, side by side, and walked to the bridge.

She shrugged one shoulder. "I had other amusements."

"Like what?"

"My books and papers. I loved making my own paper dolls."

He thought it best not to say that a normal childhood had its share of rowdy play.

"These children are very fortunate." Her voice carried a note of wistfulness.

He could name a number of ways that was true, but wanted to know what she meant, and asked her.

"They are loved by people who haven't any obligation to love them."

"That's a fact. Linette is to have a baby soon. Won't Grady feel misplaced?"

Sybil laughed gently. "Linette and Eddie aren't like that. Nor are Roper and Cassie. A child of their union won't cause them to love the other children any less."

"How can you be so certain?"

She looked into his face, studying him, perhaps wondering if there was a reason behind his question. Maybe there was. Pa had loved him, of that he was certain. But his love was on again, off again, depending on whether or not Pa felt Brand did what he wanted. And because Brand mostly hadn't, he'd often felt his father didn't really love him. Not like he did Cyrus.

Sybil rubbed her warm palm along Brand's arm. "My father taught me love is both a feeling and a choice. Even when you don't feel the emotion, you choose to love."

"That sounds pretend."

"No. It sounds real."

He decided to change the subject. "I expect there is someone back in England hoping to marry you." She'd never mentioned it, but he could imagine many suitors beat a pathway to her door.

She gave his arm a harmless tap, then withdrew her hand.

Funny how he suddenly felt cold. And alone.

"Do you really think I'd go out walking with you if someone back home had asked for my hand?"

"No. Why are you walking with me?" He wanted to slam his head against the nearest post. Why couldn't he keep his mouth shut around her?

"Why do you think?"

He turned her so the moonlight fell directly on her face. He saw uncertainty in her eyes and something more. Was it…? No. It couldn't be.

But before he could marshal a response, she tucked her arm around his elbow and drew him along the path.

"I enjoy the children here. I've never been around many before. I hope to marry someday, and have more than one child, so they wouldn't be lonely. But that's in God's hands, isn't it?"

Brand's tongue stuck to the roof of his mouth. What was in God's hands? Marriage or children?

They reached the top of the hill and stopped. She turned her face up to him with an expectant look. Did she want to be kissed? He couldn't believe that's what her glance meant. But had all this talk of children and new beginnings made her forget that Brand was a Duggan? A homeless, penniless cowboy? He'd kissed her once. Out of gratitude. If he kissed her now it would be for an entirely different reason. Would she welcome his interest? Or find him presumptuous and far too bold? He weighed his options.

She sighed and turned away. "We should be getting back."

He'd waited too long. The opportunity had passed. Probably a good thing, but he found no comfort in the thought.

He escorted her to within a few feet of the door. "Good night," he murmured. His instinct was to run down the hill, throw himself on the back of his horse and leave, while he still had an ounce of good sense left. But he was through running from the Duggan name and his fears. He'd go only if someone made it clear he should.

In the meantime, he didn't intend to walk away until Sybil was safely indoors.

"Good night," she whispered, her hand brushing his arm. "I enjoyed the evening."

Before he could pull a word or question from his brain, she stepped inside. Did she enjoy the evening because the children played tag with them or because of their moonlit walk?

Perhaps it was best not to know. That way he could allow himself to dream a few dreams.

Sybil's thoughts tangled like knotted yarn. Did Brand care about her? How could she make him understand how she felt?

Hoping to sort out her troubled thoughts, she reached for her Bible. The book fell open at Proverbs, but she continued to turn pages until she reached the Song of Solomon…a lover's song. Surely it would answer her questions.

But after a few minutes she closed her Bible, as mixed up as ever. She wrote in her notebook. *I need wisdom from above. God, please guide my path.*

She pulled out her notes on Brand. She had so many questions, but the answers weren't for her story. They were for her heart. She studied the pages. It was a good story. One her editor would like. But she couldn't bring herself to send it. What she knew about Brand seemed like a trust he'd given her. She didn't want to dishonor that.

She put the pages back in the drawer, then lay back on the bed, recalling every moment of the evening. Playing tag had been so much fun. Seeing the children enjoying each other…

A story idea sprang into her head, and she grabbed paper and pencil and wrote for two hours before turning out the lamp and crawling into bed.

Brand had asked her about her dream of publishing her stories. She'd thought the dream had died, but found it had lain dormant as it grew and matured.

Over the next couple days Sybil found it impossible to explain this drive in her, this urgency to see Brand, to spend as much time with him as possible. She stopped trying to justify it to herself and others. She stopped trying to make excuses, and simply rushed down the hill every evening to where he waited.

Sometimes the children came out and played tag with them. Always she and Brand walked. And she asked questions. What was his favorite color?

"Gold," he said. "The same shade of gold as your hair." His answer brought pleasant warmth to her cheeks.

She wanted to know the name of every place he'd worked or lived.

He hesitated at first, then told her of the many places. Some where he'd wished he could stay longer but hadn't dared. Others where he couldn't wait to move on. Only when she pressed did he admit that not everyone welcomed a stranger who wouldn't reveal his last name.

"It didn't matter to Eddie," she said.

"Eddie is a good man, a fair boss."

Then she wanted to know about every injury he'd incurred, no matter how minor. "Like the banging your leg took when Cal brought in that outlaw horse."

Brand laughed, draped his arm around her shoulders and squeezed her close. "Sybil, bumps and bruises are an everyday part of my work, and ranch life in general. I don't take note of such minor things."

She turned to observe his face. "How about the major ones?"

At first she thought he would give the same answer, then his mouth twisted in a wry grin. "They only count if they mean I can't ride."

"Do you mean ride wild horses or ride away?"

He nodded. "Yup."

She laughed and nudged him in the ribs.

He groaned and pretended to be hurt.

"How many times have you been unable to ride?"

"Twice." She heard the regret in his voice. "Once I cut my foot on a tin can someone had carelessly tossed into a pasture. It got infected and I had to rest a few days. Even when I left, I couldn't put my boot on. Carried it over the saddle horn."

She joined him in laughing about the situation, though her insides tightened at the idea of his suffering and the risk he took riding with an unhealed foot. "And the other time?"

"Well, that was entirely my fault."

"What did you do?" She pushed her shoulder against his chest as if the movement could force the words from him.

"I let myself be distracted momentarily while working with a horse. Ended up getting kicked."

"Ouch."

"Oh, the kick didn't hurt that much. But I was mad and I got back on the horse. I was not in the frame of mind I needed to be in when dealing with a wild animal. He threw me before I found my balance. Right into the boards. Knocked me out and cut my head." Brand bent and showed her where the cut had been, just above his left ear.

She parted his hair to examine his head under the light from the lantern by the barn door. She couldn't see anything, but touching him like that made the air feel light as butterfly wings. "Glad to see you survived." Her voice was husky.

"Couldn't see straight for two days. Had a sore head for a long time."

"Ah." That was all she said.

He squinted at her. "Ah? What does that mean?"

She shrugged. "Only that it explains a few things."

He caught her elbows. "Like what?" His own voice had grown low.

She pretended to try and wriggle free, though she hoped he wouldn't take her seriously and drop his hands. "Now I understand why you act so thickheaded at times."

"When have I ever done that?"

Her thoughts stalled. Only one thing came to mind and she wasn't sure she should mention it.

He shook her gently. "Tell me."

"Well, if you insist, I'd have to say that to keep running from the Duggan gang when it no longer exists is pretty thickheaded."

He dropped his hands to his sides and studied her long and hard. "I'm through running."

She touched his arm. "I'm glad."

One more question burned to be asked. "Have you ever left a brokenhearted girl behind?"

"No. Never."

"Really? No love interests?" Sybil could hardly believe it.

"Once I thought myself in love." He told her about May.

Sybil sensed how hurt he'd been, and wrapped her arm around his as they walked along the path toward the bridge, where they stopped. She raised her face to him as she did every evening, on the pretext of deep interest in something he said. It wasn't that her interest wasn't real, but what she really hoped for was a sign of growing affection on his part.

A kiss from Brand would signal he felt the same thing.

But each time, he looked ready to accept her silent

invitation…then blinked and shifted away. Perhaps he didn't share her feelings. Perhaps she was wrong in thinking he cared.

## Chapter Seventeen

Being part of a crew made Brand more nervous than riding a rank horse. He was never sure what to say. He'd forgotten how to sit at a table and make conversation. Sleeping in a bunkhouse with others made his skin twitch. But it was worth it to see Sybil every day. He often observed her helping Linette or visiting with Jayne during the day. And each evening, she joined him for a walk. He'd never known such sweet moments.

She stood before him this evening, her face upturned to him. He studied her expression, memorizing every feature, branding it indelibly on his memory. As long as he lived and drew breath he would remember these evenings with joy.

He touched a wayward curl and pulled in a breath at the satiny feel of her hair. A fine lady from high-class society. And yet she smiled at him. Tipped her face toward his touch.

"Sybil?" He whispered her name. Was he misreading the invitation in her eyes?

"Brand." She lifted a hand and pressed her palm to his chest.

"You are a fine lady."

Her smile widened. "And you are a fine gentleman."

He grinned at that. "I'm just a cowboy."

"I don't think the two are mutually exclusive."

His smile spread further. "I suppose not."

Her fingers teased the hair above his ear. Tingles of anticipation flooded his brain, even as more tingles raced up his arm and pounded through his heart. Was it possible she wanted what he wanted? A kiss? And so much more. A kiss would merely signal all the things he hoped for and dared not dream of. Love, acceptance, family, home…

"Sybil." He whispered her name, again disturbing the curl on her forehead. For a moment it held his attention.

"Yes?" Her sweet breath brushed his face.

"Sybil, would you think me overly bold if I said I want to kiss you?"

"Mostly I would think it's about time."

He chuckled, delighted at her response, and slowly lowered his head, anxious to claim her lips, but wanting the moment to last forever.

She went up on her toes and met him halfway.

Her lips were warm and welcoming. Sweet as nectar.

He would have lingered, drowning in the million sensations and delights flooding through him, but he didn't want to frighten her away, so he broke off the kiss and pressed her head to his shoulder.

She sighed.

And he knew satisfaction he'd never before experienced. He wished he could find words to describe it. "I can't remember ever feeling like this." It didn't begin to say what he felt.

"What do you feel?"

"I think…" He swallowed hard, awed by the warm

emotions flooding his heart and spreading to his limbs. Could this be love?

If he loved her, he would keep it secret. He didn't deserve someone like her. "Sybil, I'm just a poor lonely cowboy."

"Brand, I'm just a poor lonely English girl."

"Poor?"

"Did you think I was rich?" She leaned back to study him. "I'm not. When my parents died I was left almost penniless." She paused, her expression filled with questions. "Would it make a difference if I were rich?"

He studied the question. "You deserve a nice house and…"

"And what?"

"Everything that goes with it." What was the point of going into details? He had nothing. She deserved everything.

"You don't think I deserve love?" She didn't wait for him to answer. "Doesn't everyone?" Her voice was low, challenging.

Oh yes. He wanted to believe everyone did. Even a Duggan. "I'm just a cowboy," he said again.

"And I'm just a girl."

"Is that enough?"

"Do you want it to be?" She continued to watch him. Even in the silvery moonlight, her gaze probed until he had no defenses.

"Yes." He pulled her against his shoulder again and tilted his head to rest his cheek on her satiny curls.

She sighed. He imagined a pleased look on her face. One that would match his own.

A fire lit in his heart, warm and bright. But he must take her home before he gave people cause to talk about her. He didn't care what they said about him. All his life he'd been talked about. But Sybil would never bear that stigma if he had anything to do with it.

He pulled her hand around his elbow and pressed it to his side.

They walked up the hill and paused before the door. She turned, lifted her face to him, her invitation clear. He needed no more and caught her lips in a gentle, chaste kiss, then broke away.

She stepped toward the door. "Good night, cowboy."

He grinned. "Good night, English girl."

Not until he reached the bunkhouse did he force the smile from his lips.

It threatened to return the next morning even when he went to work. Eddie asked him to check all the gates, a job that gave him plenty of opportunity to watch the big house.

Twice he saw Mercy carrying water, but he couldn't see the back of the house until he went to the wintering pens. Then he was able to watch Sybil hanging laundry on the line. The wind billowed her dark blue skirt around her legs, puffed out her white top and pulled pins from her curls until they rioted around her head.

He leaned back on his heels and watched.

She emptied the basket and looked about, scanning the yard to his right.

He waited, wondering if she'd search further. She did, until she found him.

The distance was too great to see her expression, but he didn't need to. His heart leaped in greeting.

She waved.

He waved back.

Neither of them moved. For sure, he wasn't going to be the first.

Something caught Sybil's attention and she turned

toward the house, nodded, then picked up the basket, glancing again in his direction before she disappeared out of sight.

At that moment he made up his mind. He'd ask her out for a walk this evening and tell her he loved her.

He was ready to take the chance.

It was midafternoon when he finished his job. "All the gates are in good repair," he told Eddie. "What do you have for me to do now?"

"There's no point in starting another job this late in the day," the rancher said. "You're free to do whatever you like."

"Okay, boss." There was only one thing he wanted to do. He'd seen Sybil leave the house half an hour ago, headed in the direction of his old campsite. It seemed to be where she liked to go to be alone…where she read and wrote.

He washed up reasonably well, left Dawg in the barn and headed for the spot. This time it was about him and Sybil. He did not want Dawg to be part of what he had to say.

She sat against a tree, the golden leaves a bright backdrop. More leaves danced across the ground, fluttered in the air. She distractedly brushed one from her hair, lost in concentration as she wrote furiously.

He stood in the shadows, content to watch.

Her hand paused. She lifted her head, listening, and then glanced about.

He stepped forward so she wouldn't be alarmed. "Howdy."

She smiled, her cheeks rosy and her blue eyes glinting. "Howdy, yourself."

He crossed the clearing to her side and sat down. He hadn't thought this far ahead, hadn't planned how he'd do this. It didn't seem right to blurt out "I love you." Seemed something that important should be done properly. "What are you doing?"

"Yesterday when you talked to the boys about learning to ride wild horses, I thought of another story." She kept her head down.

"Why are you embarrassed?"

There was a beat of silence as she considered his question. "I suppose because my writing means so much to me."

"Are you going to get your stories published?"

"It's not that easy."

"Because you're still afraid of how people will react?" If the opinion of others mattered so much, how could he tell her how he felt? People would likely say unkind things if her name was linked to his. Would she let them influence her? He swallowed. This was harder than riding a wild horse.

"It's not so much that." She paused a moment, then went on. "Being published means someone has to be willing to publish my stories."

"And you wonder if anyone would be?"

She nodded. "I've never tried to publish fiction."

"Can I read your story?"

She handed him a handful of papers.

The story began well. Two daredevil boys with more guts than common sense decided to ride a wild mustang. He chuckled a few times as he read. He reached the end of the page and turned it over.

But the second page didn't seem to follow.

*He was known only as Cowboy. He never did give a last name before he rode into the sunset. He didn't welcome any questions about his true identity. But he was the best bronc buster in the territory. A reputation well earned.*

*It began when he was ten...*

This wasn't the same story. It wasn't about children. It was about a grown man who broke horses, a loner with no name and an ugly, but loyal, dog.

This was his story.

Brand stared at the pages. "Have you had other things published?" The words felt like blocks of ice on his tongue.

"A few nonfiction articles, but not under my own name."

He faced her, his eyes burning. "Is this one of those you've had published?" He shoved the pages toward her.

She glanced at them and gasped. "How did this get in there?"

He jerked to his feet. "So all the questions, all the interest was merely so you could write a story about a nameless cowboy?"

She scrambled to her feet. "No, Brand. Well, maybe at first. But—"

"I should have known. A fancy English miss and a nameless cowboy. Of course you had to have another reason."

She reached for him.

He stepped away.

"Brand, I never sent the story to the editor. I couldn't."

He slammed his hat on his head. "Well, don't let me stop you. I'm sure it's worth more than—" He would not say what he'd intended. *Me.* "I hope it earns you a lot of money." He strode away as fast as he could. He would not run, though his muscles twitched to do so.

"Brand, wait." She trotted after him.

He ignored her call and easily outdistanced her with

long, hurried strides. He felt as if she'd snatched the ground from beneath his feet. All her attention had been so she could get a story. How could he trust anything he'd believed about her?

Eddie was in front of the barn. Good. That would save him from finding the man.

"Eddie, I have to leave."

"Leave? Now? Is something wrong?"

Everything. He'd been a blind, stupid fool. "I have to go. I have my reasons."

"You're sure about this? I can't change your mind?"

"My mind's made up." Brand grabbed his saddle and strode toward his horse.

"I'm sorry to hear that. I'll run up to the house and get your wages."

Brand didn't want to wait, but he would need the money to buy supplies. "I'll be at the bunkhouse collecting my things."

Eddie opened his mouth to say something more, then thought better of it and jogged away.

Brand finished saddling up, and whistled for Dawg. The dog wriggled in anticipation. Guess he was ready to move on, too. Brand led the horse from the barn.

But Sybil stood in the roadway. "Brand, please."

He pretended not to hear. Dawg hesitated, turned toward her and whined. Brand whistled and the dog trotted after him.

At the bunkhouse, Brand stuffed his things into his saddlebag, rolled up his bedding and left the place without a backward look.

Eddie waited outside and counted out his wages. "I don't know what happened, but I saw Sybil with tears streaming down her face."

"I didn't do anything."

"Perhaps not, but there is obviously a misunderstanding that can't be resolved if you ride away."

"The misunderstanding was wholly on my part."

"Still."

Brand didn't reply.

Eddie shook his head. "If you change your mind, you're always welcome here."

"Thanks, but I won't be back."

Eddie held out his hand. "It's been a pleasure."

Brand shook the rancher's hand, wishing he could say the same, then mounted up. Dawg followed.

Not until he was beyond sight of the ranch did Brand stop, turn around and look back for a long time. Regret scratched through his veins. Another chapter over. Another lesson learned.

He headed down the trail. Dawg stood looking back until Brand called him.

Sybil hadn't been able to hide her tears from Eddie as she rushed to the house.

Linette saw her as she burst through the door and dashed down the hall, hoping to reach her bedroom before she collapsed.

"Sybil, what's wrong?" her friend called. When she didn't answer and continued her headlong rush, Linette hurried after her.

Sybil turned the corner and ran into Mercy.

"Whoa." Mercy grabbed her arms and steadied her. She looked at Sybil, saw the gushing tears. "Sybil, what's the matter?"

The only sounds she could make were the sobs she fought to stifle.

Linette wrapped an arm about her shoulders. "What's happened? Are you hurt?"

Sybil shook her head. Yes, she was hurt, but how was she to explain a pain without physical cause?

"It's Brand, isn't it?" Mercy sounded disgusted. "What did he do? Tell me. I'll find him and make him pay."

Sybil hiccuped and again shook her head. "He... didn't..." She swallowed back tears. "It's all a mistake."

"Then tell him. Whatever it is."

"I can't," she wailed. "He left."

Mercy held her at arm's length. "You mean he's gone? Ridden away?"

Sybil nodded.

Linette sighed. "Eddie will be disappointed. He liked Brand."

"Eddie's disappointed?" Mercy grunted. "What about Sybil?"

Sybil broke away from them and rushed to her room, buried her face in her pillow and wept.

Her friends followed her.

"I'm sorry," Linette said. "I didn't mean to be insensitive." Her footsteps tapped away down the hall. But not Mercy's.

Sybil wished she would go away and leave her to wallow in her misery, but instead Mercy sat beside her. "What happened?"

Sybil sat up and wiped her eyes. "I made a foolish mistake." She pointed at the notes about Brand.

Mercy barely glanced at them. "So?"

"He found these pages by accident. I meant to show him a story I had written about two little boys wanting to break wild horses. I don't know how these papers got mixed in. How could I have been so careless?"

"You're saying he wasn't happy about it? Why not? I'd think he'd be flattered."

Sybil kept her gaze on the pages, afraid if she looked at Mercy she'd be reduced to a fresh flood of tears. "I guess he thought I only cared about him to get more information."

"Did you?"

"No, of course not!" Then her defenses deflated. "Maybe a little at first, but just to start with."

"So what are you going to do?"

"I don't know." She tossed the offending papers into her drawer. "I should have never come here." Despite her pain, she couldn't regret knowing Brand.

"Oh, sure. You could still be living with Cousin Celia. My lands, child, why would you leave such a nice arrangement?" Mercy mocked Aunt Celia's voice.

Sybil shuddered. "I can't imagine going back. And yet I was happy enough there."

Her friend patted her shoulder in a motherly way. "Only because you didn't know how much more there was to life. You ought to send that." She tipped her head toward the drawer where Sybil had tossed the pages. "Brand's story is really good."

"I couldn't."

Mercy tsked. "This is a new world. We don't have to be chained by silly old rules."

Sybil sighed. Let Mercy think it was about rules and proper behavior, but she couldn't send Brand's story out without his permission. It would only verify his suspicions. She had no intention of doing that. Even if he never knew one way or the other. Pain pierced her heart like a spear. To never see him again… How would she endure it?

"Think about it." Mercy patted her arm and left the room.

Sybil stared toward the pages in the drawer. Yes, her

editor would love the story, but thanks to Brand, publishing it was no longer what she wanted to do. She pulled out the children's stories she'd written and looked through them.

She wanted to publish a children's book in her own name.

But did she have the courage to do so without Brand to tell her it was the right thing to do?

She fell back on the bed. Did she even want to do it without him? She turned over to stare at the wall. His leaving had taken the sunshine from her life.

# Chapter Eighteen

As Brand made breakfast, Dawg whined and paced. Breakfast didn't require a lot of work. Brand hadn't replenished his supplies, so beans were the only choice.

He offered a plateful to Dawg.

The dog sat down, stared at him and wouldn't eat.

"When did you get so particular?" he asked. Dawg gave him a baleful look. "You can forget about the kids feeding you. We won't be seeing them again." The children had started bringing table scraps to the dog.

Dawg lay down and put his head on his paws.

"Suit yourself." Brand ate the beans with the same pleasure he'd get from stabbing a fork into his thigh. Why had he let himself think he could be in love? Or maybe more accurately, why did he think Sybil's interest in him meant she loved him?

He threw away the last of the beans, downed the rest of the coffee, dowsed the fire and saddled his horse. If he rode hard and fast he could be…

Where?

He swung into the saddle and headed north, away from the ranch. The particulars of where didn't matter.

Dawg stayed by the cold campfire.

Brand whistled for him. Dawg pushed to his feet with a decided lack of enthusiasm and slunk toward Brand.

He again headed north. Dawg barked. Brand turned to see that the dog had not moved. "Come on, let's get moving."

Dawg picked up his feet and headed south.

"Wrong way, pal."

Dawg looked over his shoulder and barked.

It was a standoff. Brand meant to go north and Dawg meant to go south.

"Fine. Have it your way."

Dawg trotted away, pausing every few feet to look back and whine.

"Go. Go back to her."

Dawg yapped and took off running. The last Brand saw of him was his crooked tail disappearing down the trail.

What did a fool dog know?


Sybil had cried enough tears during the night to soak her pillow and leave her eyes puffy. She rose and washed her face. No more crying. She was done with tears. Knowing Brand had been a nice experience while it lasted. Now it was time to move on. She sighed. Words were easy and intentions were fine, but she'd never forget him.

Linette had ironing to be done so Sybil gladly stayed in the kitchen, tackling the job, while her friend sat in the front room and tended to the mending.

The stove was hot, to heat the irons, but she barely noticed the growing warmth of the room. The mindless task allowed her thoughts to constantly follow a trail north from the ranch.

Where had Brand gone? Where would he stop? Maybe

he'd change his mind and return, give her a chance to explain. *Please God, send him back.* She continued ironing, knowing God could change Brand's heart, but only if Brand didn't hold stubbornly to his anger.

Outside, a dog barked, the sound urgent, demanding. Dawg? She ran down the hall, straight out the front door. "Dawg!" She fell on her knees and hugged the animal. He licked her face and wriggled from his nose to the tip of his crooked tail.

She lifted her head and looked around. There was no cowboy on the path or in front of the door. She stood and turned full circle, but still did not see Brand. "Where's your master?"

Mercy and Jayne stepped from Jayne's cabin, saw Dawg with Sybil and looked around. Then they climbed the hill to join her.

"Where is he?" Mercy asked.

"I don't know." Sybil squeezed her hands together so hard they hurt. "But Dawg wouldn't be here without him." Her throat closed off so she had to swallow twice before she could continue. "Maybe he's hurt."

Mercy shrugged. "Or maybe he sent Dawg back."

"He would never do that." Sybil fought a suffocating sense of panic.

Mercy watched her, saw her tensing, and squeezed her arm. "I'm sure there's nothing to be concerned about."

Her words barely registered with Sybil. "Where's Eddie?" She scanned the entire ranch area visible from the hill.

Linette had joined them. "He's taken some cowboys and headed west to check on the cows."

"I have to find Brand." Sybil's voice squeaked out.

Linette took her arm on one side, Mercy on the other,

and Jayne caught her hand. They led her reluctant feet back to the house and gently pushed her into a chair.

Linette hurried away and returned in a few minutes with a pot of tea and four cups and saucers. She poured them each tea. But Sybil's arms trembled so badly Linette put the cup on a nearby table.

"If you like, once Eddie returns I'll ask him to check where Brand is."

Sybil nodded. Ten thousand protests raced through her head. Brand could bleed to death waiting for Eddie to return. He could be lying somewhere unable to move. He could…

She attempted to slam the door on all the images flooding her brain. Sometimes an active imagination was an unpleasant thing.

After a few minutes she managed to drink her tea and appear calm. All the while, her thoughts raced, until she came up with a plan.


Brand rode on and on. Every mile weighed his mind until he drew his horse to a stop and stared at the narrow trail ahead. Where was he going? And more importantly, why? What difference did it make if Sybil wrote a story about someone named Cowboy? It didn't matter to him. He no longer had to run from the Duggan gang.

His horse shuffled, uncertain what to do. Brand steadied the animal. "Just thinking, boy. Just thinking."

Maybe Dawg had it right. Life was too good at the ranch to ride away.

And Sybil?

Why, she was the best thing that had ever happened to Brand. He loved her, and even if she didn't love him back, even if her interest had only been for a story…

Well, then he could still enjoy occasional glimpses

of her. Enjoy hearing her sing during Sunday services. See her sauntering around the ranch. He might even follow her to her favorite spot and openly watch her if she didn't object.

Despite his brave talk, he knew that would never be enough. He couldn't believe she didn't care about him. She'd said he deserved love. She'd kissed him—a real, warm and giving kiss. It hadn't been begrudging in the least.

"Wahoo!" His shout sent the horse skittering sideways. Brand calmed him and turned him about to face south. Back to the ranch.

Back to Sybil. He meant to find out if that kiss meant she might have some sweet regard for him.

He grinned from ear to ear and barely restrained a happy song. This was the right thing. Somehow he and Sybil would work things out even if it took days, weeks, months. Nothing else mattered.

Lost in his happy thoughts, he didn't hear or see anything until a man on horseback appeared before him, blocking his path.

His eyes fell to the gleaming pistol the rider held in his hand, pointed directly at him. Brand's heart stalled and then he reined his horse in and slowly raised his hands in the air. He gave the man a quick once-over. He was thin, rough-shaven, with dirty blond hair and a scowl fit to rot his teeth.

"I'm just a poor cowboy," he told the stranger. All he had was the wages Eddie had given him. He sure wasn't prepared to die over a few dollars. "You can have what I've got."

"Ain't interested in your money."

The skin on the back of Brand's neck tingled at the venom in the man's voice.

"Yer one of them Duggans."

Brand's nerves went into full alarm. "The Duggan gang is dead."

"Yeah. You'd like me to believe that, but I ain't fooled. I seen them firsthand and know what they look like. Get down." He waved his gun to indicate Brand should dismount.

He did so, cautiously and slowly. No telling what this man meant to do, but shooting Brand on the spot seemed highly likely.

The gun-toting man swung down at the same time and came round to face him, the pistol aimed steadily at Brand's chest.

Brand shrugged a little, which was plenty hard to do with his hands raised over his head, but he hoped to convince this man that he was harmless. "Mind telling me what this is all about?" He kept his voice low, his tone calm, just like he did when working with frightened animals. Though he wasn't sure who the frightened one was in this situation. Was the man as nervous as Brand? Not likely, seeing as he held a gun and Brand held nothing but air.

"You no-good Duggans shot my wife."

Brand stared. Pa and Cyrus were wicked and ruthless and for that, they'd got their names on a wanted poster. He'd heard of a woman getting shot. No wonder this man was angry.

"She was an innocent bystander. You Duggans didn't care who got hurt."

Brand wished the man would stop saying "you Duggans." Except he *was* a Duggan. It appeared he'd never be allowed to forget it.

"My Isabelle died right there on the street with no

one to hold her hand. Without me having a chance to say goodbye."

"I'm sorry."

"Sorry don't mean a thing. You're going to pay. Where's your sidearm?"

"I'm not carrying." His gun was in his saddlebag. Since the demise of the Duggan gang he hadn't felt the need to wear it.

"That's downright stupid." The man waved his gun around, then steadied it on Brand's heart. "I should shoot you dead right here and now, just like you did my Isabelle. But that wouldn't give me no satisfaction." He indicated Brand should move away from his horse, then rifled through his saddlebags until he found Brand's gun belt.

The man emptied the gun of all but one bullet, then spun the cylinder. "There. You got a fighting chance. That's more than Isabelle had." He jammed the gun into Brand's waistband.

The man backed away. "Lower your arms."

Brand did so slowly, reluctantly, knowing what came next. He'd never get a chance to say goodbye to Sybil. Never be able to tell her he loved her. With blinding clarity he understood the other man's pain. "I'm sorry for how your Isabelle died."

"Don't you dare speak her name."

For a moment, Brand thought the man intended to shoot him.

Instead, he swallowed loudly and narrowed his eyes. "Go for your gun."

Sybil put aside her empty teacup. "I'm fine now. But I need to take care of Dawg." She pushed herself to her feet, willing strength into her shaking limbs. "Mercy, will you come with me?"

Her friend looked startled, then shrugged. "Sure. Why not?"

Dawg waited outside and wriggled a happy greeting when Sybil called him. "I'll take him to the barn. That's where he's used to staying." She waited until they reached the barn to turn to Mercy. "Help me saddle a horse."

"You? Why?"

"I'm going after Brand."

Mercy laughed.

"I'm serious."

Mercy squinted at her as if trying to bring her into focus. "You really are. Okay. I'll saddle a horse for you, but I'm coming, too."

Sybil hugged her friend. "I hoped you'd say that." She'd have to ride astride though she'd never done so. Regardless, she had to do this.

"Up you go." Mercy helped her into the saddle. It was uncomfortable, but she'd survive.

When they left the barn, Sybil glanced around. Should they tell someone? No men lingered about. She glanced at the big house but didn't see Linette at the window. "Maybe we should tell Jayne what we're doing."

"She'll try and stop us. Do you want that?"

"No. I must do this. Let's go." So they rode north.

It didn't take long before Sybil wondered if she had been rash. She bounced with every step. Her legs cramped. Her back cried. But they kept onward, hoping for some sign of Brand.

She saw a movement through the trees. "Stop." She pulled up so hard her horse reared.

Mercy halted and waited for Sybil's mount to settle.

"Help me down." Sybil practically fell into her friend's arms, and bit her lip as her legs took her weight. "I saw someone through there." She pointed. "It has to be Brand. Wait here," she requested. "I want to see him alone."

Mercy squeezed her arm. "You go get him."

Sybil tiptoed forward, wanting to assess the situation before she confronted him. Twenty feet in she drew to a sudden halt, her heart kicking her ribs so hard it would leave a bruise.

Brand and another man faced each other. The second man held a gun aimed at Brand, and the look on his face convinced Sybil he meant business.

"Draw," the angry man ordered.

Brand didn't have a chance at outdrawing a man with a gun already in his palm.

Her legs forgot how to work and she collapsed against a tree.

*Brand,* she silently whispered. *Don't die. Please, God, let me get a chance to tell him how much I love him.*

Brand kept his arms stretched out at his sides as if avoiding any indication he meant to draw. "I ain't gonna be part of this," he said, his voice firm and strong. Keeping his right hand far away from his body, he slowly reached with his left toward the gun in his waistband and tossed it aside.

Her heart beat so fast she felt dizzy. What was he thinking? Did he plan to die?

"You go ahead and take a shot if that's what will make things right in your mind. I ain't like my pa and brother. I won't shoot a man for any reason." Brand stood immobile. "If you think that's what your innocent wife would want you to do."

The stranger stared as the moments ticked by. Then

he slowly lowered his gun. "You ain't no Duggan. A Duggan wouldn't miss a chance to shoot someone." He stuck his gun in his belt.

"I really am sorry," Brand said. "Kind of know how you feel. When I thought I was about to die, I had similar regrets. I thought I would do most anything to make up for past mistakes, even ones I didn't make. But you can't live life backward. Only forward."

Acknowledgment flickered through the man's eyes and then he turned, swung onto his horse and rode away.

Sybil's legs folded under her and she crashed to the ground.

At the sound Brand turned. When he saw her, his expression went from alarm to concern. He hurried to her side. "How did you get here?"

"I rode a horse." She explained how worried she'd been when Dawg returned.

Brand snorted a little laugh. "He refused to follow me, so I sent him back. Then I got to thinking. If a dog can see where he belongs, maybe I should try and be as smart."

He went down on his haunches beside her. "Sybil, I want to say something I should have said before." He scrubbed his lips together before he could go on. "For a few minutes I thought I'd never get the chance to say it."

She nodded, hopeful but uncertain. After all, she had written about him without his permission, and at first, it was why she had shown interest in him.

"Sybil Bannerman, I love you. I know you're a fine Englishwoman and I'm only a poor cowboy and a Duggan at that, but I love you. You don't have to love me back. I don't expect it, but I was afraid I'd die without ever telling you."

She wondered if he was ever going to stop. It seemed

the most words he'd strung together since they'd met. She touched his lips to end his speech.

"No more apologies. Brand Duggan, I love you from the bottom of my heart."

He let out a whoop, pulled her to her feet and kissed her soundly. She kissed him right back.

Behind them, Mercy coughed.

Sybil turned without leaving Brand's arms. "I wondered how long you'd wait."

Brand held her close, filling her with pure, sweet pleasure.

Mercy drew the horses forward. "I suggest we go home before Eddie sends out a search party."

Sybil sighed and rubbed her legs. "I suppose there's only one way to get back."

Mercy's laugh rendered Sybil no sympathy. "Same way we got here. On the back of a horse." She swung up on her mount.

Brand and Sybil stood next to the other horse. She thought she had never seen such a beautiful smile as the one he wore. It sparkled in his eyes and filled her heart with joy.

"We'll take it slow," he promised.

She hoped he didn't mean their courtship. Taking it slow, being cautious, had almost cost them their chance at love.

He trailed a finger along her jaw. "The reputation of the Duggan gang might haunt me for years. Perhaps I'm not being fair to you."

"Don't you dare change your mind about loving me." She said it teasingly, having full confidence in his affections.

His laugh was short and a bit regretful, she thought.

"There might be others who want to deal with the last Duggan. Like that man back on the trail."

"Then I suppose I'll have to take shooting lessons."

He chuckled then, the sound deep in his chest.

She hugged him. "I don't intend to let you go. You'll never be alone again."

He kissed her slowly, sweetly. She was learning to appreciate his gentle ways. She would always be safe with him.

"I've always wanted a little ranch where I can break and train horses."

She laughed. "I'm sure everyone will be as surprised to hear that as I am."

He grinned sheepishly. "Will you be happy as a rancher's wife? If not, we can live in town."

"Brand, it's sweet of you to offer, but I'm finding I quite like ranch life." She brushed her hand across his cheek. "I think it will be a wonderful adventure with you."

He was about to kiss her again, but suddenly drew back. "About that story you wrote about me…"

"Forget it. I decided a long time ago I wasn't sending it to the editor."

"Here's what I think. You send it in as you've written it. About a nameless cowboy. On two conditions."

"Anything you say." She waited for him to name the conditions.

He cupped her face and looked deep into her eyes. "You write more of the children's stories and sell them in your own name."

"I promise to write them, but I can't promise someone will buy them." She knew being a woman would prove a barrier to some publishers.

"Then you'll tell them to our children."

Mercy had ridden ahead and turned to call, "Are you two coming?"

"Yes," Sybil answered. To Brand she said, "I guess we better follow her."

"Not just yet." He caught her about the waist and bent his head to kiss her, with so much tenderness her eyes stung. With the promise of a growing love, the promise of a family and a bright future, they mounted up and rode back to the ranch.

# Epilogue

*April 1883*

Sybil took one last look at the little log cabin where she and Brand had spent the winter. Eddie and the Eden Valley cowboys had built it for them as soon as Sybil said she didn't intend to wait until spring to marry.

"We both know enough about loneliness," she'd told them all last fall. "I want to share the winter with Brand even if we have to live in a tent."

Jayne's eyes had widened in shock.

Mercy had chuckled. "Whatever happened to the little Sybil who lived a safe, comfortable life?"

Sybil's smile came from the warmth of her heart. "She grew up. She found love and discovered it was worth taking risks to enjoy."

"You won't need to do that," Eddie said. "So long as you don't object to a small cabin."

"I have no objections whatsoever."

Linette had arranged for a preacher to come from the fort, and Sybil and Brand had married the last day of September. Their wedding had been simple. Just the folks from the ranch. She'd worn a new dress at Linette's and Jayne's insistence. The pair had labored over it many hours.

Sybil smiled at the remembered pleasure of that day. Honoring her wishes not to have anything fancy, her friends had made her a beautiful gown in a sunset-gold color. Its simple lines made her feel elegant.

Brand was so handsome in his white shirt and dark pants, with his hair neatly trimmed, that her eyes had stung with joy.

Her throat tightened at the thought of saying goodbye to the place where she and Brand had spent so many happy hours together.

She looked about the one-room cabin they'd shared, and prayed Brand had found their time together here as healing as she had.

The bed in the corner had been made, ready to be used by visitors. The stove was cold. She'd polished it until it was black and shiny. The shelves were almost bare. The few books and jars she left behind belonged to Linette. The unlit lamp sat in the middle of the tiny table.

"Goodbye," she whispered, and turned to wait for Brand.

He pulled a wagon to the doorstep and leaped down to lift her into his arms. He pressed a kiss to her lips before he helped her up to the seat.

Linette, Eddie, Grady and Mercy stood at the bottom of the hill. Cassie and her children waved from the foreman's house. Jayne raced out and grabbed Sybil's hands.

"You come and visit often," she said.

"And you must come and visit us." She and Brand planned to invite the Eden Valley Ranch folks as soon as the weather permitted them to gather outside.

Amid more goodbyes, Brand and Sybil drove from the yard.

She snuggled against him, eager to share her secrets as soon as they reached their own home.

Brand had purchased land from Eddie, half an hour away to the northwest. Sybil had visited the place many times as Brand worked on their house, but she hadn't been there in several days.

If not for the joy of Brand's company and the pleasure of seeing signs of spring around them, she would have found the drive endless, so eager was she to get there.

Brand pulled the wagon to a halt at the break in the trees. "There it is. Our own place. I never thought I'd ever have the privilege of being able to settle down." He pulled her close. "Nor did I imagine I would ever have a sweet wife like you."

She kissed him and rejoiced to feel how his arms no longer carried tension in them. It had taken Brand weeks to stop looking over his shoulder for his pa and brother. But now he was finally accepting that his ordeal was over.

They continued onward. Brand pulled the wagon to the front of the new house, a log cabin with a window on either side of the welcoming door. It was three times the size of the one they'd spent the winter in, with three rooms—a big kitchen, a little sitting room and a bedroom.

"We'll add more rooms as we need them," Brand had promised.

For the many children they hoped to have. Sybil pictured little boys and girls tumbling from the doorway to greet them.

Brand lifted her down. "Welcome home." His voice deepened, indicating how much he reveled in this new stage of their lives.

"Wait a minute. I have something to show you." She

retrieved the valise she'd brought from the ranch, and pulled out a book: *Western Boys and Girls,* by Sybil Bannerman.

He stared at it a moment, then understanding dawned. He whooped and swung her in a wide circle.

"I still think I should have sold it as Sybil Duggan."

"We had this argument."

"Yes, and I let you win." He thought the Duggan name might pose a barrier to her success. She'd finally relented simply because she saw how much it upset him.

"Do you still feel the same way?"

"I do. The Duggan name will always be besmirched."

She pulled his face close and kissed him soundly. "I am honored to share your name." She leaned back and studied his features. "Brand, do you think you can teach your children to be proud of their name?"

He returned her look with equal seriousness. "In time people will forget about the Duggan gang." He shrugged. "And I guess I'll learn to put it behind me, too."

"How much time do you think you'll need?"

"I can't say."

"Will six or seven months be long enough?"

His eyes stilled. "Why?"

She laughed deep in her throat. "Because in about that length of time there will be another Duggan, and I want him or her to be proud of who they are and who their father is."

He blinked. Stared. Swallowed hard. "Another Duggan?"

She cradled her arms as if holding an infant. "A very small one."

He laughed and swept her off her feet again. "Whooee. What a day this is. A new book. A baby on the way." He crossed the threshold. "And a new home." He kissed her before he set her down inside the cabin.

"A new life together as the Duggans. We will be known as a couple—a family—that loves deeply." They'd likely be known for many more things—honesty, kindness, hospitality, and above all, joy.

"Ma used to say God will always be with us," Brand murmured. "He will always guide us to a safe place. Her words have come true this day and I thank Him."

"Me, too." Clasping hands, standing forehead to forehead, they bowed, and each prayed in gratitude for God's faithfulness and love. "Amen."

They stepped into the kitchen and the beginning of a shared life together. Brand stood behind Sybil and wrapped his arms about her. He pressed his palms to the place where their child lay in safety. "Welcome home."

She leaned against his chest, so content she didn't want to move. The anticipation of shared joys blessed every thought and eased every breath.

Life as a Duggan offered a wonderful future.

\* \* \* \* \*

Dear Reader,

I hope you enjoy another visit to the Eden Valley Ranch. It is one of my favorite places. Yes, it exists only in my imagination, but I see it when I visit ranches in the foothills, when I go to museums in that area or when I see pictures that match something I've made up. Even though the stories and characters, even the settings, are fictional, I hope you find reality in how these people lived and the problems they overcame. I pray God will encourage you as you read about Sybil and Brand.

I love to hear from readers. Contact me through email at linda@lindaford.org. Feel free to check on updates and bits about my research at my website www.lindaford.org. God bless,

Linda Ford

## Questions for Discussion

1. Why does Brand feel he must isolate himself from other people? Do you think he is justified in doing so? Did he have alternatives?

2. What has Brand's past taught him about becoming friends with men? Women?

3. What has made Sybil wary about becoming friends with others?

4. Is there something in particular about Brand that makes Sybil realize he spells danger to her heart? What is there about him that gets past her barriers? What events pull them together?

5. Brand and Sybil both have secrets. Why don't they confess them to each other? Do you think they had good reasons for holding back?

6. How would you have felt if you had discovered Brand's secret the way Sybil did? Do you feel it excuses the way she judged him?

7. Was Brand justified in reacting as he did when he found the notes Sybil had written about him?

8. How do you feel about Sybil writing under a pseudonym? Of being afraid to publish her children's stories? Are her concerns justified? Do they reflect the opinion common to that era?

9. What lessons did Sybil and Brand each have to learn in order to be able to express their love for each other?

10. How was their faith challenged? Did it grow throughout the story?

11. Does their future together look rosy? Do you foresee problems? If so, how do you think they will handle them?

## THE HUSBAND CAMPAIGN
*The Master Matchmakers*
by Regina Scott

They may have married to curtail a scandal, but Lady Amelia Jacoby is certain she can persuade Lord Hascot, her guarded new husband, that even a marriage of convenience can lead to true love.

## THE PREACHER'S BRIDE CLAIM
*Bridegroom Brothers*
by Laurie Kingery

After refusing to give in to an unwanted engagement, Alice Hawthorne is determined to stake her own claim during the Oklahoma Land Rush. But when she meets Elijah Thornton, can the preacher convince her to open her heart?

## THE SOLDIER'S SECRETS
by Naomi Rawlings

Blackmailed into spying on Jean Paul Belanger, widow Brigitte Dubois soon comes to care for the gruff farmer. But is she falling for a man who may have killed her husband?

## WYOMING PROMISES
by Kerri Mountain

When Bridger Jamison arrives in Quiver Creek, he's desperate for work and a safe place to care for his younger brother. But with the town against him, his only ally is the beautiful undertaker, Lola Martin.

---

LIHCNM0314

# REQUEST YOUR FREE BOOKS!

## 2 FREE INSPIRATIONAL NOVELS
## PLUS 2
## FREE
## MYSTERY GIFTS

*Love Inspired*
# HISTORICAL
### INSPIRATIONAL HISTORICAL ROMANCE

---

**YES!** Please send me 2 FREE Love Inspired® Historical novels and my 2 FREE mystery gifts (gifts are worth about $10). After receiving them, if I don't wish to receive any more books, I can return the shipping statement marked "cancel." If I don't cancel, I will receive 4 brand-new novels every month and be billed just $4.74 per book in the U.S. or $5.24 per book in Canada. That's a saving of at least 21% off the cover price. It's quite a bargain! Shipping and handling is just 50¢ per book in the U.S. and 75¢ per book in Canada.* I understand that accepting the 2 free books and gifts places me under no obligation to buy anything. I can always return a shipment and cancel at any time. Even if I never buy another book, the two free books and gifts are mine to keep forever.

102/302 IDN F5CN

| | | |
|---|---|---|
| Name | (PLEASE PRINT) | |
| Address | | Apt. # |
| City | State/Prov. | Zip/Postal Code |

Signature (if under 18, a parent or guardian must sign)

### Mail to the Harlequin® Reader Service:
**IN U.S.A.:** P.O. Box 1867, Buffalo, NY 14240-1867
**IN CANADA:** P.O. Box 609, Fort Erie, Ontario L2A 5X3

**Want to try two free books from another series?**
**Call 1-800-873-8635 or visit www.ReaderService.com.**

* Terms and prices subject to change without notice. Prices do not include applicable taxes. Sales tax applicable in N.Y. Canadian residents will be charged applicable taxes. Offer not valid in Quebec. This offer is limited to one order per household. Not valid for current subscribers to Love Inspired Historical books. All orders subject to credit approval. Credit or debit balances in a customer's account(s) may be offset by any other outstanding balance owed by or to the customer. Please allow 4 to 6 weeks for delivery. Offer available while quantities last.

**Your Privacy**—The Harlequin® Reader Service is committed to protecting your privacy. Our Privacy Policy is available online at www.ReaderService.com or upon request from the Harlequin Reader Service.

We make a portion of our mailing list available to reputable third parties that offer products we believe may interest you. If you prefer that we not exchange your name with third parties, or if you wish to clarify or modify your communication preferences, please visit us at www.ReaderService.com/consumerschoice or write to us at Harlequin Reader Service Preference Service, P.O. Box 9062, Buffalo, NY 14269. Include your complete name and address.

LIH13R

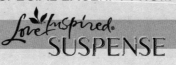
*Morgan Smith is hiding in the Witness Protection
Program. Has her past come back to haunt her?*

*Read on for a preview of
TOP SECRET IDENTITY by Sharon Dunn,
the next exciting book in the
WITNESS PROTECTION series
from Love Inspired Suspense. Available April 2014.*

A wave of terror washed over Morgan Smith when she
heard the tapping at her window. Someone was outside the
caretaker's cottage. Had the man who'd tried to kill her in
Mexico found her in Iowa?

Though she'd been in witness protection for two months,
her fear of being killed had never subsided. She'd left
Des Moines for the countryside and a job at a stable because she had felt exposed in the city, vulnerable. She'd
grown up on a ranch in Wyoming, and when she'd worked
as an American missionary in Mexico, she'd always chosen
to be in rural areas. Wide-open spaces seemed safer to her.

With her heart pounding, she rose to her feet and walked
the short distance to the window, half expecting to see a face
contorted with rage, or clawlike hands reaching for her neck.
The memory of nearly being strangled made her shudder.
She stepped closer to the window, seeing only blackness. Yet
the sound of the tapping had been too distinct to dismiss as
the wind rattling the glass.

A chill snaked down her spine.

Someone was outside.

If the man from Mexico had come to kill her, it seemed odd that he would give her a warning by tapping on the window.

She thought to call her new boss, who was in the guest-house less than a hundred yards away. Alex Reardon seemed like a nice man. She'd hated being evasive when he'd asked her where she had gotten her knowledge of horses. She'd been blessed to get the job without references. Her references, everything and everyone she knew, all of that had been stripped from her, even her name. She was no longer Magdalena Chavez. Her new name was Morgan Smith.

The knob on the locked door turned and rattled.

She'd been a fool to think the U.S. Marshals could keep her safe.

*Pick up TOP SECRET IDENTITY wherever*
*Love Inspired® Suspense books and ebooks are sold.*

Carl King scraped most of the mud off his boots and walked up to the front door of his boss's home. Joe Shetler had gone to purchase straw from a neighbor, but he would be back soon. After an exhausting morning spent struggling to pen and doctor one ornery and stubborn ewe, Carl had rounded up half the remaining sheep and moved them closer to the barns with the help of his dog, Duncan.

He opened the front door and stopped dead in his tracks. An Amish woman stood at the kitchen sink. She had her back to him as she rummaged for something. She hadn't heard him come in.

He resisted the intense impulse to rush back outside. He didn't like being shut inside with anyone. He fought his growing discomfort. This was Joe's home. This woman didn't belong here.

"What are you doing?" he demanded.

She shrieked and whirled around to face him. "You scared the life out of me."

He clenched his fists and stared at his feet. "I didn't mean to frighten you. Who are you and what are you doing here?"

"Who are you? You're not Joseph Shetler. I was told this was Joseph's house."

She was a slender little thing. The top of her head wouldn't reach his chin unless she stood on tiptoe. She was dressed Plain in a drab faded green calf-length dress with a matching cape and apron. Her hair, on the other hand, was anything but drab. It was ginger-red, and wisps of it curled near her temples. The rest was hidden beneath the black *kapp* she wore.

He didn't recognize her, but she could be a local. He made a point of avoiding people, so it wasn't surprising that he didn't know her.

"I'm sorry. My name is Elizabeth Barkman. People call me Lizzie. I'm Joe's granddaughter from Indiana."

As far as Carl knew, Joe didn't have any family. "Joe doesn't have a granddaughter, and he doesn't like people in his house."

"Actually, he has four granddaughters. I can see why he doesn't like to have people in. This place is a mess. He certainly could use a housekeeper. I know an excellent one who is looking for a position."

*Pick up THE SHEPHERD'S BRIDE*
*wherever Love Inspired® books and ebooks are sold.*

## OPEN TO LOVE?

After refusing to give in to an unwanted engagement,
Alice Hawthorne is determined to stake her own claim during
the Oklahoma Land Rush. But when she meets Elijah Thornton,
can the preacher convince her to open her heart?

**BRIDEGROOM
BROTHERS**

*The Preacher's Bride Claim*

by

# LAURIE KINGERY

*Available April 2014 wherever
Love Inspired books and ebooks are sold.*

LIH28259

# *Love Inspired*®

### Cowboy, wanderer… Father?

Nate Lyster and Mia Verbeek are in perfect agreement—that
letting someone new into your heart is much too risky.
Left on her own with four kids, Mia can't let just anyone
get close, while wandering cowboy Nate learned young that
love now means heartbreak later.

But when a fire turns Mia's life upside down, Nate is the only
one who can get through to her traumatized son—and her heart.
If Nate and Mia can forget the hurts of their pasts, they might get
everything they want. But if they let fear win, a perfect love could
pass them by….

# A Father in the Making
### by
# Carolyn Aarsen

*Available April 2014 wherever*
*Love Inspired books and ebooks are sold.*

Find us on Facebook at
www.Facebook.com/LoveInspiredBooks